WILLOW AND THE WOLF

THE SHIFTERS SERIES, BOOK ONE

ELIZABETH KELLY

EK PUBLISHING INC.

WILLOW AND THE WOLF

(The Shifters Series Book One)

She's not afraid of the big bad wolf.

Wolf shifter, Malcolm Burke, lives an ordinary life, and that's just the way he likes it. Until Willow Tanner waltzes into his office and his life. Perky, odd, and human – his new receptionist is definitely not what he's looking for. So why does his wolf so vehemently insist Willow belongs to him? And why does he find it so difficult to resist her sweet kisses?

Willow Tanner knows what she wants, and what she wants is the grumpy but deliciously sexy Malcolm Burke. The wolf shifter makes her entire body tingle, and she's not going to let a silly little thing like him being a paranormal stop her from coaxing him into her bed.

Determined to prove she's no ordinary human, Willow uses her unique abilities to help Mal and his partners at the security firm. But when her curiosity and eagerness to help land her in trouble, Mal will do whatever it takes to keep her safe.

CHAPTER 1

"So, uh, Ms. Tanner – you've worked for Harvey Snow for the last two years, is that right?" Bishop tugged anxiously at his tie as he scanned the paper in front of him.

Mal sighed. Bishop was sweating through his suit jacket, and he looked distinctly uncomfortable. Calling Bishop the strong, silent type was the understatement of the century. Grizzly shifters were known for their fierceness and strength, not their interviewing abilities. Bishop was the muscle of their small security company and rarely spoke to their clients. He wasn't afraid of getting his hands dirty, and while Mal trusted him with his life, he didn't trust that Bishop would get through the interview without passing out or throwing up.

He wished for the hundredth time that Kat was here to spearhead the interview. She was a jaguar shifter, and while not that talkative herself, she at least could ask questions without looking like she was going to faint. She had led the other three interviews, but a client emergency had forced her out of the office.

He forced himself to concentrate on the slender brunette sitting in front of them. She was a tiny little thing. He doubted she was taller than 5'4", and if she weighed a hundred pounds, he would be surprised. Her dark hair was pulled into a bun high on her head, and her light blue eyes sparkled with intelligence and humour. He idly wondered what she would look like with that dark hair drifting down her back and frowned to himself. The woman was not his type. One - she was human, and two – as a wolf shifter, he preferred to take bigger, stronger women to his bed. This one looked like a strong wind would blow her over.

"That's right." She smiled at Bishop. "Harvey is a great boss."

Bishop pulled at his tie again. "So, uh, why are you leaving?"

"Just looking for something different," she said cheerfully. "I suspect that working for your security firm would be more exciting and challenging than working for Harvey."

"Uh, right." Bishop shuffled the papers in front of him as he searched for something else to say.

"Ms. Tanner?" Mal figured it was time to rescue Bishop.

She turned toward him and gave him a dazzling smile. "Call me Willow."

"I'll be brutally honest. We've never hired a human to work for us before."

"So why are you interviewing me?" she asked.

"Harvey highly recommended you, and frankly, we're a bit desperate. Our last receptionist had to leave rather abruptly, and we've been scrambling to find her replacement. Our clients are mostly paranormal, and you'll see a great deal of oddity if you work for us."

"I don't mind," she said. "I enjoy odd things. It makes the world more interesting. Don't you think?"

"Uh, yes. I guess," he said.

"Harvey has paranormal clients, Mr. Burke. I've dealt with shifters and the fae, even a vampire."

He smiled thinly at her. "Harvey's clients are a bit more refined than ours."

She laughed, a soft and low vibration that made his wolf sit up and take notice. "I imagine they are. Harvey is a rather high-profile lawyer. His fees alone generally bring in a snootier class of people and paranormals."

"Right." He reached out and took the papers from Bishop's sweaty hand, smoothing out the wrinkles as he scanned her resume. "So, why don't you tell us what you know about our firm?"

She sat up straighter and smiled again at Bishop. The bear shifter blushed and stared at the floor as she said, "You and Mr. King started the firm seven years ago. Three years ago, Ms. Frost became a partner in the firm. You provide personal security for a large portion of the paranormals in our city. Considering how small our city is, quite a few paranormals live here. Wouldn't you agree, Mr. Burke?"

He shrugged. "I never really thought about it."

"I have. The number of paranormals that have gravitated to our city is extraordinary. I think it's because of the fault line."

"Excuse me?" Mal frowned at her.

"The paranormal fault line. It lies directly across our city. Haven't you heard of the fault line?" she asked.

He shook his head. "The fault line is a myth, Ms. Tanner."

"Maybe, maybe not," she said. "I can assure you, Mr. Burke, that I am excellent at my job. I'm organized, great with clients, and type over a hundred words a minute. I understand that your firm will require working strange hours from time to time, and I have no problem with that."

"Even if it means working in the middle of the night to accommodate a vampire or coming in at dawn for the fae?"

"Yes," she said. "I don't need much sleep."

"You must have an understanding husband."

He could have punched himself. Why the hell had he said that? His wolf growled happily as Bishop stared at him in disbelief.

"I'm not married." She raised her hand and wiggled her bare ring finger at him. "I can do what I want, when I want, with whomever I want."

An image flashed through his head of Willow in his bed, naked and on her hands and knees with his hand wrapped in that long dark hair. He cleared his throat. "Okay, well, thank you for coming in, Ms. Tanner. We'll get back to you in the next couple of days."

She blinked in surprise at his abruptness, then stood and smoothed her short skirt. He eyed her slender legs before his gaze drifted to her small, perky breasts draped in her pink, silk shirt. Beside him, Bishop stood and extended his massive hand.

"Nice to meet you, Ms. Tanner," he said.

She shook his hand before extending her hand to Mal. He stood and shook her hand, ignoring the little shiver that went down his back at the touch of her soft palm.

"Nice to meet you both. I look forward to hearing back from you," she said in that same cheery voice.

She left the room, and Bishop punched him in the arm when Mal stared at her tight ass. "Stop it," he grunted.

Mal growled at him as the door shut and sank back into his chair. "We're not hiring her."

Bishop rolled his eyes. "She'll never agree to work for us anyway – not with the way you were eyeing her. Jesus, Mal, I thought you were going to try to mate with her right in front of me."

"I don't know what the hell you're talking about," Mal said.

"Whatever, man." Bishop took her resume and scanned it. "She's the best candidate."

"She's human, Bishop. We were only interviewing her as a favour to Harvey, remember?"

"Yeah, I remember. I don't know what the big deal is about hiring a human, anyway."

"Because humans and paranormals don't mix," Mal said.

"You hate humans," Bishop snorted.

"I don't," Mal protested. "I'm trying to protect the humans. A human always gets hurt when they start messing around with paranormals. You know that. It's why that asshole senator tried to pass that law forbidding us to have anything to do with humans."

"Don't tell me you supported that?" Bishop glared at him.

"Of course, I didn't. It was a ridiculous law created by an actual damn racist. But you have to admit he has a point. Plenty of humans have been hurt or killed when dealing with paranormals, and some of them are out for our blood."

"You think I don't know that? Protecting our kind against humans is eighty-five percent of our business, Mal," Bishop said. "It doesn't mean all humans are against us."

"I'm not saying that," Mal said. "I'm just saying that hiring this human female is a bad idea."

"Is it a bad idea because she's human or a bad idea because you want to mate with her?" Bishop raised his eyebrows at him.

"I don't want to mate with her!" Mal snapped.

"Sure, you don't." Bishop pulled off his tie and gathered the resumes together. "I'm telling Kat we should hire her."

"The Gorgon! What about the Gorgon? She was great," Mal said a bit desperately.

"Are you kidding? She has the voice of a lumberjack, and she wants ten dollars more an hour than we're offering. And what happens the first time it's the Gorgon mating period? Do you want to find yourself pinned against your desk while she tears off your clothes and has her way with you?"

Mal paled. "We'll just give her some time off during the mating period."

Bishop snorted and headed toward his office. "I'm recommending the human, Mal, and you know Kat will agree with me. She didn't like any of the other candidates. Just keep your paws to yourself, okay?"

"THANK YOU SO MUCH, MR. KING! YOU WON'T REGRET hiring me, I promise." Willow ended the phone call and grinned delightedly at her best friend. "I got the job, Ava!"

"Congratulations!" Ava hugged her hard. "I knew you'd get it. When do you start?"

"Next Monday. Oh, Ava, I'm so happy. It's finally my chance to work with actual paranormals. Mama would be so pleased for me."

"She would be," Ava agreed. "Now, tell me about your new job."

"It's just a reception position. I could probably do it in my sleep, but once I show them what I can do, I'm hoping they'll move me up in the company," Willow said.

"I'm sure they will. How big is the office?" Ava poured more tea and followed Willow into the small, cluttered living room. She moved a pile of laundry from the armchair and curled her curvy body into the seat.

Willow flopped down on the sofa, rested her feet on a pile of papers on the coffee table and took a sip of tea. "The company is called Burke, King, and Frost Security. There are three partners, Bishop King, Katarina Frost, and Malcolm Burke. They have a dozen employees that are in and out of the office, according to Mr. King."

She pulled absentmindedly on her lower lip. "I didn't meet Ms. Frost, just Mr. King and Mr. Burke."

"What were they like?"

"Well, Mr. King is a massive bear shifter. He's the biggest man I've ever met in my life, Ava. I wouldn't be surprised if he were over seven feet tall. He seemed nervous. I don't think he's very comfortable around women."

"What about the other one?"

"Mr. Burke? He's a wolf shifter, and he seemed - I don't know - grumpy. I'm pretty sure he didn't like me." She laughed.

"He doesn't even know you," Ava said indignantly.

"I know, but you know how some paranormals are. They don't like humans. He made sure to point out that they had never hired a human before. It's why I was so surprised that -"

She stopped as her breath plumed out in front of her like smoke. Ava shivered and leaned back in the chair as Willow turned and stared behind her.

"I can't help you if you don't tell me what's wrong," Willow said.

The room grew steadily colder, and Ava looked around anxiously. "Willow? Who is it?"

Willow shrugged. "I don't know. He won't talk to me."

Ava clutched her tea mug and stared at the corner that Willow looked into. "That's weird."

"Yep, it is," Willow said. She stood and approached the corner, holding her hands out in a friendly manner. "Will you at least tell me your name? Don't be shy."

Ava watched as Willow inched closer. "I want to help you. Let me – no! Don't go!"

She sighed discouragingly and turned around. "He's gone."

The room warmed up again, and Ava shivered before curling deeper into the chair. "God, I hate it when that happens."

Willow grinned. "I love it."

"I know you do. You're a weirdo."

"Oh c'mon, Ava. It's not a bad thing. Think of how

many spirits I've helped cross to the other side. They're hurting, and I can help them. How is that bad?"

"It's not bad. It's just creepy," Ava said. "And what happens when you run into a not-so-nice spirit?"

"I've been seeing the dead for almost my entire life, and not once have they ever been malicious or evil," Willow said.

"What about that girl two years ago? She didn't seem so nice," Ava said.

"Courtney? She was perfectly nice."

"She broke every dish in your house, Willow!"

"She was just misunderstood, that's all. She was angry and upset, and she didn't know how to express it."

"So, she expressed it by shattering all of your dishes?"

"Hey, you'd be angry too if your boyfriend cheated on you with your mother."

Ava rolled her eyes. "I'd need to have a boyfriend for that to be a possibility, and with a body like this, we both know that's not going to happen."

"Oh hush, Ava. I hate it when you talk badly about yourself." Willow frowned at her. "Besides, it has nothing to do with your body and everything to do with your self-confidence. You're gorgeous and sweet, and you just need to get over this ridiculous idea that all men want a skinny stick in the sack."

"Says the girl who wears a size two," Ava said.

Willow snorted. "I'd gladly take your curves." She grabbed her small breasts and gave them a shake. "You think these little molehills are grabbing any man's attention? I'd kill to have your mountains."

Ava blushed and crossed her arms over her chest.

"Yeah, and my carrot-coloured hair and pale, freckle-covered skin."

Willow laughed. "I only wish I could pull off red hair. Now, let's go shopping. I need a couple of new outfits for my new job."

CHAPTER 2

"Good morning, Mr. Burke!"

Willow's voice, way too chipper for this early in the morning, floated into his office, and Mal groaned inwardly. He didn't look up from his computer as Willow set a coffee on his desk.

"I brought you a coffee, a white mocha for your sweet tooth."

He could hear the grin in her voice, and keeping his eyes on the screen, he said, "I keep telling you that you don't have to bring me coffee in the morning, Ms. Tanner."

"And I keep telling you to call me Willow," she said. "I've been working here a month, you know. Maybe it's time to stop with the formalities."

"Maybe," he said. He knew damn well it was a month. It had, in fact, been the longest month of his life. The smell of the coffee did nothing to dampen Willow's scent. A scent that haunted his dreams and made it nearly impossible to sleep without jacking off every night like a horny teenage wolf.

He knew he was in trouble the first day she worked for them. She arrived in the office wearing a knee-length skirt that clung to her firm ass, and he'd spent most of the day wondering if the nylons she wore were thigh-highs. Her delicious and intoxicating scent had quickly filled the entire office. Finally, in desperation, he'd shut the door to his office and opened the window.

It was ridiculous even to want a human and even more foolish to want this particular human. She was too small and fragile for the likes of him, and besides, she was annoyingly cheerful. She had quickly won over Kat and Bishop and seemed bound and determined to win him over as well, no matter how cold he was to her.

"Is that everything, Ms. Tanner? I'm swamped this morning." He risked a glance at her, and his wolf growled happily. Although it was just after eight, it was already warm in the office, and she had shed her suit jacket. The dark blue tank top she wore was modest, but even just the sight of her bare, tanned arms was enough to make his cock stir in his jeans.

She gave him a broad grin and shifted the tray of coffees in her hand. "Right, sorry, Mal."

God, even the way she said his name turned him on.

"Oh, before I forget – Mr. Danson is going to be fifteen minutes late for his appointment this morning."

"Thanks."

"You're welcome."

She still stood in his office, giving him that same damn sweet smile she gave him every morning, and he said, "As I was saying, I -"

"Morning, Mal." Kat's low, smooth voice was a

welcome distraction from his inappropriate obsession with their new receptionist.

"You're late," he growled.

"Pshh, I'm five minutes late and besides, Bishop isn't here either. Morning, Willow."

"Hi, Kat! How was your date last night?" Willow leaned her hip against the side of his desk, and Mal scootched his chair away.

"It was a bust. I knew better than to go out with a lion shifter, I swear to God they're the most egotistical paranormal on the planet, but my mother set us up. She had the guilt turned high for this one. He's a doctor, Katarina. He's from a good pride back in New York, Katarina. Do you want me to die without ever holding a grandkitten in my arms, Katarina?"

Kat rolled her eyes as Willow laughed and handed her a coffee. "Here, I brought you a coffee."

"Oh my God, you're such a sweetheart. I don't know how we got along without you." Kat took the coffee lid off before inhaling deeply. "Thanks, Will."

"No problem."

"Did you and your friend go to that movie?" Kat sat down in the leather chair across from Mal's desk and crossed her legs.

Mal groaned again. The two of them were settling in for a nice long chat, and he'd go crazy if he had to keep inhaling Willow's scent.

"Nah. Ava has come down with a bad cold. We'll probably have lunch today if she's feeling better, but last night she stayed at home with a bottle of Nyquil and the first season of *Mad Men*."

"I love that show," Kat said. "I'm only on season three, but I'm planning on doing a marathon this weekend."

Mal rolled his eyes. He had always thought of Kat as being quiet, but since Willow's arrival, she was becoming much chattier and outgoing. It was Willow's influence. He was certain of it. Hell, even Bishop could sit and have a conversation with her, and the grizzly hated talking to anyone. She had coaxed his entire life story out of him one evening when they were all working late. Since that night, he was almost as bad as Kat when it came to his inability to resist Willow's infectious chatting.

It was time to take control of the situation. "Hey, do you think you guys could -"

"We talkin' about *Mad Men*?" Bishop strode into the office, making the pictures shake and dropped into the second chair. "I just watched it last night and -"

"Stop!" Kat cried. "You know I'm only on season three, Bishop."

"Sorry, I forgot," he said sheepishly.

He growled happily when Willow handed him his coffee. "No whip, right, Willow?"

"Of course," Willow said. "Non-fat latte, no foam, no whip. Although honestly, Bishop, you don't need to watch your weight."

He leaned back in the chair and patted his abdomen. "We grizzlies gotta be careful, Will. It's not so bad in the summer but come winter, I can gain thirty pounds easily."

"Do you hibernate?" Willow asked. "I keep meaning to ask."

Bishop shook his head. "No, not really."

Mal snorted, and Bishop frowned. "What? I don't."

"You go to bed at seven every night and get up at noon during the winter cycle," Mal said.

"I work a few hours a day," Bishop shrugged, "so I'm not hibernating."

Willow grinned and took a sip of her coffee. "You've got to meet my friend Ava. I swear she sleeps more than any human I've ever met. Maybe she's got some bear shifter in her."

The phone rang before Bishop could reply, and Willow left Mal's office. Mal breathed a sigh of relief and slumped in his chair before taking a drink of coffee. His wolf growled happily at the sweetness, and he gave the other two a defensive look when he realized they were staring silently at him. "What?"

"You need to get laid, Mal," Bishop said.

"Excuse me?"

"You need to get laid. Go find a pretty little wolf bitch and get your rocks off. You've been a total asshole lately." Bishop sipped at his coffee as Mal gaped at him.

"Bishop!" Kat scolded. "That's not true."

"Thank you, Kat," Mal said. "I appreciate -"

Kat held up her hand. Her nails were long and painted a fiery red, and she leaned forward and tapped them against his desk. "Don't get me wrong, Mal. Bishop isn't wrong about you being an asshole lately or about you needing to get laid. You are, and you do. But you don't need some random wolf - you need to get laid by Willow."

"Kat!" Mal scowled at her before glancing at his open door. "Keep your damn voice down."

Kat shrugged and sat back in her chair. Every move she made was a testament to her jaguar. She was tall and curvy, and she moved with the lithe grace of a cat. She smoothed down her dark hair before taking another drink of coffee. "Oh, please, Mal. You think Willow doesn't know you want to bend her over your desk?"

"Shut. Up. Kat." Mal growled at her, and she hissed in return.

"What's your problem?" she asked. "Willow's a nice girl, too nice for you now that I think about it, yet she doesn't seem to dislike the idea of taking you to her bed."

"Has she told you that?" Mal couldn't help himself. He needed to know.

Kat shook her head. "No. But it's obvious."

He was holding on to the edge of his desk so tightly that his knuckles were turning white. He forced himself to relax. "Since when have you and Bishop felt the need to shove your noses into my sex life?"

Bishop snorted. "What sex life? Rubbing one out to the latest issue of 'She-Wolf' ain't a love life, buddy."

"You're one to talk," Mal said. "You haven't had a girl-friend in years. At least I can talk to a woman."

The bear shifter growled. "I can talk to women."

Kat held her hands up. "Okay, okay. You're both virile, incredibly sexy men who can get whatever woman they want."

She leaned forward again. "You want Willow, and she wants you. Go for it, Mal."

"Have you gone mad, Kat? She's our receptionist. I'm not sleeping with an employee. Have you thought about what would happen if it didn't work out?"

Kat frowned. "Huh, not really. Christ – Willow would probably leave."

She stared at Mal in panic. "Forget what I told you. Do

not sleep with Willow. Do you hear me? Do not sleep with her."

"I wasn't planning on it," Mal said through gritted teeth. "Now, would the two of you get the hell out of my office? I've got work to do."

"Hi, Willow."

Her nose red and her voice husky from her cold, Ava walked into the office and leaned against the reception desk.

"Hi, honey! How are you feeling?" Willow asked.

"Better. I know I look terrible, but I feel much better than I did last night. I'm sorry I had to bail on our movie night."

"Don't even worry about it." Willow bent under her desk and picked up her purse as the door to Bishop's office opened. "We can always go on the weekend if -"

She straightened when she heard Ava gasp in surprise.

"Bishop?" Willow blinked at him. "What are you doing?"

He stood directly behind Ava. The curvy redhead turned to face him, and despite her height, the bear shifter dwarfed her. His large hands gripped the reception desk, trapping her between his massive arms, and Willow watched as he leaned down and buried his face in Ava's long red hair.

"Willow?" Ava squeaked out as Bishop inhaled deeply. A deep rumbling growl started in his chest, and he inhaled again, nuzzling his face into her hair as Ava made another frightened squeak.

"Wh-what do I do?" she whispered to Willow.

MAL STEPPED OUT OF HIS OFFICE AND STARED IN SURPRISE at his best friend. Bishop had a tall redheaded woman trapped against the reception desk with his face buried deep in her hair.

"Wh-what do I do?" the woman whispered to Willow.

"Bishop!" Mal's voice rang out, and the bear shifter stiffened before abruptly pulling away.

He stared silently at the woman, his face reddening as Willow said, "Bishop, this is my best friend, Ava Lewis. Ava, this is Bishop King."

"H-hello." Ava held her hand out. It trembled lightly, and Bishop stared at it for a moment before backing away.

"I'm, uh, I'm so sorry," he muttered. The part of his face not covered by his dark beard was beet red, and he took another stumbling step backward, flinching when he ran into Mal.

"Bishop." Mal gave him a warning look, and the big man turned and lumbered back to his office, slamming the door shut with a bang.

"Sorry about that." Mal extended his hand to Ava. "I'm Malcolm Burke."

"It's nice to meet you." Ava shook his hand. "I've heard a lot about you."

"All good, I hope," he said.

"Nope, not a single good thing." Willow grinned at him as she came out from behind the desk and linked her arm around Ava's. "Come on, Ava. I want to get to the café before it's too crowded."

She led the redhead toward the door before glancing over her shoulder at Mal. "Do you need something to eat, Mal?"

An image of Willow, her pale thighs parted and her voice moaning his name as he thrust his tongue deep into her wet pussy, flashed in his head.

"What?" he croaked.

"I asked if you wanted something from the café. I can bring you back some food," Willow said.

"Uh, no. No, thank you," he said.

"Okay." She winked at him and shut the door behind her.

He ran a shaking hand over his forehead before walking into Bishop's office. "What the hell, Bishop? Have you gone mad?"

Bishop sat at his desk with his head buried in his large hands. He groaned and stared at Mal in embarrassment. "I – I don't know what happened, Mal."

"Don't know what happened? I thought you were going to throw that poor girl over your shoulder and carry her off like some damn caveman."

Bishop slammed his fist onto his desk. The wood cracked beneath his hand, and he stared at it before glancing up at Mal. "I don't know what happened," he repeated. "I was just sitting at my desk, and then I could smell this most delicious scent, and the next thing I knew, I was standing in front of her, sniffing her like a dog."

He stared at Mal pleadingly. "You smelled it, didn't you?"

Mal shook his head. "No. She smelled like a regular human, Bishop."

"Did she?" Bishop asked hoarsely. He traced the crack

in the wood with one callused finger. "I can't believe I did that."

Mal clapped Bishop on the shoulder. "It's okay. Willow will smooth it over, I'm sure. But maybe keep your sniffing to yourself the next time you see Ava."

Bishop's panic was apparent. "I'm not going to see her again! Why would I see her again?"

"Calm down, Bishop." Mal could barely keep the grin from his face. He had spent the last month lusting over Willow and her scent, and, truthfully, it cheered him a little to see Bishop suddenly suffering the same agony.

He couldn't resist poking the grizzly a little. "She's Willow's best friend. I'm not sure you'll be able to avoid her."

Bishop groaned loudly. "We need to make a new rule in the office. No friends dropping by. Do you hear me, Mal?"

Mal laughed and squeezed Bishop's shoulder. "Yeah, I'll let you explain that new rule to Willow."

"AVA? HELLO, AVA?" WILLOW REACHED OUT AND poked Ava.

"What?" Ava asked irritably, and Willow grinned.

"You seem distracted."

"Wouldn't you be distracted if a giant grizzly shifter had just sniffed you?"

"I told you he was a big man." Willow stabbed a tomato with her fork and popped it into her mouth.

"Yeah, you did." Ava stirred her soup before pulling

out a tissue and wiping at her nose. "But you don't get it until you see him in person."

"He certainly seemed fond of you," Willow said. "It took a solid two weeks before he would even look me in the eye, and he's certainly never sniffed me."

Ava blushed furiously. "I'm sure he was just sniffing me because…."

Willow laughed. "You should ask him out."

Ava stared at her in horror. "What? No way! I am not asking him out."

"Why not? The worst that can happen is he says no."

"Yeah," Ava said, "and then I die of humiliation in front of him."

Willow rolled her eyes. "You need to take a chance. You need to -"

"Why didn't you tell me that Mal was so friggin' hot?" Ava said.

Willow shrugged. "Is he? I hadn't noticed."

"Bullshit," Ava said. "Let's see…." She held up her hand and ticked the points off her fingers. "He's big, maybe not as big as that grizzly shifter, but he's over six feet for sure. He has gorgeous green eyes, a smoking body, a jawline to murder for and the perfect, and I do mean perfect, amount of stubble."

Willow snickered and ate another bite of salad. "Fine," she mumbled around the lettuce, "he's friggin' hot."

"Yeah," Ava sighed before spooning soup into her mouth.

"He's also arrogant, grumpy, and completely immune to my charms," Willow said. "I did some research on shifters before I started working for them, and bear shifters are supposed to be the grumpy ones. Bishop is a complete sweetheart compared to Mal."

"What are wolf shifters known for?" Ava asked.

"They're loyal, protective, and apparently make excellent husbands. They believe in mating for life. Out of all the shifters, they prefer to stick to their kind the most. In fact, there's only a few recorded instances of a wolf shifter mating with a human."

"Really?" Ava raised her eyebrows.

"Yup," Willow confirmed. "Not that they don't have sex with humans – they're notorious playboys – but they don't generally settle down with them and raise wolf babies."

"Is that why you're pretending not to be interested in him?"

"Oh, I'm interested in him. I'd give a month's pay to see that man naked, but he is my boss, so…."

She stared at her salad for a moment. "Not to mention that he really, really doesn't like me."

"Don't worry. You'll win him over." Ava patted her hand. "You always do."

"I do, don't I?" Willow grinned at her. "I'm tough to resist. I'll just have to try harder with Mr. Malcolm Burke."

"God help him," Ava said.

"KAT! YOU HAVE TO COME WITH ME. YOU KNOW MRS. Belfry doesn't trust wolf shifters. We've been working for years to break into corporate security, and this is our best chance. Her import company is the largest in the city, and we need this contract."

"What do you want me to do, Mal? My flight leaves in exactly two hours, and I can't miss my own sister's wedding." Kat scowled at him. "I told you I was leaving today. It's not my fault you didn't remember."

"Kat, I can't go there by myself. You know that. She won't let me through the fucking door," Mal said.

"So, take Bishop with you," Kat suggested.

"Like that will help. She hates bear shifters almost as much as she hates wolf shifters," Mal said.

"Why the hell is she even agreeing to meet with us then?" Kat asked.

"Because she knows you're a jaguar shifter, and she's married to one. She's willing to give us a chance based on that alone."

"I'm getting on that flight, Mal," Kat said.

"Kat -"

"How does she feel about humans?" Willow stepped into his office.

"What?" Mal scowled at her.

"I said, how does she feel about humans? I can go with you," Willow said.

"No," Mal said.

"Hold on. That might be a good idea. Mrs. Belfry has over a dozen humans working for her, so obviously, she doesn't hate them. Willow has excellent people skills," Kat said.

"I said, no," Mal growled.

Kat hissed at him. "You don't have much choice, Mal. Either go by yourself and hope she lets you in the house or take Willow with you. You said it yourself, this contract could make us."

Mal raked his hand through his short dark hair. He wanted to howl with frustration. "Fine. We're leaving in ten minutes."

"Great! I'll just freshen up," Willow said.

She disappeared from his office as Kat stood and smoothed her long skirt. "There, problem solved."

Mal glared at her, and Kat grinned saucily. "Try not to maul Willow when you're alone with her, okay? She's the best receptionist we've ever had, and I'll be pissed if she quits because you keep trying to shove your tongue down her throat."

"Out, Kat! Now!" He grabbed the ruler sitting on his desk and snapped it in two as Kat laughed.

"See you in a few days, Malcolm." She blew him a kiss and sauntered from his office.

"I love your car." Willow smoothed her hand over the dashboard.

"Thanks," Mal said.

He opened the window and had to restrain from sticking his head out into the breeze. Willow's scent was everywhere, and he could barely concentrate on driving. Her scent would cling to him for the rest of the day and drive his wolf mad with need.

"Maybe I could drive on the way back?" Willow said.

"No."

"Why not?"

"Because you're too little to handle this type of power."

She laughed and rolled her eyes. "Please, I've been driving cars like this since I was sixteen."

"Really?"

"Yup. My dad was a mechanic and a collector of fast cars." She stared out the window. "He taught me how to drive when I was twelve."

"Twelve?" He couldn't keep the disbelief out of his voice.

"Yes. Mama wasn't pleased about that. She gave him the biggest lecture when she found out. She was worried I'd get in an accident. Of course, it was fine. Daddy was a very safe driver, and he taught me to be safe as well."

He grunted in reply, and she smiled at him again. "So, what do you say? Can I drive on the way back?"

"No."

She wrinkled her nose at him. "Meanie."

"Did you just call me meanie?"

"Yes. What? Is everyone too afraid of the big bad wolf to tell him the truth about his personality?"

"I'm not a meanie," he protested.

"Well, you're definitely a grumpy," she said.

"You don't know anything about me," he said.

"That's true. But whose fault is that? Not mine. I've been trying to get to know you over the last month," Willow said.

"You don't need to know anything about me. You're my employee, nothing else."

"That doesn't mean we can't be friends."

She pouted adorably, and he had to clench his hands around the steering wheel to stop himself from pulling the car over and kissing away the pout. "It sort of does."

"Ridiculous," she said. "I think you just dislike humans."

"I don't dislike humans," he said.

"No? Then it's just me?"

"Ms. Tanner, I don't -"

"You know what I think? I think you just don't know enough about me. Once you get to know me, you won't be able to resist me, Mal." She wiggled her eyebrows at him, and he almost groaned out loud when she wet her bottom lip with her small, pink tongue.

"So, here are the facts about Willow Blossom Tanner. I'm twenty-five, I -"

"Your middle name is not Blossom," he said.

"It totally is. My parents were hippies. Did I forget to mention that?" She giggled.

He didn't reply, and she continued. "As I was saying, I'm twenty-five, single – but you already know that – and my best friend is Ava. What was up with Bishop and the sniffing, by the way?"

"Uh…" He didn't know how to respond.

"He certainly seemed to like her smell. Is that a bear shifter thing or a shifter thing in general?"

"Most shifters have an excellent sense of smell. They use it to figure out all sorts of things about other paranormals and humans."

"Like what?"

He shrugged. "Where they live, what they do for a living, how old they are, their emotions at the time."

"Really? How old they are?"

He nodded. He was suddenly sweating, and he hoped Willow wouldn't notice. From a single sniff, most shifters could tell if a person was hungry or happy, or frightened or – he swallowed thickly – aroused.

"That is so cool," she said thoughtfully. "Paranormals are so lucky. Imagine being able to sniff someone and instantly know if they were happy."

"Not all paranormals can do it," he reminded her. "Some have better senses than others."

"I suppose something like a penguin shifter wouldn't be able to smell your happiness," she said.

"There is no such thing as a penguin shifter."

"How do you know?" She countered immediately. "Just because you've never seen one doesn't mean they don't exist. They wouldn't live here, would they? It's much too warm for them."

"Penguin shifters do not exist," he said through gritted teeth.

"Do you believe in spirits?"

He blinked at the abrupt change in topic. "What?"

"Spirits? Do you believe in them?"

"You mean ghosts?"

"Ghosts, spirits, ethereal beings – whatever you want to call them." She shrugged.

"There is no such thing as ghosts."

She frowned at him. "You know, for being a paranormal, you have an awfully restricted view of the world."

He rolled his eyes. "I'm just not prone to ridiculous thoughts and ideas, Ms. Tanner."

"You think I'm ridiculous?" She gave him a hurt look.

"I didn't say that. I'm just implying that you have ridiculous *ideas*."

She mulled that over. "I suppose you have a point. To the unbeliever, I would come across as ridiculous."

"The unbeliever?"

"Yes. You know, someone like you. You're much too practical for your own good, Mal. You have to open your heart and your head to the possibility that there are things in this world that can't be explained."

"I prefer to be seen as normal, thanks. It's better for business."

She laughed. "True. I blame your upbringing."

"You know nothing about my upbringing," he said.

"I know your parents aren't hippies like mine were."

"Were?" He glanced at her.

For the first time since he'd met her, the cheerful look on her face dropped away. "My parents died two years ago in that plane crash. You know the one."

He nodded. It had been all over the news. One hundred and twenty-five humans and forty paranormals died instantly when their plane crashed into the ocean. "I'm sorry."

"Thanks. I miss them terribly. I'm an only child, and neither of my parents' siblings is still alive."

She stared out the window for a moment. "It gets pretty lonely, you know? Thank God for Ava."

She fidgeted with the buttons on her shirt. "I thought maybe I would see them again. Thought that maybe they would make an appearance just to say they loved me but that never happened. I shouldn't be surprised. Both my parents were extremely happy people. There was nothing left to keep them in this world. Still... I hoped they would want to see me one last time."

"What are you talking about?" Just when he thought she was normal, she threw out random crap like that.

"Nothing," she said cryptically. "Where was I? Oh yes, we were telling each other about our personal lives. It's your turn now."

He shook his head. "We weren't talking about our personal lives - you were talking about your personal life."

"Oh c'mon," she wheedled. "Throw me a bone, would you? I want to know something about the big bad wolf."

He snorted, and she grinned at him. "Maybe I can guess."

She studied him for so long that he could feel a blush creeping up his neck. "Stop staring at me."

"I'm just trying to figure you out."

"It's rude to stare."

"I suppose it is. Maybe I should sniff you instead."

Before he could stop her, she leaned over and nearly buried her face in his neck. She inhaled deeply, and he stiffened and leaned away.

"It's even ruder to smell someone without their invitation," he snapped.

"Man, I've got a lot to learn about shifters. I thought shifters would be cool with the sniffing." She sat back in her seat. "That didn't tell me anything, anyway. Other than you wear great cologne."

He blushed, and she clapped her hands with unrestrained glee. "I made you blush!"

"No, you didn't!" he snapped again.

"Of course not. Your natural colour is bright red," she said.

He stopped the car at a red light, and she grinned impishly. "Maybe you should smell me."

"Definitely not," he growled.

"Oh c'mon…it'll be fun!"

She unclicked her seat belt and leaned in until he could feel her small breasts pressing against his arm. He stared at her in panic as she tilted her head up.

"Go on, Mal. Sniff me," she said.

"Ms. Tanner, this isn't -"

"Are you a chicken?" She smacked him playfully on

one broad thigh. "I've never seen you in your wolf form. Maybe you're actually a chicken shifter."

He growled and pressed his face into her soft throat. He inhaled deeply, his cock hardening against the worn fabric of his jeans as her scent washed over him. He inhaled again and again as Willow waited patiently.

"Well? What can you tell about me?" she asked.

"You showered this morning."

"Obviously. I shower every morning. C'mon, wolf boy, tell me something you couldn't possibly know."

"You had strawberries and wine last night for dinner. You wear vanilla body lotion, but not this morning, you were excited by something last night, and you're twenty-six, not twenty-five."

She leaned back a little and stared at him in wide-eyed wonderment. "That's amazing! I did totally lie about my age!"

A grin crept across his face, and her eyes sparkled happily in response. "Do me again, Mal!"

"I – what?" he croaked out. He couldn't stop the immediate mental image of yanking up Willow's skirt, tearing off her panties, and making her straddle him while he fucked her senseless.

"Sniff me again! Tell me something else!"

"Uh, no, I don't think -"

He groaned out loud when she shoved her throat eagerly into his face. This time she rested one warm hand on his thigh, and he was helpless to stop from cupping the back of her head and holding her steady while he breathed in. His traitorous tongue licked her soft skin, his balls tightening when she moaned softly in response. Her hand clenched on his leg as he licked her again.

"Does – does taste tell you something as well?" she squeaked out.

"Yes," he muttered. Her arousal was strong and overpowering in the small car, and his wolf howled with delight when he nipped her neck.

"Oh!" She jerked against him, and he gripped her neck and forced her head to the side before licking from the hollow of her throat to her earlobe.

"What does it tell you?" she asked breathlessly.

"That you taste good," he whispered.

"Why do I get the feeling that the big bad wolf wants to eat me right up?" She laughed nervously.

He sucked on her earlobe. "Oh, he does, Willow. He wants to eat your sweet pussy until you're begging him for mercy. Until you've come so many times, you can't -"

The loud blaring of a car horn jerked them apart. The light had turned green, and as the horn blasted again, he waved in apology and stepped on the gas.

He didn't dare look at Willow. His wolf was begging to be free, begging for him to pull over the car and take the little human who so obviously wanted him to. He controlled it fiercely, breathing in shallow breaths to try to avoid the smell of her need.

"So, um, that got a little weird, yeah?" Willow said.

"I'm sorry," he said hoarsely. "That was incredibly inappropriate of me and I -"

"Don't worry about it," she said. "It was my fault anyway. I was the one who practically sat on your lap and forced you to sniff me."

He shook his head. "I want you to know that I understand how this must make me look, and I promise you, I'm not the employer who – who hits on his staff."

"I know," she said. "Listen, if you keep my actual age a secret, I'll keep your inappropriate licking a secret. Deal?"

He stole a glance at her. She acted calm, but he could still smell her excitement and see her flushed skin. If he wanted to, he could take her right now. She was wet and more than ready for him.

He growled and slammed his fist against the steering wheel.

"Hey, don't do that!" Alarm threaded through her voice, and she patted him on one broad shoulder. "Seriously, it's fine. I'm not going to sue you for harassment or anything like that."

He blew his breath out. He had licked Willow and, even worse, talked about eating her pussy. He didn't know what the hell he was thinking. He wasn't – that was the problem. His dick was doing all the thinking. Christ, he was in trouble. Willow said she would keep it quiet, but the girl never stopped talking. Kat and Bishop would find out, and he'd never live it down.

"Hey, Mal?" Willow's hand touched his tentatively, and he jerked it away.

"Yeah?" he said.

"I meant it when I said I wouldn't say anything. I know I talk a lot, but I can keep a secret, sometimes," she said.

"Yeah, I know. It won't happen again, I promise you."

"Right."

He was almost sure that was disappointment in her voice, but before he could consider that in too much depth, she was talking again. "So, tell me about Mrs. Belfry."

"She's sixty-seven and a multi-millionaire. She took

over the import company eight years ago when her second husband died."

"What do they import?"

"Clothing, mostly. Specifically – clothing for para-normals."

"You need your own type of clothing?" she asked.

"Sometimes. A bear shifter like Bishop has a tough time finding clothes that fit in normal stores, and many shifters are big into the tear-away clothing."

"Tear-away clothing?"

"Yes. The clothing is put together with small, nearly invisible strips of a new and more durable Velcro, rather than being stitched together. When a shifter changes to their animal form, the clothing isn't ruined."

"I never even thought of that. I just assumed that shifters took off their clothes before shifting."

"If they have any type of control, they do," he said.

She grinned. "Let me guess. You've never Hulked out and ruined a t-shirt. Is that right?"

"I have excellent control, Ms. Tanner."

"Oh please, Mal. Not five minutes ago, you were talking about eating my pussy. I think you can drop the Ms. Tanner thing, don't you?"

He blushed furiously, and she giggled like a mad woman. "I'm sorry." She giggled again. "Oh my God, the look on your face. I'm sorry."

"No, you're not." He frowned at her.

"I'm really not." She laughed. "Tell you what, you promise to call me Willow instead of Ms. Tanner, and I promise not to mention how badly you want to have a taste of my sweet girlie bits."

"Please stop talking about your girlie bits," he muttered.

"Do you promise to call me Willow?"

"Yes, dear God, yes!" he nearly shouted.

"Great! So, does Mrs. Belfry's company do well or was she a millionaire before?"

He blinked at the sudden change in topic and wiped away the sweat from his forehead before turning off the highway. "She comes from money, but the company is the reason she's a millionaire. The company was on the brink of bankruptcy for years, but when Mrs. Belfry took it over, she turned things around."

"Interesting. What else should I know about her?"

"Two years ago, she married her third husband, a jaguar shifter named Garrett Finnigan. He's younger than her by nearly sixteen years, but the rumour is that he does love her. She has two children from her first husband. They're lion shifters named Keegan and Koren."

"So, Mrs. Belfry is a lion shifter?"

He shook his head. "No, she's a lizard shifter."

"Really? Keegan and Koren are half-lion, half-lizard?"

"No. When two different species of shifters mate, their offspring only take on one of their species characteristics."

"Do they take on the more dominant one?" Willow asked.

"No. It's a fifty-fifty chance what species they'll be. Both her boys just happened to inherit their father's lion genes."

"That's so interesting," Willow mused. "What kind of shifter was her second husband?"

"Tiger."

"Wow. I'm not sure why you're so worried she won't like you. She loves pussy just as much as you do."

He growled fiercely at her while she snorted laughter and wiped at the tears starting in her eyes.

"I'm sorry. I won't mention pussy again. I promise, Mal."

"I don't believe you," he sighed.

"Cross my heart, hope to die. Pinky swear." She crossed her finger over her heart and held her pinky finger out to him.

He stared at it. "What?"

"Pinky swear." She wiggled her pinky at him, and he shook his head at her before returning his gaze to the road.

"You need to relax more, Mal. You won't live past fifty if you stay this wound up all the time. How old are you, by the way?"

"Thirty-two."

"Seriously?"

"Yes, why?" he asked.

"You act a lot older," she said.

He grunted in reply, breathing a sigh of relief when he turned into the driveway of the Belfry mansion.

CHAPTER 4

Willow watched as Mal knocked firmly on the front
door. Her heart thudded heavily in her chest, but
it wasn't nerves. When Mal had growled in her ear that he
wanted to eat her pussy, she had almost come in her pants.
His warm tongue and his breath on her heated skin was
one of the most erotic moments of her life.

She took a deep breath and forced herself to concentrate on the task at hand. Sure, she wanted Mal, and now it
was more than evident that he wanted her, but he was her
boss. Plus, the shifter liked routine and order – the guy
organized his pens in his pen jar for God's sake – and her
life was nothing but chaos and weirdness. Just the way she
liked it.

Still, she mused to herself, she wouldn't turn down the
chance to take him to her bed, even if it did break every
rule of the employee/employer relationship. Rules were
meant to be broken.

The door swung open, and a thin, balding man in a

tuxedo gave them a polite but distinctively nervous look. "Can I help you?"

"Yes, I'm Mr. Burke, and this is my associate Ms. Tanner. We have an appointment with Mrs. Belfry." Mal smiled at him, and the man's eyes widened a little. His nervousness was readily apparent, and Willow silently applauded him when his back straightened.

"Please follow me, Mr. Burke." He nodded stiffly, and they followed him down the wide hallway into the sitting room. It was stuffed with furniture, the wood gleaming in the bright sun flooding through the large windows. Willow sat gingerly on the old, fragile-looking couch as Mal settled into a navy wingback chair.

"Mrs. Belfry will be right with you." The man made another stiff nod, and Willow smiled at him.

"Thank you so much…." She raised her eyebrows at him, and he hesitated.

"Jeffries, ma'am," he finally replied.

"Thank you, Jeffries." She grinned again at him, and with a final anxious look at Mal, he exited the room.

As soon as he left, she dissolved into giggles. "Jeffries? She has a butler named Jeffries? That can't be real."

"Hush," Mal said. "Someone's going to hear you."

"Right, sorry. Hey, why was he so nervous around you?"

"He's a chicken shifter. They're always nervous around my kind."

Her mouth dropped open, and she stared wide-eyed at him. "You're kidding me."

"What?"

"There are not chicken shifters."

"Of course, there are," he said. "You know, for

someone who professes to love the paranormal stuff, you don't know a lot about us."

"That's true," she said. "But in my defense, I lead a very strange life, and it doesn't leave a whole lot of time for Googling. It's partly why I wanted to take this job. I figured the best way to learn more about you was just to throw myself into the midst."

"Why are you so fascinated with us anyway? Most humans avoid us," he grumbled.

"That's not true. I know plenty of humans who interact with paranormals every day. Heck, more and more humans and paranormals are getting married and raising families."

"I thought you didn't know anything about us."

"I watch 'Entertainment Tonight'. Did you know they have a paranormal segment every show?"

"Yeah," he said. "Most of it is bullshit."

"I thought so. That's why I'm working with you so I can find out the real scoop. Although you're so uptight and private that it's difficult to figure you out."

"I'm not uptight." He scowled at her.

"Eh, the jury's still out on that one." She grinned at him.

"Why are you so interested in us?" he repeated.

"Are there really chicken shifters?"

"Yes," he said a bit impatiently. "There really are."

"Uh oh." She could feel her face paling.

"What's wrong?"

"I love chicken." She stared at him anxiously. "Now I'm wondering how many chickens I've eaten have actually been shifters."

He laughed. "Chicken shifters don't look like regular

chickens, Willow. Trust me – you haven't eaten a chicken shifter."

"That's a relief." She cocked her head at him. "How do they look different? Do they have giant teeth lining their beak or something?"

"No. They're just bigger and faster. They have a longer wingspan, and they fly very well."

"Neat." She eyed the doorway. "Do you think I could convince old Jeffries there to shift so I could see him?"

He snorted laughter. "No. They're notoriously shy."

"That's too bad. I'd like -"

A woman swept into the room, and Willow followed Mal's lead when he stood. The woman was tall and slender with bright yellow eyes and skin that looked tough and weathered with age. Her dark hair was pulled back into a severe bun, and she wore a long black dress with a high neckline. Willow pulled self-consciously at her short skirt as the woman eyed her appraisingly.

"Mrs. Belfry, I'm Malcolm Burke, and this is my associate Ms. Willow Tanner. It's nice to meet you."

Mal stepped forward and held his hand out as Mrs. Belfry gave him a withering look. "Where is Ms. Frost?"

"I'm afraid she had an out-of-town commitment. However, I can assure you that -"

She shook her head, and Willow wondered if it was her imagination or if Mrs. Belfry's long, thin tongue had flicked out delicately and tasted the air in front of Mal.

"I don't deal with wolf shifters, Mr. Burke. The agreement was that Ms. Frost would meet with me. I'll have Jeffries show you to the door."

Mal's face reddened as Mrs. Belfry turned and marched to the door. She pressed a button next to the doorframe as Mal stared frantically at Willow. She shot him a thumbs-up and rushed after the old woman.

"Mrs. Belfry?"

The woman turned and frowned at her. "Yes?"

"I'm so sorry that Ms. Frost isn't here. Her sister decided to get married on the spur of the moment, and Kat flew down for the wedding. She hated to miss this meeting, but you know how it is with family commitments. I know you're not fond of wolf shifters, and, frankly, I don't blame you." Willow smiled at her. "Just between you and me, Mr. Burke is a real challenge to work for."

A look of amusement flashed across Mrs. Belfry's face. "Is he?"

"Oh yes. Do you know he doesn't even believe in spirits? Who doesn't believe in spirits?" Willow said.

Mrs. Belfry blinked rapidly, Willow was certain that she had lower eyelids instead of upper, before glancing at Mal.

"Wolf shifters are the worst," she said. "They're so dull and uneducated."

Willow laughed. "Well, in Mr. Burke's defense, he is extremely bright."

"But dull?" Mrs. Belfry raised her eyebrow at her.

"He does have a well-organized pen jar. Sometimes I go in after he's left the office and rearrange them. Just to mess with him. It's good for him, you know?"

"Indeed. What did you say your name was again?" Mrs. Belfry asked.

"Willow. Willow Tanner."

"And how did you find yourself working with Mr. Burke? Wolf shifters don't care for humans."

"You're telling me. Honestly, I think it was Ms. Frost's

influence. I just find jaguar shifters to be so much more accommodating and open to the wilder side of life. Don't you?" Willow said.

"I'm married to one."

"Are you? Well, then you know exactly what I mean, Mrs. Belfry," Willow said.

"You may call me Marika." Mrs. Belfry said.

"And please, call me Willow." Willow shook the old woman's hand. Her skin was as rough as it looked and scraped across her palm like sandpaper.

Jeffries appeared in the doorway. "Yes, Mrs. Belfry?"

Marika stared appraisingly at Willow for a moment. "Bring our guests some tea, please, Jeffries. And some of the lemon Danishes."

"Of course, ma'am." Jeffries bowed slightly and disappeared down the hallway as Mrs. Belfry held her arm out to Willow.

"Come, we will sit together and hear what your wolf shifter has to say."

Willow took her arm and, as they walked toward the couch, gave Mal a smug grin and stuck her tongue out at him. He rolled his eyes, and her grin widened.

"YOUR SECURITY FIRM IS RATHER SMALL, MR. BURKE, and my company is large. How do you propose to provide an adequate service?"

"Our team of security is very good at what they do, ma'am. We only hire the best paranormals for the job. They all have a background in providing security, whether personal or corporate, and a few are ex-military.

Depending on your current need, we can always hire more employees to accommodate you."

As Mrs. Belfry considered his answer, Mal took a sip of the hot tea. He hated tea, it tasted like deer piss to him, but he forced himself to take another drink without grimacing. On the couch beside Mrs. Belfry, Willow licked her fingers clean of the sugary, sweet Danish she had just eaten. He looked away hurriedly. He needed to concentrate on the matter at hand, not on what it would be like to have Willow's mouth sucking his dick.

"Up until a month ago, our security issues were non-existent," Mrs. Belfry said slowly. "We had a night security guard for the entire warehouse, and that was more than adequate. However, over the last few weeks, we've had a few acts of vandalism that are rapidly growing worse."

"What have they done?" Willow asked.

"At first, it was small things. Some clothing was strewn about, a few windows broken, and the air let out of the tires on a few of our shipping trucks. We hired a second security guard, but over the last week or so, things have escalated in a very unpleasant manner."

She smoothed her dress with one rough hand. "Four nights ago, a truck with an entire shipment of clothing was set on fire. The security guards had just finished their rounds outside and swore they saw nothing. As well, the security cameras revealed no one. One moment the truck was as it should be, and the next, it was fully engulfed in flames. The following night, an entire room of clothing was slashed to pieces. And last night, one of the security guards was injured."

"How?" Mal set his tea on the side table and leaned forward.

"We're not entirely sure. The guard was doing his rounds inside the building and woke to find himself tied to a chair in the main office with his chest slashed in numerous places."

"How awful," Willow said with a genuine look of horror. "Did he survive?"

"Yes. He's a bear shifter, so the wounds are healing fairly quickly, all things considered."

"A bear shifter?" Mal frowned. "Someone overpowered a bear shifter?"

"Is that unusual?" Willow asked.

Mal nodded. "Bear shifters are incredibly strong and have a powerful sense of smell. Few shifters can harm them."

"Bentwell has no memory of the attack at all. As well, there were no signs of forced entry into the building. There is video surveillance covering every inch of our warehouse, yet nothing was revealed. We have footage of Bentwell doing his walk-through of the office, and then he's suddenly tied to a chair, unconscious with blood pouring out of him," Mrs. Belfry said.

"What did the police say?" Willow asked.

"We haven't gone to the police. This is a shifter matter, and we'd like to keep it that way."

"But," Willow frowned, "there are shifters in the police force. Aren't there?"

"Yes," Mrs. Belfry said, "but the chief of police is human, and I do not believe the rumour that he is in the senator's pocket to be only a rumour. My generation remembers well the trouble we had with humans."

She glanced at Mal. "As I'm sure your grandfather does."

"You know who my grandfather is?" Mal said.

"Of course. At the time, I found him both extraordinarily brave and dismayingly stupid. Does he have regret?"

"Yes."

Mrs. Belfry nodded. "I imagine he does. Terrible things were done to our kind those first few years. Still, we couldn't conceal ourselves forever, could we?"

"No, ma'am," Mal said.

"You have humans who work for you." Willow touched her arm. "I thought you liked them."

"There are good and bad humans, Willow. Surely you realize that? Do I look like the type of person who would judge someone based on the action of others?" Mrs. Belfry asked.

Willow stole a quick peek at Mal, and Mrs. Belfry laughed. "Wolf shifters are the exception. I've never met one who wasn't an arrogant ass."

She sighed and took a sip of her tea. "Our workers are afraid. Even during the day, strange occurrences are happening. Clothing is being moved or falling from the racks for no reason. Every dish in the kitchen was shattered one morning. Our employees heard the crashing and ran in to investigate. The dishes were all smashed to bits on the floor."

An odd look crossed Willow's face. "Did anyone see the dishes being smashed?"

Mrs. Belfry shook her head as Mal studied her thoughtfully. "Have you considered that it's someone working for the company, Mrs. Belfry?"

"Of course, we have," she snapped. "However, we're very thorough with our background checks, and besides, most of our employees have been with us for years. No one would stoop to this kind of destruction."

"Sometimes, people can surprise you."

She huffed angrily at him, and Willow said, "Maybe it's spirits."

Mal groaned inwardly as Mrs. Belfry said, "I'm sorry?"

"Spirits," Willow replied. "You know, ghosts. Not all spirits leave the earth, you see. Perhaps these are some that are trapped in our realm and are acting out."

Mal gritted his teeth and gave Mrs. Belfry a strained smile. "Forgive my associate, Mrs. Belfry. She has, from time to time, some odd ideas."

"Frankly, at this point, I'm willing to consider just about anything, Mr. Burke," Mrs. Belfry said.

"Well, I can assure you it isn't spirits," he glared at Willow, "but if you hire us, we'll not only keep your company and workers safe, but we'll discover who's behind the vandalism."

"Will you?" Mrs. Belfry said.

"We will."

There was a moment of silence, and then Mrs. Belfry clapped her hands together briskly. "You're hired, Mr. Burke."

"Thank you, Mrs. Belfry. I can assure you that -"

"Mother?" A tall man with shaggy blond hair and light blue eyes stuck his head into the room. "Keegan and I were just heading to the warehouse. Do you -"

He paused and raised his head, inhaling delicately before dropping his gaze to Willow. "Well, hello there. And who might you be?"

Ignoring Mal completely, he crossed the room and held out his hand as Willow stood. "I'm Willow Tanner."

"It's nice to meet you, Ms. Tanner. My name is Koren Belfry." He took her hand and raised it to his mouth, pressing his lips against her knuckles in a warm caress.

Unable to stop himself, Mal jumped out of his chair and crossed the room to stand behind the lion shifter. A growl escaped his throat, and Willow peeked over Koren's shoulder before tugging her hand free. "Mr. Belfry, this is Malcolm Burke."

"Call me Koren." The lion shifter smiled at Willow before turning and extending his hand. "It's nice to meet you, Mr. Burke."

Mal shook his hand as Mrs. Belfry stood. "I've just hired Mr. Burke's company to act as security at the warehouse."

Koren stared at her in surprise. "Really? A wolf shifter? How very progressive of you, Mother."

"Indeed. What were you saying earlier?" she asked.

"Keegan and I are heading over to the warehouse. Perhaps Mr. Burke and Ms. Tanner would like to join us for a tour?"

The old woman nodded. "That's a good idea. What do you say, Mr. Burke?"

"I can do that. However, I think Ms. Tanner should return to the office. It's -"

"Nonsense," Willow said. "I'd love to see the warehouse."

"Then it's settled," Koren said. "Why don't you travel in our vehicle, Ms. Tanner? Mr. Burke can follow us."

"Oh uh, sure," Willow said. "That sounds nice."

"It does sound nice." Koren grinned at her, revealing

white teeth, and Mal could see the fascination on Willow's face as a beard appeared on Koren's jaw. Mal growled again, the sound rumbling out of his chest.

Mrs. Belfry rapped Koren on the arm with her knuckles. "Behave yourself, please, Koren. You and your brother."

"Of course, Mother," Koren said. "We always do."

"I WANT YOU TO RETURN TO THE OFFICE, WILLOW."

Koren had disappeared to find his brother, and Mal used the opportunity to lead Willow outside. They stood next to his car, and he stared down at her. "I don't need you at the warehouse."

"I'd like to go," she said. "I have a feeling that if my suspicions are correct, I'll be very helpful."

"What do you mean?" he asked.

"It's kind of hard to explain, and, besides, you won't believe me anyway."

"Are you ready to go, Ms. Tanner?" Koren called. He stood just outside the doorway of the house, and Mal growled again when he heard Willow inhale sharply.

"Goodness. Those lion shifters are something else," she mumbled.

His brother had joined Koren, and she scanned Keegan up and down as Mal clenched his hands into tight fists. Keegan was even larger than his brother, his hair a dark gold instead of light blond, and he gave Willow the same hungry look that his brother did.

"Willow?" Mal said.

"What?" She continued to stare at the lion brothers.

"Stay away from the lion shifters. They're no good."

"What do you mean?"

"You don't want to get involved with them. Lion shifters are known for doing everything together. Including their women."

"Really? How deliciously kinky." She wiggled her eyebrows at him, and he bit back his howl of frustration. He thought telling her the brothers would want to share her would be enough to end her interest. Instead, it seemed to have piqued it, and he tamped down the hot jealousy flowing through him.

"Willow, it's not good to mix business with pleasure," he said. "This contract is important to the firm. If we lose it because -"

"Relax, wolf boy," she said airily. "I'm not going to boink the clients. Besides, my preferences run toward the canine fellows, not feline."

He tried not to let the relief he felt show on his face. For all he knew, Willow was just trying to appease him, and she'd be in the middle of a lion shifter sandwich by tonight. The thought filled him with wordless anger and an odd sense of possessiveness.

As she turned away, he took her arm and swung her back around to face him. She gave him a startled look as he yanked her against his hard body and cupped the back of her head.

"Mal, what -"

He tugged her head back and, without stopping to think about it, rubbed the rough stubble on his jaw across the left side of her throat and then the right. He straightened and released her arm, breathing harshly through his nose as she stared at him.

"Um, what was that about?" She touched the delicate skin on her throat. He hadn't been gentle, and her skin had reddened.

"Nothing," he said.

"Okay, then." She gave him a look that suggested he was crazy before walking away.

He clenched his hands into fists again as he watched the two lion shifters give her greedy looks. He restrained his howl of anger as she climbed into the truck with them.

CHAPTER 5

"Are you mating with your boss, Ms. Tanner?"

"Excuse me?" Willow stared at Keegan. She sat between the two brothers in the front cab of the truck. Keegan drove, and he grinned carelessly before turning his attention back to the road.

Koren laughed and nudged her gently. "Forgive my brother. He can be very blunt at times."

"I've noticed," Willow said.

"The thing is," Keegan turned left onto the highway and glanced at her again, "we like you, Willow – can I call you Willow? – but we're not interested in stepping on the wolf's toes."

"Are the little pussy-cats afraid of the Big Bad Wolf?" Willow grinned at him.

Both he and Koren laughed again. "Let's just say that it's never wise to be on the bad side of an angry wolf. Especially one as big as your Mr. Burke."

"I'll remember that," Willow said. "Why do you think

we're, uh, mating?" For no discernible reason, she blushed.

"Well, he marked you," Koren said.

"He what?" she asked.

"He marked you back at the house."

When she continued to stare blankly at him, he said, "Have you ever been with a wolf shifter before, Willow?"

"No," she admitted.

"A wolf shifter marks his mate, either with his scent or with his bite."

"His bite?" Her eyes widened, and Koren shrugged.

"It's not, like, a rip-you-open kind of bite. More like a love bite."

"Yeah, a bite that leaves a permanent scar." Keegan rolled his eyes. "Wolf shifters are so old school. It's ridiculous. Now lion shifters – they know what a woman wants and needs. They would never mark a woman just to keep other shifters away. They understand that she needs her freedom."

He gave her a sexy little grin, and Willow said, "I'm sure you do. Although I'm wondering how many women are into being tag-teamed by a couple of lion shifters."

Koren roared laughter. "Someone's been telling stories about us."

"Are you telling me that you don't both like to have a go at the girl together?" Willow asked.

Keegan shrugged. "We're not against it. Especially if that's what our woman wants. Is that what you want, Willow?"

"A girl never reveals her secrets, Mr. Belfry."

He chuckled and rested one big hand on her nylon-covered thigh. "Call me Keegan. Listen, we're not into commitment, let's get that out of the way right now, but if you're interested – we're definitely interested. Lions are well-known for their abilities in bed, by the way."

"How charming." She pushed his hand from her leg. "But can I point out that one - you're a client, and I never mix business with pleasure, and two – according to you, I've been marked by a wolf shifter."

"You certainly have." Koren leaned into her and sniffed delicately at her neck. "Really marked. I'm surprised he didn't bite you right there in the yard."

She touched her throat, feeling the slight tenderness that Mal's stubble had left on her skin.

"Normally," Koren continued, "wolf shifters only mark during mating. Unless, of course, they really want to warn other shifters away."

"So, are you telling me that now I smell like a wolf?" Willow asked.

"Well, you smell like Mr. Burke's wolf. Don't worry, though – only other shifters can smell it. You'll smell exactly like you always smell, to humans."

"Lovely," Willow said.

Koren leaned over and smelled her again. "Whew. He must have been really riled up to leave such a heavy mark."

She frowned at him. "Exactly how long am I going to smell like Mal?"

He shrugged. "At least a week or so."

"Fantastic," Willow said.

Keegan grinned at her. "Your boss must really want to fuck you, Willow."

"That's rude, Keegan."

He shrugged. "Doesn't make it any less true."

WILLOW COULD SEE THE ANGER ON MAL'S FACE WHEN HE joined them at the entrance to the warehouse. The lion brothers flanked her, and she didn't protest when Mal took her arm and drew her away. He kept her against his side as the brothers grinned.

"Ready for the tour?" Koren asked.

"We sure are." Willow smiled and tried to tug her arm from Mal's hard grip discreetly. He growled softly and tightened his hand on her arm before leading her into the warehouse.

"This is the front office area," Koren said as they entered a large reception area. The walls were a warm honey colour, and the floors were a rich, dark wood. It was decorated sparingly, but the high-quality reception desk and the art on the walls screamed money.

"Hello, Layla."

"Good morning, Mr. Belfry," the receptionist said. She was a young woman with blonde hair and dark brown eyes, and she glanced at Willow before smiling warmly at Mal.

Jealousy shot through Willow, and she snorted inwardly. She was being ridiculous.

"Layla, this is Malcolm Burke and Willow Tanner. Mr. Burke owns the new security company we've hired."

"It's so nice to meet you!" Layla stepped around the desk, and Willow felt another surge of jealousy. The woman was gorgeous, long-limbed and stacked on top, and Willow was suddenly too aware of her small breasts.

Layla shook Mal's hand. "I feel safer already, knowing that a wolf shifter will be providing security." She spoke in a soft purr, and Willow instinctively knew that she was some kind of cat shifter.

Burying her jealousy and irritation, Willow stepped forward and held out her hand. "Hello, Layla!"

"Oh, hi." Layla tore her gaze from Mal's face and shook Willow's hand. "It's nice to -"

She stopped and inhaled deeply, staring hard at Willow before a look of disappointment crossed her face. "It's nice to meet you, Ms. Tanner."

"Please, call me Willow." Willow couldn't stop the smug smile from crossing her face. Mal marking her might mean other shifters would stay away from her, but it seemed it worked the same way for him.

Mal had dropped her arm to shake Layla's hand, and Willow curled her hand into the crook of his arm and leaned against him with an easy familiarity. He gave her a startled look as Layla returned to her desk.

"Mother's office is to the left, and my office is to the right." Koren led them down a short hallway to a door marked 'warehouse personnel only', and he used a card key to open the door. "Keegan runs the warehouse, and his office is in the actual warehouse."

"What is it that you do for the company, Koren?" Willow asked.

"Oh, a little of this, a little of that. Whatever needs to be done, really." He winked at her, and Mal snarled under his breath as the brothers led them into the warehouse.

"So, what do you think, Mr. Burke? Will your company be able to provide the security we need?" Keegan asked.

It was half an hour later, and they had ended up in the staff kitchen after finishing the warehouse tour. Willow stood a little apart from them, trailing one hand along the cement wall as she stared up at the ceiling.

Mal nodded. "Yes, more than capable. Based on the trouble you've been having, we'll start with a team of five. Once we find out who's doing the vandalism and stop them, we'll lower the number to two."

He pulled out his phone and made a quick note. "We can have the five-person team in the warehouse by tomorrow night. We'll need to set them up with key cards, obviously, and I'll email you their background checks and credentials when I return to the office. Do you have -"

"Willow?" Koren said. "Where are you going?"

Without answering, Willow darted out of the kitchen. Staring curiously at each other, the three shifters followed her.

"Do you feel that?" Keegan frowned at Koren, and his brother nodded.

There was an odd chill in the air, and Mal grunted with surprise when he could see his breath.

"What the hell?" Koren asked.

"Wait! Please, wait!" Willow said in a frantic soft voice as she nearly ran into the main area of the warehouse. She disappeared down an aisle, and Mal hurried after her with strange anxiety in his chest. He strode into the aisle and skidded to a stop. The lion shifters were close behind him, and he grunted in irritation when they ran into his back.

"Please don't hide," Willow said. She stood in the middle of the aisle and stared at the shelving to her left. "I want to help you, I promise."

Mal moved behind her. The air was bitterly cold, and he put his arm around Willow. Her body shook from the cold, and he drew her back against his chest. "What's going on, Willow?"

"Shh," she said before staring at empty space again. "It's okay. My name is Willow, and this is Mal, and neither of us will hurt you. Why don't you tell me why you're here?"

A whispering, sighing moan made the hair on the back of his neck stand up, and a shiver went down his spine.

"That's right. Come out," Willow said. Her gaze switched to the middle of the aisle, and she held her hands up in a soothing motion. "Tell me your name, sweetheart."

There was another whispering moan that he felt more than heard, and a growl escaped his throat when something ice-cold flew by him. Willow twisted out of his grip and stared behind him.

"Wait! Don't go!" she called. "Why are you -"

She gasped when a towering stack of clothing on the top shelf suddenly tipped over and landed on the two lion brothers. They both growled in surprise, and identical beards grew on their faces as the weight of the clothing dropped them to their knees.

"No, stop!" Willow cried. She started to run down the aisle, and Mal grabbed her arm and yanked her behind him. He had no idea what was happening, but his wolf was howling at him to protect Willow. He ignored her frustrated scent and kept her firmly behind his back.

"Who's there?" he shouted.

There was nothing but silence as the brothers struggled to their feet.

"What the hell just happened?" Keegan said.

"Mal, let me go." Willow still struggled behind him, and he yelped when she bit him on the back. He dropped her arm, and she darted around him and ran toward the brothers. She ducked past them and scanned the ceiling frantically before sighing. "She's gone."

"Who?" Koren asked.

"I don't know. She wouldn't tell me her name."

Koren and Keegan glanced at Mal. He could see the question in their eyes, and he smiled grimly. "Please forgive Ms. Tanner. It's been a long day."

Willow scowled at him and turned to the brothers. "She was petite with dark brown hair and hazel eyes. She wore a pink blouse and blue jeans. Do either of you know her?"

The brothers glanced at each other uneasily, and Willow studied them. "Do you know her?"

"No," Koren said.

Willow continued to stare at them. "I don't believe you."

"Willow!" Mal said. She ignored his pointed look.

"I think you know her. Tell me her name," she said.

"Know who?" Keegan said in exasperation. "There was no one there, Willow."

"There was," Willow insisted. "I can see spirits, ghosts if you want, who haven't left our realm. Something has happened, something that's angered or upset her so badly that she can't let go. If you can tell me what it is, I can help her. Once she's free, she'll stop causing trouble in the warehouse."

"You're nuts, right?" Koren turned to Mal. "She's nuts, yeah?"

Mal didn't reply. He stalked past the brothers and gripped Willow's arm. "We need to return to the office. I'll send you the information for the security team by email and call you tomorrow."

Without another word, he dragged Willow from the warehouse.

"WHAT WERE YOU THINKING, WILLOW?" MAL SAID. They'd been driving in silence for nearly twenty minutes, and she stared stonily at him before turning to stare out the window again. "Answer me, please. You came very close to costing us the contract back there."

She sighed. "I can see ghosts, Mal. I've been seeing them since I was two years old. They come to me for help."

"They come to you for help," Mal repeated slowly.

She nodded. "Yes. Like in that movie with that little kid who saw dead people. Do you remember it?"

He nodded in acknowledgement, and she toyed with the edge of her skirt. "I see dead people. And just like in that movie, all they want is some help to move on. Something has gone wrong, they need something changed or fixed, and I help them do that."

"There are no such things as ghosts," he said.

She scowled at him. "You felt her presence back in the warehouse, Mal. Don't try to tell me you didn't."

"I felt something," he muttered.

"Have you ever been walking along on a beautiful

warm day, and you hit a patch of air that feels like it's been doused in ice water?" she asked.

He looked at her cautiously, and she nodded. "That's a spirit, Mal. They're everywhere. Most humans and para-normals can't see them, but I can. They're so lost and so frightened, it hurts my heart to see them sometimes."

"Let's say that I believe you. Let's say that there are ghosts just walking around, waiting to bump into you and have you save them. What about the nasty ones? The serial killers and the rapists and the murderers. What happens when you run into one of those poor lost souls? Huh, Willow? If it was a ghost back there, she managed to somehow drop an entire stack of clothing onto the lion brothers. What happens if the next ghost you meet decides to drop a – a tree on your head?"

She burst into giggles. "A tree? Why on earth would they drop a tree on my head?"

He stared impatiently at her. "You know what I mean, Willow."

"I've never met a mean or harmful spirit yet. If they're acting out, like the girl was today in the warehouse, then it's because they're agitated. Once I find out what it is that's upsetting them and fix it, they move on."

"Move on to where?"

"Heaven, I guess," Willow said. "And those lion shifters know more than they're admitting. They knew who I was talking about when I described the girl to them. We need to find out what they're hiding."

Mal sighed in frustration. "If - and I'm not saying it is - but if it is a ghost that's in that warehouse, then she's a hell of a lot more upset than any other ghost you've met. She carved up a bear shifter's chest, remember?"

Willow frowned. "That is kind of weird."

"Kind of weird? Kind of weird?" Mal thought his head would explode. "This – this ghost of yours has serious anger issues, and you're not going back to that warehouse."

"I have to!" Willow glared at him. "I'm the only one who can help her. If it is her doing those violent things, then I need to stop her before it gets worse."

"No, Willow. You're not going back there," he said.

She scowled. "Just because you marked me doesn't mean you can tell me what to do."

He stared at her in embarrassment. "I don't know what you're talking about."

"Bullshit, Mal! The lion brothers told me all about you wolf shifters and your marking. They said I stunk to high heaven of your wolf. What the hell did you mark me for anyway?"

He blushed furiously. "Because those damn lion shifters were looking at you like they were going to devour you, Willow! You have no idea what lion shifters are like, and I had to do something to keep them away from you."

"So, you rubbed your scent all over me? Couldn't you have just, I don't know, punched them like a normal man?"

"I'm not a man. I'm a wolf shifter," he pointed out.

She sighed and seemed to deflate against the seat. "Yeah, I know."

"I'm sorry, Willow. I shouldn't have marked you like that. Again, it was inappropriate of me, and I have no excuse for my behaviour. Your, uh, love life is none of my business."

"It isn't," she agreed. Her hand rubbed lightly at the faint redness on her throat. "I suppose I should just be happy that you wolf shifters don't mark a girl by peeing on them."

"That's disgusting, Willow!"

She shrugged. "I'm just saying – there are probably shifters out there who do mark their territory by peeing on it."

"You're not my territory." He frowned at her. "You're free to do what you want, when you want, with whomever you want, remember?"

"Except for the fact that any shifter who gets close to me for the next week is going to smell Eau-de-Mal and beat a hasty retreat."

He swallowed. "Yeah, but, uh, humans can't tell."

"Well, thank God my sex partner is human." She clapped her hand to her heart dramatically.

His wolf made an undignified whine, and Mal stared anxiously at her. "Who are you sleeping with?"

"That is so not any of your business, Mal."

"It's my business if it keeps you from doing your job."

"Keeps me from doing my job? Since when did sex ever keep someone from doing their job?"

"Just tell me who the human is that you're sleeping with!" he shouted.

"Oh, for Pete's sake! No one. I'm not sleeping with anyone. Does that make you feel better, wolf boy?"

"Yes, it does," he said primly, and she burst out laughing.

He gave her a small grin, and she shook her head before staring out the window. "Sooner or later, you'll have to admit that you want to fuck me. You know that, right?"

"I don't have sex with humans," he said.

"Why not?" she asked.

"Human women are too fragile. You, especially. You wouldn't be able to handle me."

She turned and gave him a slow seductive smile that made his cock harden. "You'd be surprised at what I can handle, Malcolm Burke."

He stared out the windshield, his pulse pounding and lust coursing through his veins.

"I don't have sex with humans," he muttered again before turning on the radio and blasting the music.

CHAPTER 6

"Hey, how'd it go? Did we get the contract?" Bishop was standing in the reception area when they returned.

"We did. Thanks to Willow," Mal said.

The bear shifter's face lit up in a huge grin. "That's great. Way to go, Willow!" He raised his fist, and she bumped it with her own.

"No problem, Bishop."

"So, what are the details? Are we -"

Bishop stopped and stared at Willow for a long moment before leaning down and inhaling.

"Oh, shit." He turned and glared at Mal. "Kat's going to kill you, Mal. She told you not to sleep with Willow. What the hell? Did you just pull the car over and bang her on the way to the client's?"

"I didn't sleep with her!" Mal said. He could feel his face reddening yet again.

"Like hell, you didn't! Your damn scent is all over her." Bishop growled.

65

"He didn't," Willow said. "He didn't, Bishop."

He turned to face her with a confused look on his face. "Willow, his scent -"

"All he did was mark me to keep a couple of randy lion shifters from tag-teaming my vagina," she said. "I can assure you there was absolutely no boss/receptionist coitus. Although there was some licking."

She turned and disappeared into their small kitchen as Bishop's mouth dropped open. He gawked at Mal. "Did she just say 'tag-teaming my vagina'?"

"Yeah." Mal strode into his office and slammed the door shut.

"HI, WILLOW." AVA STUCK HER HEAD INTO THE OFFICE and glanced around. "Where's, uh, Bishop?"

"He's in the conference room with a client. No need to worry about random sniffing attacks," Willow said.

It was three days later, and she still hadn't convinced Mal to let her return to the warehouse. She had poked and probed and questioned him about the warehouse until he had admitted that there were no weird activities in the two days and nights that their team had been watching the warehouse.

"There's no need for you to go, Willow. We have it under control," he'd finally snapped at her before ordering her from his office.

Ava leaned against the reception desk. She still wore her scrubs, and dark circles were under her eyes.

"You okay, sweetie?" Willow asked.

She nodded and rubbed at the back of her neck. "Just

tired. I did a double shift at the hospital. I'll be better once I get some sleep and get rid of this damn cold."

Willow reached out and patted her hand. "You work too hard, honey. You know you're not the only nurse in the ER, right? They can find someone else to work overtime."

"I know, but I love it."

"I know you do." Willow smiled at her.

"Why is it so warm in here?" Ava fanned herself with her scrub top.

"The stupid air conditioning is on the fritz. I've got a call into maintenance, but who knows when they'll show up," Willow said.

Ava glanced at the closed door of the conference room. "Are you ready to go for lunch?"

"Yes. Just give me a minute."

The door to the conference room opened, and a short man with rat-like features and a nervous demeanor came bouncing out.

"Thank you so much, Mr. King!" he squeaked. "My wife and I can finally sleep at night again."

"You're welcome." Bishop joined him in the reception area.

Willow studied Ava. Her best friend looked like she couldn't decide if she should run away or stay frozen to the spot.

The bear shifter shook the rat-like man's hand. "Anytime you need us, just call. We're happy to -"

He stopped, lifting his head and sniffing the air before his eyes widened, and he turned toward the reception desk. He stared unblinkingly at Ava, and she smiled weakly at him. "Hello again."

Without replying, he backed into the conference room.

"Thanks, Mr. Tilton!" Willow hurried around the reception desk and guided him toward the front door. "If you need us, just call. Okay?"

"I – okay." Looking a little confused, Mr. Tilton left the office, and Willow shut the door behind him.

Ava stood at the desk with her body trembling lightly. Willow smiled at her. "We should probably go."

"What?" Ava continued to stare at the doorway to the conference room.

"I said we should probably go for lunch. Unless there was something you wanted to ask Bishop?"

"Uh, no. Of course not." Ava fumbled for her purse and then gasped at the loud bang from the conference room.

"What the hell?" Willow ran to the room as Ava stumbled after her.

"Bishop? What happened?" Willow said.

"Nothing. Just, uh, accidentally broke a chair, uh, accidentally." His back to them, Bishop held one of the conference chairs in his massive hands. The chair was broken in half, and he clutched the pieces tightly as Ava peeked over Willow's shoulder.

Bishop's back stiffened, and he said, "It's fine. Go for lunch, Willow."

"Are you sure? I can help clean up if you want."

"No," he said in a loud and panic-tinged voice. "I can do it. Enjoy your lunch."

"Okay. See you in an hour, Bishop." Willow grabbed Ava's hand, and the two women quickly left the office.

"DAMMIT, WILLOW! DID YOU EVEN CALL MAINTENANCE?" Mal walked into the reception area. His t-shirt was damp and sticking to his body, and she tried to ignore the way it clung to his abdomen muscles as he glared down at her.

"Yes, I called them. And no, I don't know when they're going to show up," she said.

The heat in the office was horrendous, and in desperation, she'd stripped off her shirt and wore just her bra and camisole. It was inappropriate for the office, but she was past the point of caring. Besides, it was nearly quitting time, and no clients were scheduled to come in.

She sighed with irritation as she stared at her computer. It'd been acting up all afternoon, and after the damn thing had crashed for the seventh time, she was about ready to throw it out the window.

"Where's Bishop?" Mal barked.

"He left. He couldn't take the heat any longer," she said.

She groaned as the blue screen of death appeared on her computer and slammed her hand on the desk in frustration. "Have you guys thought about upgrading your damn computer system? It's impossible to get anything done!"

MAL STARED CAUTIOUSLY AT WILLOW. HE'D NEVER SEEN her like this - grumpy and looking like she was ready to tear off his head - and he wasn't quite sure what to do. "Is your computer not working?"

She smacked her desk again. "Obviously. Do you know how much time I've wasted this afternoon trying to work around it?"

"Here, let me take a look at it," he said.

She boosted herself onto the desk beside him as he sat down in the chair before crossing her legs and sighing. "I'm sorry, Mal. I didn't mean to snap. I just – I hate the heat."

"Why don't you head home? It's almost quitting time, and I can handle any calls that come in," he suggested.

She shook her head. "No, I'll stay. It's fine."

He gritted his teeth. She was very close to him, so close he could feel her body heat. He could barely concentrate on the computer in front of him. He had deliberately kept his distance from her for the last three days, and being so close to her now was wearing down his defenses. His scent still clung to her, and his wolf stirred within him. It wanted him to finish the job of marking her. It wanted him to take her hard and rough until she screamed with pleasure, and Mal was tired of denying his wolf.

He groaned to himself when she shifted on the desk. She re-crossed her legs. The delicate sound of her nylons rubbing together made his cock harden, and the faint scent of her pussy drifted to him. She smelled delicious, and he flattened his hands on the desk, afraid that if he didn't, he would reach for her.

"Mal? What's wrong?"

"Nothing," he gritted out.

"There's something wrong. Look at me, please," she said.

He raised his gaze to her, and her lips parted as she gasped. He knew what he looked like, knew that his eyes glowed a bright green and that his usual stubble had thickened to a dark beard, but he was helpless to stop it.

"Mal?" she whispered. He watched the answering call

of lust in her own eyes as she picked up on his want and his need, and he swallowed heavily.

"I want to taste you, Willow," he said.

"I want that too," she breathed.

His wolf howled with mad delight when she deliberately uncrossed her legs and spread her thighs on the smooth desk. He made a low moaning noise of need, and she reached out and traced his cheek with one slender finger. "Please, Mal."

He slipped to his knees on the floor in front of her and gripped the bottom of her skirt. He tugged it upward as she braced her hands on the desk and lifted her hips. He growled with delight at the sight of her thigh-highs and smoothed his hand over the top of them before reaching for her lace panties. She lifted herself again, and he made himself remove the scrap of fabric with infinite care. He pulled them down her legs and dropped them to the floor before placing a soft kiss on her knee.

"Your skin is so soft," he said.

She licked her lips and widened her thighs. "Taste me."

"Yes," he agreed. "Yes."

He pulled her forward and buried his face between her thighs. She moaned, her hand cupping and pulling at his short hair as he licked the swollen, wet lips of her pussy.

"You taste delicious," he growled.

"Ohhh…" She moaned again as he stroked the edge of her nylons with his warm, hard hands, then shoved her thighs wide apart.

"Mine," he muttered before sliding his tongue between the lips of her pussy and sweeping it across her clit.

Willow cried out and arched her pelvis into Mal's face. She could hardly wrap her head around what was happening. It was like a switch had flipped in his head. When he stared at her, his eyes glowing brightly with pure primal need, her body had responded immediately. Her core had gushed liquid, and she was instantly overcome with the same hard, sweet bite of lust that had overtaken Mal.

He growled softly, and she gasped as the sound vibrated against her sensitive skin. His hot, wet tongue was licking and darting and tasting, and she was already on the verge of an orgasm. She pushed his face deeper into her and tightened her thighs around his head as her nipples hardened and a warm tingling began in her lower body.

"Oh God," she whispered. "Mal, I'm going to -"

She moaned with dismay when her breath puffed out like grey mist in front of her. The room was icy cold, and she wanted to scream with frustration when she turned her head and saw the old man standing next to her.

"You seriously need to work on your timing," she groaned.

Mal lifted his head and frowned up at her. "Willow, what's wrong?"

He froze when he realized he could see his breath. "Shit. Not again."

"Now?" Willow shook her head in disbelief. "Now you want to tell me your story? You can see I'm kind of busy here, right?"

She shoved her skirt down as Mal rose to his feet and stared into the empty space.

"Fine," Willow said. "I'm listening."

"Willow -"

She pressed her hand against his and gave her head a quick shake. "I'm sorry, Mal. Just – can you be quiet for a minute?"

He nodded and leaned against the desk, watching in silent amazement as she had a conversation with thin air.

CHAPTER 7

"So, you're telling me that this Rich guy was -"

"Mitch. His name is Mitch, not Rich," Willow said patiently.

Mal paced back and forth in the reception area. "Mitch, Rich – whatever. This old man was murdered for his secret stash of money."

"No, he was just murdered. I think. That part's a little confusing."

"But before he was murdered, he hid his secret stash of money, and now he wants you to tell his wife where it is."

"Exactly!" Willow said breezily. "Easy-peasy!"

"It is not *easy-peasy*, Willow," he said.

"Of course, it is. Mitch told me where he lives, and I'll simply go to his wife and give her the message he gave me."

"The guy was murdered, Willow. What if the people who murdered him killed him for his money and are now watching his house? What if they find out that you know where the money is?"

"But I don't know where the money is," she said. "Mitch wouldn't tell me."

"So, he wants you to help him, but he doesn't trust you enough to tell you where the money is."

"You can't blame him. He doesn't know me from a hole in the ground, does he?" She shrugged.

This time he was sure his head was going to explode. "Then how are you going to tell Mitch's wife where the money is?"

She smiled at him. "Mitch said to tell her the money was where they first fell in love. He said she would know what that meant. Isn't that so romantic?"

He gripped the reception desk. "Does Mitch know who murdered him?"

Her face darkened. "No. The dirty bastard snuck up behind him. Who murders a sweet old man? That's what I want to know."

"You don't know that he's sweet. For all you know, his secret stash of money is from selling drugs." Mal scowled at her.

She laughed and patted him on the hand. "Oh, Mal. You're so cute. Mitch is nice. I can tell. He wasn't a drug dealer or a bad man, okay? Don't worry. I do stuff like this all the time, and it'll be just fine."

"Willow, promise me you won't go to see that woman until I've looked into this. Just give me a couple of days to look into this guy's murder and -"

She shook her head. "Nope. I can't do that, Mal. Poor Mitch is trapped in our realm until I give his wife the message, and she finds the money. Do you have any idea what it must be like to be trapped on earth when you should be playing the harp in Heaven?"

"Willow..." He stared at her in exasperation as she gathered her purse and headed for the door. "Just don't go tonight, okay?"

She nodded. "Fine. I won't go tonight."

"And don't go by yourself!" he said as she opened the door to the office.

"Oh, for the love of Pete! I do this stuff all the time, Mal," she repeated. "I'll be fine."

"I'll go with you."

She shook her head. "No way. It'll be hard enough to convince the poor woman that I have a message from her dead husband without your disbelieving aura clouding up the room."

"My aura?" He sighed. "Willow, do not go by yourself to this woman's house."

"Fine. I'll take Ava with me."

"Ava isn't going to be able to help you if -"

"Enough, Mal! Honestly!" she suddenly snapped. "It's been a long, hot day, and I'm tired, and I want to go home. So, unless you want to finish what we started before good old Mitch interrupted us, I'm leaving."

His nostrils flared at the memory of her taste and the sound of her soft moans. "Willow, what we started wasn't a good idea. I'm sorry."

She sighed. "Surprise, surprise. You're a tease, Malcolm Burke. A terrible, horrible tease, but I'll be damned if I can resist your fine ass. Have a great weekend. I'll see you on Monday."

She blew him a kiss and disappeared into the hallway, shutting the door behind her.

"Explain to me again why I'm spending my Saturday afternoon following our receptionist?" Bishop asked grumpily.

He was crammed into Mal's small car, and he pulled irritably at the seat belt that cut into his chest.

"I told you, Bishop. Willow is in way over her head with this 'I can see ghosts' thing, and she's going to get hurt." Mal scanned the road in front of him. Willow's car was a few cars ahead of them, and he flicked on his signal light when she turned right.

"You don't honestly believe that she can see ghosts, do you?" Bishop frowned.

Mal shrugged. "I don't know. Yesterday in the office, there was something there with us, and Willow certainly believes it so...."

"Why didn't you just go with her then?"

"I told you – she won't let me. She says my disbelieving aura will make it harder to convince the old woman."

"We don't even know that she's going to see her. We've spent the last hour following her to the bank, the grocery store, and the drug store," Bishop grumped. "I could be at home watching football."

Mal didn't reply. Willow had pulled up in front of a large grey apartment building, and he parked a few car lengths away and peered out the windshield. Willow didn't exit her car, and after a few minutes, the door to the apartment building opened. Ava, wearing jeans and a light green t-shirt that hugged her large breasts, came hurrying out.

Beside him, Bishop inhaled sharply before clapping his hand over his nose. "Uh-uh. No way, Mal.

I'm done. You didn't tell me she was going to be here."

Mal quickly pulled into the street as Ava climbed into the car, and Willow drove away. "That's because I knew you wouldn't come with me if I did."

"Asshole," Bishop said.

Mal glanced at him. "You don't have to cover your nose, Bishop. I know you've got one hell of a sense of smell, but I'm pretty sure that you can't smell her with the windows rolled up."

Bishop lowered his hand before sniffing the air gingerly. "Drop me off, Mal."

"No. What is up with you and this woman, anyway?"

"Nothing."

"Bullshit. You can barely control yourself around her."

"You're one to talk. I've never seen you get this worked up over a woman before, let alone a human woman," Bishop said.

"This isn't about me. This is about you and Ava," Mal said.

Bishop sighed. "I don't know, okay? She … her scent is intoxicating."

"What does she smell like to you?" Mal asked.

"Nothing special - just all of my favourite things."

"So, chocolate and sex, then?"

"Pretty much," Bishop said morosely.

"I KNOW THIS IS HARD TO UNDERSTAND, ELISE, BUT PLEASE believe me that I really did see Mitch. He wants you to have the money. He's worried about you because he let his life insurance lapse, and he's afraid you'll lose your home. Until he knows that you'll be okay, he can't leave our realm." Willow reached out and took the old and frail-looking woman's hand gently. "I know it's a lot to take in."

The old woman stared at the floor before glancing at Willow. Tears shone in her eyes, and she blinked them back rapidly. "You really did see my Mitchell?"

"I did."

"But Mitch and I didn't have that kind of money. There's no way he had a hundred and fifty thousand dollars. He was murdered because he was in the wrong place at the wrong time, not because of our wealth."

Willow squeezed her hand. "Mitch said to tell you that he's sorry he kept the money from you. He didn't say anything because he won it at the track a few weeks earlier, and he knew how much you disliked his gambling."

"Oh, Mitch," Elise sighed shakily and wiped at the tears. "He was a good man, Ms. Tanner. He really was."

"I know he was." Willow glanced at Ava. "He said to tell you that he hid the money in the place you first fell in love. Do you remember where that is?"

"Of course, I do," Elise said. "It's back at my parents' old farmhouse just off Route Twelve. Mitch told me he loved me and proposed to me under the apple tree in the backyard."

"That's so beautiful." Willow smiled at her.

"Thank you." Elise struggled to her feet, gripping her cane firmly, and Willow stared at Ava in alarm when the old woman swayed on her feet.

"Elise? Are you okay?" Ava hurried forward as Willow stood and steadied Elise.

"Are you having pain anywhere? Do you feel weak or lightheaded?" Ava's fingers searched for her pulse, and the woman shook her head.

"No, no. I feel fine." She smiled weakly at her. "I just – I need to get out to that farmhouse, but it's so difficult for me right now. I'm not very mobile." She gestured to her cane.

"Elise, if you tell us where the farmhouse is, we'll go out there and find the money for you," Willow said.

"Really? You would do that for an old woman?" Elise said.

"Of course. I want to help Mitch cross, and I want to help you as well," Willow said.

"I – well, if you're sure you don't mind," Elise said.

"I don't mind at all. Give me the address, and we'll be back in less than an hour," Willow said.

"Thank you, my dear. You're so kind to help me." Elise patted her cheek. "Let me get a pen and paper."

ELISE WAVED TO WILLOW AND AVA AND CLOSED THE front door. She leaned against it for a moment before turning and peering down the hallway. "You can come out now."

The two men popped out of the kitchen and stared at her. "Do you believe her, Aunt Elise?"

Elise scowled. "How the fuck should I know? But if that rat bastard did hide a bunch of money at that farmhouse, I want it."

"We want our cut." The smaller of the men, he was

dark-haired with multiple tattoos across his meaty fore-arms, said immediately.

"Yes, yes, I know," Elise said.

"Don't give me that look, Aunt Elise." He scowled at her. "We did your dirty work, we killed Uncle Mitch so you could get his life insurance, and we were promised a cut of it."

"Is it my fault the idiot didn't pay our premiums?" Elise snarled.

"You could have checked before we killed him."

"Shut the hell up. I want you to follow that stupid bimbo to the farmhouse. If she finds the money, take it from her, and get rid of her and her friend."

The taller man was fair-headed and had a large round hoop pierced through the middle of his lower lip. He gave her a sullen look. "You want us to kill more people, we're going to need a bigger cut."

"No one fucks you over like family," Elise said. "Just get out there and see what she finds, Dwight."

"Why the hell didn't you just tell her thank you and show her the goddamn door?" Dwight glared at her. "What possessed you to tell her where the money was?"

"Are you that fucking stupid?" Elise snarled. "Do you think that Mitch's ghost is talking to her? The woman is a nutcase, but obviously, she knew Mitch somehow."

"That's why you shouldn't have told her where it was!" Dwight shouted.

"What if she knows that we killed him? Did you ever think of that? What if she's waiting for me to take the money, and then she's talking to the cops, telling them that I had my nephews kill my husband for the hundred and fifty grand? The farmhouse is out in the middle of nowhere, and it's been abandoned for years. You can kill the two girls and dump their bodies in the woods if the money is there. It'll be months before anyone finds them."

"This is a ridiculous plan. There's no way that bitch knows anything," the dark-haired man said. "You've gone fucking crazy, Aunt Elise.

Elise slapped him viciously across the face. "You shut the hell up, Billy, and do what I fucking tell you! Now get out there and bring me my money!"

"THAT BLUE CAR AHEAD OF US. THEY'RE FOLLOWING Willow and Ava as well," Bishop said in a low voice.

"Yeah, I know," Mal said.

"Where the hell are they going?" Bishop asked.

"I have no idea," Mal said. They had driven through the city and were rapidly approaching its edge.

"This doesn't feel right to me, Mal."

"Me either." Mal looked at Bishop. "Something is -"

"Look out!" Bishop shouted.

Mal cursed and slammed on the brakes. A large delivery truck had backed out of an alley right in front of them. They were mere inches from the truck, and the driver flipped him the bird before slowly backing up.

"Fuck! Get out of my way!" Mal shouted uselessly. The driver ignored him, and Mal clenched his hands on the steering wheel and waited anxiously as the driver took his sweet time backing up before driving away. He searched the street ahead of them, but both cars were gone.

"Where the hell did they go?" he asked.

Bishop rolled down his window and stuck his head out.

He repeatedly inhaled before pointing to a street on their left. "Go that way."

"You can smell Ava?" Mal asked.

"Yes." Bishop nodded. "We got lucky – she has her window rolled down."

"Are you sure?"

"I'm sure. Go quickly, Mal. Her scent is fading fast," Bishop said impatiently.

CHAPTER 8

"Is this the right place?" Ava peered at the decrepit old farmhouse as Willow shut off the car.

"It must be," Willow said. "It's the only farmhouse out here."

The two women stepped out of the car, and Ava shivered. "It's creepy out here, Willow."

They were in the middle of nowhere. The farmhouse loomed in front of them, the front porch sagging, and the windows boarded up. To their left was an equally weary-looking barn. It was once a bright red, but the paint had peeled and faded to a soft greyish pink.

"No, it isn't. Come on – let's check out the backyard."

Holding hands, they waded through the weeds past the farmhouse, and Willow peered into the yard. "Look! There's the apple tree!"

She grinned delightedly at Ava, and the two women hurried over to the tree. Willow scanned the tree and the ground before giving a soft squeal of happiness. "The ground here has been disturbed." She kicked at the dirt. "I bet this is where he buried the money."

She squatted and scraped at some loose dirt with her hands before hesitating and glancing at the barn. "I'm going to look for a shovel in the barn. I'll be right back."

"Willow, I -"

"I'll be right back, Ava. Don't worry." Willow pinched her cheek lightly and hurried off to the barn. She pulled the door open, making the hinges squeal. She disappeared into the building.

Ava crossed her arms over her chest. She was anxious and unsettled but didn't know why. She glanced at the apple tree, a small smile crossing her face before she walked forward and ran her hand over the carving nearly hidden beneath one of its large branches. A heart was carved into the bark with the words "Mitch + Elise" in its center, and she traced the lettering with one finger.

It was romantic, she decided. Willow was right. She only hoped that she would have the type of love that Mitch and Elise had one day. It wasn't –

"Hello, pretty lady."

She whirled around, her heart thumping like a drum in her chest and stared at the dark-haired man standing in front of her.

"Wh- who are you?" She took a step back, feeling the comforting solidness of the tree against her back.

"That doesn't matter, does it?" He grinned at her, keeping his hands folded neatly behind his back.

Adrenaline pumped through Ava's veins.

The man glanced at the ground at her feet, staring at the rough patch of dirt and snorted. "The old bastard did hide some money. Christ."

"I have to be going now," Ava said. She was afraid. She didn't want to be, but she could smell her damn fear rolling off of her in waves.

"No, I don't think so." The man smiled at her again, and she moaned when he produced a long, sharp knife from behind his back. "Tell me, how did your little bitch friend know about my Uncle Mitch and his money? Was she fucking him?"

Ava didn't reply. She glanced behind her at the woods less than ten feet away. If she could make it to the trees, she might be able to lose him. She groaned to herself. She couldn't leave Willow.

The man made a slight tsking sound. "Don't bother running, sweetheart. You won't get very far. I'm fast, and you're too fat to outrun me."

"Fuck you!" she said, and he laughed.

"Did I hurt your feelings?" He looked her up and down, and fresh fear poured into her. "I don't mind the fat girls. Gives you something to hang on to when you're pushing. If you know what I mean."

"If you touch me, I'll kill you," she said with a bravery she didn't feel.

"Sorry, sweetheart. You're the only one dying out here today." The man grinned at her, and Ava opened her mouth to scream.

The man lunged forward and clapped his hand over her mouth, cutting off the scream before it began and placed his knife at her throat. "Hush now, sweetheart. Screaming won't help anyway. There's no one around for miles."

He traced her throat with the edge of the knife. "My brother will bring your little friend out, and we'll dig up the money. Once we have it, you and your friend will go for a walk in the woods with us. Doesn't that sound nice? Doesn't that sound -"

He frowned as Ava's terrified gaze shifted to the left. Her eyes widened, and the man stiffened when he heard the loud growling. He turned, a soft moan escaping his throat and urine darkening the front of his pants when he saw the giant grizzly behind him.

"Oh shit," he whispered. He dropped the knife and stumbled backward. "Good bear, good -"

With a roar that made Ava throw her hands over her ears, the bear swung one meaty paw into the man's chest and knocked him flying. He landed on his back with a loud thud. His head slammed into the hard ground, and blood seeped through his shirt as his entire body shuddered and he went limp.

Terrified, Ava stared up at the bear standing on his hind legs in front of her. He was enormous, standing over nine feet tall, and his fur was a dark rich brown. She stared petrified at his long sharp claws as the bear leaned closer and sniffed at her long red hair.

She moaned when she felt the bear's hot breath on her throat, and tears slid down her cheeks. He stepped back, and she watched in amazement as the bear shifted into Bishop. Fur turned to skin, claws became nails, and his fangs slowly receded until he stood naked and fully human in front of her.

Her frightened eyes dropped downward, her cheeks flushing at the size of his penis. It grew half-hard under her gaze, and she licked her lips nervously before forcing herself to look up.

"You're – you're naked," she whispered. She groaned

inwardly at her stupidity as Bishop pushed his body against hers and pressed her roughly against the tree.

"I want you naked," he rumbled into her ear. "I want you naked and under me, while I make you mine."

"Um, sure, okay," she replied breathlessly as lust roared to life in her belly.

He growled happily in response, and then his mouth was on hers. He kissed her hard, his tongue pushing past her lips and teeth to slide against her own. She returned his kiss eagerly, throwing her arms around his broad shoulders and pressing her soft curves against his warm, naked body.

She gasped, her hands clutching at his short hair as he licked a searing path up her collarbone. He grabbed the hem of her t-shirt and tugged it over her head, dropping it on the ground next to them. His hot gaze landed on her tits, and her nipples hardened against the silk material of her bra as he made another growl of happiness.

His big hands moved to her hips, and he lifted her easily. She wrapped her legs around his waist and arched her pelvis when he rubbed his hot, heavy erection against her jean-covered core. He rested her against the tree and kissed her again as he cupped one heavy breast in his large hand. He squeezed it roughly, rubbing his thumb over her hardened nipple before sliding both hands up her back to her bra. She whimpered eagerly as his fingers reached for the clasps.

***

"AH-HA!" WILLOW GRINNED TRIUMPHANTLY AND GRABBED the shovel out of the empty stall. She headed out of the stall, smiling happily to herself.

"Hello."

She shrieked in surprise and staggered to a stop, staring suspiciously at the blond man in front of her. "Who are you?"

"I think the question is – who are you? And how do you know my uncle? Better yet – how do you know about his money?" he asked.

Willow took a step back, gripping the shovel like a weapon in front of her. "Mister, I don't know who you are, but you'd better get out of my way."

He grinned. "I'm Dwight. I like your shovel."

"Thanks. I like your lip ring." She smiled thinly at him.

He ran his tongue over the ring before stepping toward her. "Were you fucking my uncle?"

"That's none of your business," Willow said. "I've asked you to get out of my way."

"I'm afraid I can't do that." He sprang forward, and she swung the shovel at him. He blocked it with his arm, cursing angrily when it hit him with a heavy thud. He grabbed both of her wrists and twisted harshly. She squealed with pain as the shovel fell from her suddenly numb fingers.

"Be a good girl, now." He smiled at her.

"Of course," she said sweetly and then kneed him in the balls.

The man grunted with pain and released her wrists before grabbing his crotch, sinking to his knees. "You fucking bitch!" he wheezed. "I'll kill you!"

Quickly, she reached out and grabbed him by his lip ring. She yanked on it, and he screamed.

"Touch me again, and I'll rip this ring right out of your face, I swear to God," she said.

"Bitch," he gasped.

She pulled on his ring a second time, smiling when he shrieked. "Didn't your mother teach you that it's not nice to call people names?"

He stared sullenly at her, and she gave the ring a friendly tug. "We seem to be at a standstill, don't we?"

"Let go, and I'll walk out of here," he mumbled.

She laughed. "Oh, I don't think that's going to happen. In fact -"

A loud growling interrupted her, and the man at her feet whipped his head around. The ring pulled free of his lip with a wet tearing sound, and he screamed shrilly as blood poured down his chin.

"Oops!" Willow stared at the bloody ring in her hand before tossing it to the ground and walking toward the grey wolf standing in the barn. "Hey, Mal."

He barked at her, and she shrugged. She didn't actually understand him, but she had a pretty good idea of what he'd said. "I have no idea who he is. He just showed up."

He barked again, this time in a warning. She whirled around to see that Dwight had lurched to his feet and lunged for her. She took a quick step backward and stuck out her right foot. Blood still pouring from his lip, Dwight tripped over her foot and went sprawling.

She winced when his skull connected with the stall door. He released his breath in a soft sigh and collapsed on the floor of the barn. She prodded him with her foot, and when he didn't move, she kicked him in the ass before grinning at Mal. "He's unconscious."

She blinked in surprise when Mal abruptly shifted.

"Good gravy," she said as she scanned his naked body. "You're friggin' hot, Mal."

He scowled at her and gripped her arms before giving her a gentle shake. "What did I tell you, Willow? I told you it was too dangerous for you, and yet here you are, out in the middle of nowhere, about to be attacked by some asshole!"

"I was fine." She grinned at him. "I handled it."

"You handled it?" He shook her again. "Do you have any idea what kind of danger you put yourself and Ava into? There's another guy out there, and he -"

"Ava!" Alarm shot through Willow, and she wrenched herself free and sprinted from the barn.

"Willow, wait!"

Willow stopped just outside the barn, staggering forward when Mal ran into her. He caught her around the waist. "Willow! What's wrong?"

"Now that's hot," she said and pointed toward the apple tree.

A naked Bishop had a shirtless Ava pushed up against a tree with her long legs wrapped around his thick waist. They kissed enthusiastically as Bishop cupped Ava's breast before reaching behind her back.

"Bishop!" Mal shouted.

The bear shifter froze and looked behind him as Ava's face turned a brilliant shade of red.

Willow tried to keep the smile from her face as Bishop slowly lowered Ava to the ground. She snatched her t-shirt from the soft dirt and struggled into it as the bear shifter backed away from her.

"I'm sorry," he said before turning and fleeing. He thundered past them, ignoring Mal when he called his name and disappeared down the driveway.

"Where's he going?" Willow asked.

"Probably back to the car," Mal said as Ava walked slowly toward them.

"Hey, Ava. You okay?" Willow grinned at her.

"Um, yes." Ava rubbed a shaking hand across her forehead as she avoided looking at Mal's naked body. "There was this, uh, guy, and he had a knife, and Bishop saved me, and then I was just um...."

"Saying thank you?" Willow suggested. "With your bosom?"

Ava groaned as Mal pulled Willow's phone from her back pocket.

"Sorry, honey." Willow put her arm around Ava. "This isn't the time for jokes. Are you sure you're okay?"

"I'm fine." Ava leaned against Willow and closed her eyes.

"Who are you calling?" Willow asked Mal. "And you do realize you're naked, right? I mean, I'm not complaining," her eyes drifted over the granite muscles of his abdomen, "but your ass is going to get bit to hell by mosquitos."

"I'm calling the police." He glared at her. "My clothes are in the car. Once we get finished here, you and I will have a very long talk about personal safety. Do you hear me, Willow?"

She rolled her eyes. "Yes, sir."

CHAPTER 9

"Wait, so why did this woman even tell you where the money was?" Kat took a sip of her coffee and leaned against the reception desk.

It was Monday morning, and Willow had spent the last fifteen minutes filling Kat in on the events of Saturday.

Willow shrugged. "The nephews said she had gone crazy. As soon as the police showed up, they turned on their aunt and confessed everything. I guess good old Elise had convinced her nephews to kill Mitch for his insurance money. Only, as I said, he didn't have any."

"Unbelievable." Kat shook her head. "So, they arrested the aunt?"

"Yup, and the nephews. Ava and I will have to testify and Mal and Bishop too, but that won't be for a few months."

Kat studied Willow for a moment. "You really see ghosts, Will?"

"I really do," Willow said.

"Okay."

"You believe me? Just like that?" Willow asked.

"Just like that." Kat smiled at her.

"You really should talk to Mal. I still don't think he believes it."

Kat laughed. "Mal doesn't put much trust in the supernatural stuff. If he can't see it, smell it, or tear it apart with his teeth – he's suspicious."

"How on earth does he not die of boredom?" Willow said.

"Speaking of Mal," Kat said, "you two had sex, huh?"

"We didn't," Willow said.

"Yeah, um, Willow, you should know that when you mate with a shifter - especially a wolf shifter who likes to mark - their scent is all over you."

"We didn't have sex, Kat. I swear. He just marked me in a fit of temper to keep the Belfry brothers away."

Kat's mouth dropped open. "You're kidding me?"

"I'm not," Willow said.

"What the hell has gotten into Mal? I've never seen him act like this before," Kat said.

"Why does he have such a thing about humans and paranormals mating anyway?" Willow asked.

"Mal's grandfather was one of the first of the paranormals to reveal himself publicly. I don't know if you know much about our history, but the humans weren't exactly pleasant to paranormals when they were first discovered."

A scowl crossed Willow's face. "I know. I remember reading about it in school. Christ, we're lucky you guys didn't wipe us off the planet for some of the things we tried to do."

Kat shrugged. "Humans don't like change. Besides,

there were plenty of paranormals who did terrible things to humans."

"Both our species suck," Willow said.

"Anyway, Mal doesn't hate humans, but after what his grandfather went through, he's leery about interacting with them. He says it's because paranormals can too easily hurt humans, and sooner or later the humans will grow tired of it, and there will be an all-out war between us."

"Do you believe that?" Willow asked.

Kat shrugged. "Humans are always looking for a reason to fight. If not with us, then with each other. Keeping ourselves segregated won't change that. Besides, I don't believe that's why Mal keeps away from humans. He grew up listening to his grandfather speak of the horrible things humans have done to our kind. That would have a strong influence on him."

"I can't believe he's even willing to have anything to do with us," Willow said.

"His mother is a well-known human and paranormal equal rights activist. Mal says she's very fond of humans. I'm sure her beliefs helped balance out some of the anger and hatred his grandfather would have shown him."

"Poor Mal," Willow said somberly. She hated that Mal didn't believe humans and paranormals should have anything to do with each other, but she at least understood his reasoning a little better now.

Kat touched her hand. "Listen, I'll talk to Mal for you, Willow. I don't want you to quit because he's marking you and making unwanted sexual advances."

"Are you kidding me?" Willow said. "They are not unwanted sexual advances. Trust me."

Kat blinked at her before giving her low, throaty laugh. "Oh, okay then."

"Hell, I'm worried I'm going to get fired for sexually harassing my boss. I've said way too many inappropriate things to him," Willow said.

"I won't let Mal fire you." Kat grinned. "I happen to think you're good for him and that he needs a free spirit like you in his life. He's way too uptight, and his life is ridiculously boring."

Willow laughed. "Maybe, but he's so mouth-wateringly delicious looking."

"Eh, I don't see the appeal," Kat said. "Wolf shifters are just way too possessive of their mates. I like my mate to give me some freedom."

"Yes, well, I -"

Willow broke off as the office door opened, and Bishop stuck his head in. He looked around cautiously but didn't enter the room. "Is it just, um, you two in the office?"

"Are you expecting someone else?" Kat asked.

Before Bishop could answer, Willow stood and grinned at him. "Ava isn't here, Bishop. She's working at the hospital."

He turned bright red and nodded before nearly running to his office. He slammed his office door as Kat stared at Willow in confusion. "What was that about?"

Willow laughed. "After Bishop saved Ava from that idiot nephew, they totally made out."

"They did not." Kat stared at Bishop's closed office door.

"They did," Willow said, her excitement pitched her voice higher. "Bishop knocked the guy flying, and then he shifted to his human form and told Ava that he wanted to see her naked."

Kat's jaw dropped. "I don't believe that."

"It's true, I swear. Ava was all – okay, sure," Willow laughed again, "and the next thing you know, he's got his mouth and hands all over her like she was a jar of honey."

"I don't know what to say," Kat said.

"Is it weird for Bishop to have a crush on Ava?" Willow asked.

Kat shrugged. "Bishop is, well, I've just never seen him go after any woman – paranormal or human. Grizzly shifters are loners. They rarely take a mate and prefer to spend most of their time alone. Plus, I'm sure you've noticed that Bishop's kind of shy."

"I'll say. I thought I'd never get him to look me in the eye. You should have seen him at the interview. He nearly sweated through his suit," Willow said. "If they don't mate, how do they stop from going extinct?"

"Well, some of them will find a mate, but mostly they just get together for sex, and the woman raises the baby alone."

"Really?"

Kat nodded. "Most of the time. As I said, there are exceptions, and grizzly shifters who do mate with one woman are often more protective and possessive than the wolf shifters. I've never seen a grizzly mate with a human for life, though. And Bishop doesn't strike me as the type of guy who wants to be mated for life."

"Well, he's got a definite thing for Ava," Willow said. "Mal said when they were tailing us, they lost us at one point. The only reason they arrived at the farmhouse in time was because Bishop followed Ava's scent. How crazy is that?"

"Grizzlies' have an incredible sense of smell," Kat said. "Still, I'll be amazed if anything comes of Bishop's crush. Especially since you told me that Ava is shy."

"I'll work on them both." Willow grinned. "They make a cute couple."

Kat laughed as the door to the office opened, and Mal strolled in. He held two coffees and sat one down in front of Willow without speaking.

"Where's mine?" Kat raised her eyebrow at him.

"Throwing me to the lizard and the lions officially strikes you off the coffee list," Mal replied. "If it hadn't been for Willow, we wouldn't have got the contract."

"Nice work, Willow," Kat said.

"Of course, she got it for us by commiserating with Mrs. Belfry about how awful wolf shifters were." Mal gave Willow a mock scowl.

"Hey, you have to work with what the client gives you. Besides, you know I didn't mean it. I adore you and your hot, tight ass," Willow said.

Mal rolled his eyes and escaped to his office.

"See, I told you," Willow said to Kat. "I'm going to be fired for sexual harassment. I can't seem to stop myself. It's like an addiction now."

Kat laughed. "I maintain that it's good for Mal, and I know Bishop will back me up on it."

Willow squeezed her arm. "I'll be sure to continue torturing him then. Now, how was your sister's wedding?"

"Good afternoon, Willow." Koren entered the office and leaned against the reception desk. "How are you?"

"I'm good, thank you." Willow closed the document she was working on and smiled at the lion shifter. "How are you?"

"I can't complain. See any ghosts lately?" He wiggled his eyebrows at her.

"Not lately. How about you? Has your lady friend returned to the warehouse?" Willow asked.

Koren shrugged. "I have no idea what you're talking about."

"I'm sure you don't." Willow could barely hold in her urge to scoff.

Mal's office door opened, and he hurried into the reception. "Mr. Belfry, what's wrong?"

"Nothing. Can't a client stop by the office?" Koren asked.

"Of course. Would you like a cup of coffee?" Mal started toward the kitchenette, and Willow stood up.

"I'll grab it for him, Mal."

"No thanks. I've only got a minute. I'm here to invite you to a small party we're throwing at my mother's place," Koren said.

Mal stared at him. "A party?"

"Yes."

"Well, that's very kind of you, Mr. Belfry, but generally speaking, we don't mix business with pleasure."

"Yes," Koren sighed dramatically, "your lovely receptionist has already informed me of that. Unless you've changed your mind?" He gave Willow a hopeful look, and she shook her head.

"Definitely not, Koren."

"Pity." Koren shoved his hands into the pockets of his suit pants. "Regardless, Mother insisted we invite you, and I'm sure she'll insist you go. You may not have noticed this about her, but my mother can be very adamant about getting what she wants."

"What kind of party is it?" Willow asked.

"Oh, you know, the usual boring type. All the big wigs in the paranormal world will be there." He at Mal. "In fact, it might be an opportunity for you to expand your clientele. Unlike most people, my mother encourages business talk at her parties."

"Why exactly are we invited?" Mal asked.

"Well, it's certainly not because of your charming personality, wolf shifter." Koren laughed. He glanced at Willow. "My mother didn't share her reasons, but if I had to guess, it's because she's quite fond of your receptionist. You made a rather charming impression on her, Willow."

Willow smiled. "I like your mother a lot."

"Good. The party is Friday night, around seven. Please extend the invitation to Ms. Frost and Mr. King. The dress is formal so you," he glanced at Mal's jeans and t-shirt, "rent a tuxedo and you," his gaze swung to Willow, "wear something shiny."

Willow burst out laughing. "Something shiny? Really? That's your suggestion?"

Koren grinned at her before reaching across the desk and taking her hand. He brought it to his lips, kissing it gently as Mal growled behind him. "If you need my help picking out something suitable from your closet to wear, I'd be more than happy to drop by your place."

Mal stalked around the reception desk and pulled

Willow's hand free of the lion shifter's grip. He rested his hand possessively on the back of her neck and glared at Koren. "Is that everything, Mr. Belfry?"

"Oh, I could chat to Willow all day, but I think I should go before you wolf out and mark the poor girl again," Koren said with a grin as Mal flushed.

"One more thing," Koren paused at the threshold of the door, "you're all welcome to bring a date with you. Although," he winked at Willow again, "keep in mind that I'll be going solo to the party."

Mal's hand tightened on her neck until she gasped. She whacked him gently on the thigh and stared pointedly at him. He loosened his grip but didn't release her fully until the still grinning Koren left the office.

She rubbed her neck. "Ease up, wolf boy. I'm going to have bruises."

"I'm sorry." He studied her neck anxiously before cursing under his breath. "I didn't mean to do that."

"I know. Just try to control yourself the next time I'm eyed up by the lion brothers, okay?"

He nodded as she sat back down at her desk.

"Are you bringing a date to the party?" he asked.

"Are you?"

"I asked you first."

She rolled her eyes. "Good God, it's like being in grade school all over again. If you make Bishop pass me a note asking me if I like you, I'm going to punch you. I swear it."

"Are you bringing a date or not?" He frowned at her. "Tell me, Willow."

"No, I'm not bringing a date," she said. "Does that make you happy?"

"I was just curious," he said.

"Sure, you were." She laughed. "Are you bringing a date?"

"No."

"Excellent. Maybe we can sneak off and have a make-out session in a closet somewhere," she said. "I'm sure there are, like, a hundred closets in the Belfry mansion. One of them will undoubtedly be big enough for the both of us."

She watched with amusement as he stared at her with red cheeks before shaking his head and walking back to his office.

CHAPTER 10

"God, I hate these things," Bishop grumbled as he pulled at the collar of his shirt. "I can't breathe with this stupid bowtie around my neck."

"I know, but this party is an opportunity for us, Bishop. You know that," Mal said.

"I didn't need to come. You and Kat could have handled it by yourselves. Hell, Kat could have handled it alone. She's a natural at this shit."

Mal's gaze drifted to Kat. The jaguar shifter looked gorgeous in a long, form-fitting red dress. Her dark hair was piled high on her head, and she was smiling and talking animatedly with the owner of one of the most prominent paranormal-run restaurants in the city.

"She is a natural," Mal said. "But it looks better if all three of us are here."

"Yeah, yeah." Bishop pulled at his collar again as Mal scanned the yard. When they arrived, Jeffries had led them through the house and to the backyard. The yard was large and impressive, with towering trees surrounding it. Tiny twinkling lights were strung through the trees, and they cast a welcoming glow as the sun slowly set. Tables covered in crisp white cloths and laden with food were set up around the yard. In the center of the immaculate lawn, a massive water fountain with multi-coloured lights flowed into a pool that was larger than Mal's living room. Large Koi fish swam lazily in its depths.

"Mrs. Belfry certainly spares no expense for her parties," Mal said.

Bishop stared at the small group of musicians playing in the far corner of the yard. "Who hires live musicians for a 'small' party?"

Mal snorted and gazed at the hundreds of paranormals milling around the yard. "If this is her version of a small party, I'd hate to see what a large one looks like."

He straightened as Mrs. Belfry appeared in front of them. "Good evening, Mr. Burke."

"Good evening, Mrs. Belfry. I'd like to introduce you to one of the partners in our firm, Mr. King."

Bishop held out his hand, and Mrs. Belfry shook it briefly. "It's nice to meet you, ma'am."

"You as well." Mrs. Belfry smiled thinly. "I'm surprised you're here, Mr. King. I know how bear shifters hate large crowds."

Bishop cleared his throat. "It's my pleasure to be here."

"I'm quite sure it isn't," Mrs. Belfry said. She studied Mal closely. "For a wolf shifter, you clean up very well, Mr. Burke."

"Thank you, ma'am."

"Where is your associate, Ms. Tanner?" Mrs. Belfry glanced around the yard. "You did tell her she was invited as well, didn't you?"

"I did. She'll be here shortly," Mal said.

Beside him, Bishop inhaled sharply, and Mal and Mrs. Belfry followed his gaze.

"Ah, there she is." Without saying goodbye, Mrs. Belfry hurried away.

Mal stared at Willow. He felt like he'd been punched in the gut, and his wolf was positively howling. For the first time since he'd met Willow, her hair wasn't in her usual bun. Instead, it fell in soft waves around her face, and he wanted to bury his hands in its dark length. She wore a tight black dress with a high neckline and short sleeves. He sucked in his breath when she turned and revealed the back of her dress. The soft material stopped just above her ass, leaving her entire back naked, and he studied her smooth skin. He was struck with an almost undeniable urge to go to her and throw his jacket over her shoulders. He didn't want anyone but him seeing that creamy expansion of delectable flesh.

He watched as Willow smiled at Mrs. Belfry before kissing her on both cheeks. The old woman talked animatedly to her as Bishop elbowed him hard in the side.

"Why didn't you tell me she was going to be here?" he growled.

"Who?" He couldn't take his eyes off of Willow.

"Who do you think, Mal? Have you gone blind?" Bishop snarled.

He finally pulled his gaze from Willow, and he grunted with surprise. Ava stood next to Willow. Her long red hair was pulled into a twist, and she wore a dark green dress cut low in the front that showed off her ample cleavage.

Mal grimaced. "I didn't know, Bishop. I swear. Willow said she wasn't bringing anyone to the party."

"I have to get out of here," Bishop said, with one hand already covering his nose.

Mal grabbed his arm. "You can't leave. Pull yourself together, man."

"I can smell her already," Bishop groaned. "I can't be this close to her, Mal."

He yanked free of Mal's grip, and Mal watched in disbelief as the grizzly shifter ran across the yard and disappeared behind the fountain.

———

"YOU SAID YOU WEREN'T BRINGING ANYONE."

Mal's low voice sent tingles of awareness up and down her spine. Willow turned from the dessert table and smiled up at him. "No, I said I wasn't bringing a date. I'm not dating Ava."

"Where is Ava?"

She pointed across the yard. A tall, thin man with a horse-like face had his shirt sleeve rolled up to show Ava a large black mole on his forearm.

Willow giggled. "Mrs. Belfry introduced her to Mr. Handen, and the minute he found out she was a nurse, he started showing her all of his suspicious moles and freckles."

"You should have told me you were bringing her." Mal frowned at her. "I needed to warn Bishop."

She shrugged. "Bishop just needs to relax and talk to Ava. If he took the time to get to know her instead of just sniffing her and making out with her, he'd probably not be so nervous around her."

"Bishop's a grizzly shifter, Willow. He isn't interested in making small talk with the woman he's lusting after."

"So, he tries something new." Willow shrugged again. "It won't kill him."

"Yeah, well, you'll be lucky if he doesn't kill you for bringing Ava tonight."

"Oh, please. Bishop's a big old softie, and we all know it. He wouldn't hurt a fly," she said.

"That isn't true. You don't -"

"Are you going to tell me how nice I look tonight or not, Mal?" she said.

"I – what?"

"You're being awfully rude. I wore this dress for you, and you haven't said a single thing about it." She gave him that adorable pout again.

"You look very," he hesitated, "pretty tonight."

"Pretty?" She arched her eyebrow at him. "That's the best you can do?"

"Fine. You look sexy and damn hot, and I want to throw you on that table and fuck you."

She grinned happily at him. "Now that's more like it. Maybe we should find that closet. What do you think?"

"I think you're killing me, Willow," he groaned.

"I know." She studied him in his tux before moving a little closer. "You're looking very handsome tonight."

"Thank you." He rested his hand on the small of her back and stroked her delectably soft skin. She shivered delicately.

"That feels nice, Mal."

"Nice? That's the best you can do?" he asked.

She giggled and leaned against him. "Do you like my dress?"

"Yes, but I think I should give you my jacket to wear."

"Why? It's not cold."

He made small circles with his fingertips against the middle of her back. "I know, but as soon as those damn lion shifters see you, I'm going to have to kill them."

"Killing the clients is a bad idea, Mal."

"Watching them stare at you in this dress is a bad idea."

"I told you – I'm not interested in the pussy-cats. It's the big bad wolf I want," she said.

He growled happily before leaning down and pressing his face against her hair. "I like your hair down. You should wear it this way more often."

"It gets in the way when I'm working."

"It's so soft." His hand crept up from the small of her back and threaded through the long dark locks. He gently tugged until she looked up at him.

"Do you have any idea how many times I've pictured you naked in my bed with your hair down and wrapped around my fingers?" he said in a low voice. "I can barely sleep at night thinking about all the ways I would take you. Wondering how you would look and sound as I slid my cock into you and made you mine."

She released her breath in a harsh rush. "Jesus, Mal. Seriously – we need to find a closet ASAP."

He moved behind her and pressed his erection against the small of her back. "I can smell how wet you are," he breathed into her ear.

She made a soft, gasping moan as he placed his hands on her hips. "I want you, Willow. I want to -"

"Willow! When did you get here?" Kat joined them. "You look great. I love your hair."

"Thanks. You're looking pretty hot yourself," Willow said.

Kat frowned at her and then at Mal. "What's going on?"

"Nothing," Willow said quickly. "We were just discussing Mrs. Belfry's closets."

"Mrs. Belfry's closets?" Kat said in confusion.

"Yes. I think there has to be at least a hundred in that giant house, but Mal says fifty, tops," Willow said. "What do you think?"

"I think you two are weird and that it's more than obvious you're about three seconds from tearing off each other's clothes. We could drum up a lot of business at this party, so do you think you two can control your hormones for the night?" Kat said.

"Yes. We're sorry," Willow said.

"Good." Kat held out her hand. "Come with me, Willow. I have yet to meet Mrs. Belfry, and I hear she likes you, so why don't you introduce me?"

———

AVA TOOK A DEEP BREATH AND CLEARED HER THROAT. SHE had finally escaped Mr. Handen and his moles, and she gathered her courage and approached the bear shifter. Bishop stood with his back to her, but she had an odd feeling that he knew she was there. "Hello, Bishop."

He turned and stared at the ground. "Hey."

He held a plate in his massive hand with a giant piece of chocolate cake, a wedge of apple pie, and a thick slab of brownie piled on it. Ava smiled tentatively.

"You like the sweet stuff, huh? Me too. Obviously." She took a quick look at her chubby body.

When he didn't reply, she cleared her throat again. "So, I, um, just wanted to say thank you for the other day. I never really got the chance to tell you thank you for saving my life, so, uh, thank you."

"You're welcome." He finally raised his gaze to hers, and she gave him another tentative smile.

"I don't know what would have happened if you hadn't been there, and I am very grateful to you."

He blushed, and his hand squeezed the plate so hard she was afraid he was going to break it. As she watched, he raised his free hand to his face and covered his nose for a moment before lowering it and breathing through his mouth.

"Are you okay?" she asked.

"Yeah. Are you?"

"I'm great. Really great," she said. "Some party, huh?"

"I don't like parties. Too many people," he said.

"I'm kind of a homebody myself. I like to stay in my pajamas and just hang out on my couch. Kind of boring, I know." Her laugh was high-pitched and nervous.

"I like that too," he replied.

"It's a lot more comfortable than this dress." She ran her hands over the fabric and her face flushed when Bishop's gaze dropped to her breasts.

"You look beautiful," he rasped.

Her cheeks flamed red, and she touched his thick arm. "You look beautiful too."

There was an awkward silence, and Ava groaned to herself. She had just told a bear shifter he was beautiful.

Her heart racing, she looked around the yard, anxious to break the weird tension between them.

The musicians played a soft, slow song, and a few couples were dancing in the grass. She threw caution to the wind. "Would you like to dance with me, Bishop?"

He stiffened, and this time the plate in his hand did break. The desserts fell to the grass with a wet plop, and she gasped and grabbed at his hand. "Bishop, are you okay? Did you cut yourself?"

He yanked his hand away from her. "No, I'm fine. I don't dance. I'm sorry. I need to go."

He hurried away, nearly knocking over some of the party guests. Embarrassment seeped through her as they stared first at the retreating Bishop and then at her. She was an idiot for thinking the bear shifter might be interested in her. Hell, for all she knew, shifters just got really horny when they nearly killed people, and that's why he had made out with her. She raised a shaking hand to her forehead and rubbed gently. She shouldn't have come to the party, but she had wanted to see him again. And then she had gone and ruined it by being her usual awkward self.

"Hello there. I don't believe we've met." A low voice spoke behind her, and she turned around to see a large, blond man smiling at her. "What's your name, beautiful?"

"Ava."

"That's a lovely name, Ava. I'm Keegan." He held his hand out to her, and she shook it as he gave her another slow smile. "Can I get you a drink?"

"Yes," she said.

He held out his arm, and she tucked her hand around it as his smile widened and he led her toward the bar.

CHAPTER 11

"Ms. Frost, Willow, I'd like you to meet my husband Garrett Finnigan," Mrs. Belfry said.

"It's nice to meet you, Mr. Finnigan." Willow held her hand out, and he shook it quickly. The jaguar shifter was handsome with hazel eyes and sand-coloured hair.

"Please, call me Garrett." He gave them a warm smile before shaking Kat's hand. "I haven't heard of the Frost family in the jaguar community. Do your parents live here in the city?"

"They do," Kat said. "Do you work at the warehouse as well, Garrett?"

"Oh no, no." He laughed before putting his arm around his wife's waist. "I'm not clever enough for that."

Mrs. Belfry frowned. "Don't be ridiculous, Garrett." She smiled proudly at her husband. "Garrett works in computers. He was a life saver when our entire warehouse system crashed."

"Yes. We would have been lost without him," Koren said with a hint of sarcasm.

Mrs. Belfry glared at her son, but he held his hand out to Kat before she could say anything. "Ms. Frost, I would love it if you danced with me."

Kat hesitated and then took his hand. "Sure."

Willow grinned to herself. From the moment Koren had laid eyes on Kat, he'd lost all interest in her and had spent the last half hour using every last bit of his considerable charm on the jaguar shifter.

As Mal and Bishop joined them and Mrs. Belfry introduced them to her husband, she searched for Ava. She frowned a little. Ava was standing near the bar with Keegan. She smiled shyly at him as he handed her another glass of wine and stroked her arm.

She would have to warn Ava about Keegan. Not that she didn't want her to have fun, but she was certain that a romp with a commitment-phobic lion shifter wasn't a good idea for her best friend. Ava wasn't the type of girl to just fall into bed with someone.

"So, Mr. Burke, my wife tells me there haven't been any issues since your company has taken over security for the warehouse."

Mal nodded. "It's been very quiet."

"Perhaps the presence of your security team suggests this is an inside job. After all, employees would be less willing to cause problems with your team in place," Garrett said thoughtfully.

Mrs. Belfry frowned. "I told you, Garrett. This isn't something our employees would do. They can be trusted."

"I know, my dear, but some people are excellent at hiding their true natures. Wouldn't you agree, Mr. King?"

There was no reply, and Mal elbowed Bishop in the

ribs. The bear shifter was glaring at Ava and Keegan, and he jerked his gaze away from them.

"Uh, yes, I suppose so." He gave Garrett a strained smile.

Mal cleared his throat. "I've had my team question the warehouse employees and -"

"I know you have," Mrs. Belfry said. "They scared some of them half to death." She glowered at Mal.

"I'll make sure to speak with them about being gentler in their questioning," he said.

"You don't need to question them at all, Mr. Burke. I told you – they have nothing to do with this," Mrs. Belfry barked.

Garrett rubbed her waist soothingly. "Do not get yourself so worked up, my dear. You know what the doctor said about your blood pressure."

"My blood pressure is just fine," Mrs. Belfry said. She looked over Willow's shoulder and her scowl deepened. "Oh, good Lord, what is he doing here?"

Willow glanced behind her at the man walking toward them. He was short and unbelievably round. His body was squeezed into a tuxedo that looked about two sizes too small, and she studied his features as he stood next to Garrett. His face was red, his eyes a dark brown and beady looking, and his nose bore a remarkable resemblance to a snout. Pig shifter, she decided. He had to be.

"Good evening, Marika. Lovely party."

"Indeed. I don't remember inviting you, Mr. Howell," Mrs. Belfry said frostily.

He snorted laughter, and Willow tugged on Mal's arm. He bent his head down, and she breathed into his ear. "Pig shifter?"

"Close enough," he breathed back. "Boar shifter."

"Oh, please, Marika. We've known each other for years. When are you going to start calling me Craig?"

"Perhaps when you stop pestering me to buy my company, Mr. Howell."

He laughed again. "You can't blame a man for trying. I was certain when your husband died that you would be more than willing to get rid of the company. It was, after all, a financial strain."

"Was, Mr. Howell, was. I think even you will admit that it's done well under my guidance," Mrs. Belfry said. "Why are you here?"

I'm the guest of the lovely Ms. Parkens." Mr. Howell pointed behind him, and Willow looked over at the tall, skinny blonde woman. She had a bulging forehead and wide-set eyes, and her teeth were large and an unfortunate shade of yellow.

"Surprise, surprise," Mrs. Belfry said. "Horse shifters have always had the common sense of a stalk of corn."

"No need to be unkind, my dear," Garrett said quickly.

"Ms. Parkens and I enjoy a very close relationship," Mr. Howell said.

Willow pressed her lips together to stop from laughing as Mrs. Belfry sniffed haughtily. "Yes, well, her close relationship with you has lost her a spot on my future guest list."

Mr. Howell changed the subject. "I hear you've been having some problems at the warehouse as of late, Mrs. Belfry. Some nasty, childish pranks, yes? I heard a bear shifter was wounded badly."

"Nothing we can't handle, Mr. Howell."

"Is that why you hired the security company of Burke,

King, and Frost?" Mr. Howell raised his eyebrow at her before turning to Mal and holding out his hand. "Craig Howell."

"Malcolm Burke." Mal shook Craig's hand. "This is Bishop King and our associate Willow Tanner."

"Lovely to meet you." Craig gave her a brief, disinterested look before returning his gaze to Mal. "I hear good things about your company, Mr. Burke."

"Thank you."

"I run a food import business. Specializes in bringing in some of the more exotic foods that paranormals enjoy."

"I've heard of it," Mal said.

"I'm sure you have. We've done quite well for ourselves. We service every major paranormal specialty restaurant across the city, as well as half the grocery stores."

He gave Mal and Bishop a scrutinizing look. "Perhaps you'd like to come by our corporate office this week. With all the trouble Marika's been having lately, I've been considering upping our security. Shall we say Tuesday at nine?"

Mrs. Belfry made a snort of disgust, and Willow watched as Mal and Bishop glanced at each other. A type of silent communication rippled between them, and then Mal said, "I'm afraid we'll have to decline, Mr. Howell."

"Decline? Are you joking?" Mr. Howell said.

"No. Our plate is full with Mrs. Belfry's company and our other clients."

"You're making a mistake, Mr. Burke. I have many connections within the paranormal business community."

"I'm sure you do," Mal said.

"Well," Mr. Howell straightened his back and smoothed the front of his jacket, "if you'll excuse me."

He turned and waddled away as Mrs. Belfry gave Mal a cool look. "You may not be that bad after all, Mr. Burke."

"Thank you, Mrs. Belfry." Mal grinned at her, and a ghost of a smile crossed her lips before she squeezed Garrett's arm.

"Come, dearest. We cannot ignore our other guests." With a nod to the three of them, she led Garrett toward a large group of people clustered around the fountain.

***

As Mrs. Belfry walked away, Mal hoped like hell he and Bishop had made the right decision to deny Mr. Howell the chance to offer them the job. As well connected as the boar shifter was, Mrs. Belfry was the more prominent business figure in the paranormal community.

Willow tugged on his arm. "I think there's some tension between Koren and Garrett."

"Why do you say that?"

"Before you and Bishop joined us, Marika was telling us how Garrett's computer skills came in handy when their system crashed. Koren seemed less than impressed."

"Interesting. I wonder if that's why Garrett doesn't work at the company," Mal mused. "It might be worth speaking to Koren and Keegan about. If -"

He was interrupted by Bishop's loud growl. The bear shifter stared across the yard, and Mal and Willow followed his gaze.

Keegan was dancing with Ava. His large body held hers firmly against his as they danced, and Bishop's growl grew louder when he bent his mouth to her ear and whispered something. Ava blushed, and when Keegan's hand on her back dipped to the top of her ass and stroked lightly, the beer bottle Bishop held in one large hand shattered. Beer flowed down his hand, and he winced before picking out a large piece of glass embedded in his palm.

"Jesus, Bishop. Cool it," Mal said.

"If he keeps touching her like that, I'm going to kill him," Bishop said.

"Oh, for Pete's sake!" Willow pressed a napkin to his hand to stem the trickle of blood. "You need to ask her out, Bishop. Ava likes you. She'll say yes."

"I don't date." Bishop glared at her. "And I definitely don't date humans."

"Yes, you and Mal both," Willow said in annoyance. "You're both acting ridiculous. How is denying yourself what you want any fun at all? You need to learn to relax and enjoy life. Both of you are way too uptight for your own good."

Bishop glared at her again, and she stared defiantly at him. "Ava's a sweet girl, and you should take her for coffee. I'm not saying you need to get married, just maybe get to know her. If you don't do something soon, that damn lion shifter is going to have her in his bed."

Bishop snarled, and Mal frowned at Willow. "Stop pissing him off, Willow. Are you trying to make him shift?"

"Of course not. But Ava's not going to wait around forever for him to get his head out of his ass," Willow said.

"My head is not in my ass," Bishop bit out.

"Really? Because from over here, it looks like it's pretty firmly wedged in there."

Mal snickered despite himself, and Willow grinned at him as he clapped Bishop on the back. "She does have a point, Bishop. If you like Ava, you should just go for it."

"Mr. Pot, have you met Mr. Kettle?" Willow said.

"It's completely different, Willow," Mal said. "Ava doesn't work for us."

"Yeah, because Willow working for us is the only reason you haven't slept with her," Bishop snorted.

"Shut up, Bishop," Mal said through gritted teeth.

"Uh oh." Willow gripped his arm.

"What's wrong?"

She stared at the Belfry brothers, and Mal realized with a bite of dismay that he could see his breath. "Oh shit, not again."

"Did it just suddenly get a hell of a lot colder?" Bishop asked.

"Hey!" Willow turned to stare at a spot just to her left. "Honey, look at me. My name's Willow. What's yours?"

Bishop nudged Mal. "What's she doing?"

"Talking to a ghost," Mal said.

"No, no, honey, don't do that." She turned to Mal, her eyes wide. "Um, we might have a problem."

"What do you mean?"

"The girl is pissed. She's -"

She flinched when the table next to them suddenly tipped over. Food and dinnerware crashed to the ground as the party patrons quieted and turned to look in their direction.

"Oops, my bad," Willow said loudly. Her hand dug

into Mal's arm. "We need to get the Belfry brothers out of here, right now. Do you hear me?" she said in a low voice.

"Willow, what -"

"Too late!" she groaned.

One by one, the tables began to flip over. One of them rose high in the air before flying forward and smashing into the stone edge of the fountain pool. People screamed and ran for cover as plates and cutlery smashed into the side of the house. The path of destruction headed in the direction of the brothers.

Mal cursed when Willow darted toward the Belfry brothers. "Willow! Stop!"

Beside him, Bishop had stiffened and squeezed his hands into fists. "Ava?" he said

With a confused look on his face, Keegan stepped away from the redhead and toward his brother. Koren had left Kat, and the two brothers huddled together. Koren shouted something into Keegan's ear, and he shook his head immediately. The wind was howling now, and Ava backed away a few feet, her hands clutching nervously at her dress.

Mal chased after Willow. As he reached out and snagged Willow's arm, he could hear the thundering footsteps of Bishop behind him. He pulled Willow to a stop, and she struggled and twisted in his grip.

"Mal! Let me go! She's going to hurt them!" she shouted.

"You're not going anywhere near them!" he shouted back as Bishop ran by them.

She stared at him in frustration before booting him in the shin. He barked in pain and dropped her arm.

"I'm sorry!" she shouted before turning and running after Bishop.

"Koren! Keegan! Watch out!" she hollered.

The brothers turned toward her as a table, spinning crazily in the air, was thrown directly at them. They ducked in unison, and Willow screamed in horror as the table skimmed over them and hurtled toward the frozen Ava.

"Ava!" She screamed again.

FAINTLY, AVA HEARD WILLOW SCREAM HER NAME AS SHE stared at the table flying toward her.

Move, you fool! Her mind shrieked.

She took a single, stumbling step backward before throwing her arms over her face. Arms encircled her, and she was yanked against a hard, wide wall of flesh and muscle. There was a splintering crash, and the person holding her bellowed in pain as they were sent flying. He landed on her with a hard thud, and her eyes flew open. Bishop, bits of wood in his hair and a cut on his cheek stared worriedly at her.

"Ava? Are you okay?"

"I – yes," she said. She touched the cut on his face. "You're hurt."

"It's nothing." He was still covering her with his body, and he ran his hands over her head and face. "Are you sure you're not injured?"

"I think so." She struggled to get out from under him. He was so large she could barely breathe. He stood before pulling her roughly to her feet. She peeked around him.

The table laid in pieces on the ground, and she stared wide-eyed at him. "The – the table? It hit you."

"I'm fine." He put his arms around her and sheltered her against his large body. "We need to get you out of here and somewhere safe."

He suddenly yanked her back to the ground. She squeaked in surprise, and he rolled her onto her back, covering her body with his as a large silver serving platter whipped by them. It hit a tree with enough force to embed itself deep within the wood, and Bishop cursed under his breath.

A deafening roar made Ava cringe. In their lion forms, the Belfry brothers bounded past them and into the trees that surrounded the yard. Willow - Mal and Kat hot on her heels - chased after them.

Bishop continued to lie on top of her. The wind had died down, and the party guests were rising to their feet and looking around with dazed expressions at the destruction.

"Bishop?" Ava wheezed. "I'm sorry, but I can't breathe."

He blushed and quickly stood up. "Sorry."

He helped her to her feet, and she smiled shakily. "Thank you."

"You're welcome. I should probably go help Mal and Kat, so, uh, bye."

He turned away from her, and she gasped in horror. She grabbed his arm and squeezed. "Bishop!"

"Yeah?"

"There's a piece of the table in your back!"

"What?" He twisted his head and looked over his

shoulder at the piece of wood jutting out of his lower back. "Huh, look at that."

"Look at that?" Ava said in disbelief. "You need to go to the hospital right now."

He shook his head. "No, it'll be fine. I'll just pull it out."

"You can't do that! It could have severed some nerves or muscles."

"It's fine," he repeated. "I'm not going to the hospital."

She stared at him in exasperation before suddenly grabbing his hand. He stiffened at her touch but didn't resist when she linked their fingers together. "Come with me."

"Where are we going?" he asked as she pulled him in the direction of the house.

"I'm a nurse, Bishop. If you won't go to the hospital, then at the very least, you're going to let me look at it."

CHAPTER 12

"**B**ishop, come in here so I can look at your back," Ava coaxed.

Bishop stood in the hallway and stared into the tiny bathroom. His face pale, Jeffries had shown them to the guest bathroom and found them a first-aid kit. Ava rifled through the kit, pulling out bandages and tape and a pair of scissors.

"You'd think for a house this large, they'd have a bigger bathroom," Bishop grumbled.

"I need to look at your back and assess the damage," Ava said. "I know you don't believe you need to go to the hospital, but I'm fairly certain you do. Please, Bishop. Let me look at it, okay?"

He sighed and stepped into the small room. With his size and Ava's curves, he could barely avoid touching her. He bit the inside of his cheek when her breasts nearly brushed against his chest.

"Turn around, please," she instructed.

He turned obediently, and she studied his back. "I'm

sorry, but I think I'll have to cut off your jacket and shirt. It'll be easier and safer than trying to take them off around the table piece."

He snorted impatiently, and she gasped in horror when he reached behind his back and pulled the piece of wood out of his flesh with a hard tug.

"Shit!" she shouted. "Bishop, what are you doing?"

Her hands yanked his jacket from his body, and he grunted in surprise when she whipped him around with surprising strength and hurriedly removed his bowtie before unbuttoning his shirt.

"You shouldn't have done that!" she scolded him fiercely as she pulled off his shirt and dropped it to the floor. "You could bleed to death. Turn around."

Her hands were already tearing open the gauze packages, and he turned again so she could press the gauze against the wound in his back. He could feel blood oozing down his back, but his skin was tingling, and warmth was surging through the wound. His body was healing itself like it always did. He rested his hands against the wall in front of him and gritted his teeth when he felt Ava's warm breath on his skin.

"You're definitely going to the hospital now!" she scolded him again. "You'll have nerve damage. You'll need stitches -"

"It's already healing," he said.

"I wonder if we should call an ambulance or if it would be faster to take my car. Although I'm not sure you'll fit in my car." Ava pressed more gauze against the wound. "Maybe we should – what did you just say?"

"I said it's already healing. You know paranormals have healing abilities, right?"

"Of course, I know," she said. "But you're not immortal. I've seen plenty of paranormals in the ER, and I've seen a few of them die. This is a bad wound, Bishop, and -"

"It's not that bad," he said. "Honestly. The wood was barely stuck in there. Check for yourself."

He could hear her muttering under her breath as she eased the gauze away from his back. She gasped in surprise, and he twitched when he felt her soft fingers brushing against the bare skin of his back.

"Oh my God," she said. "That's amazing. I mean, I've seen a paranormal's wounds heal quickly but never like this."

He shrugged. "Grizzly shifters are better than most at healing."

She wet a towel and gently wiped the blood from his back before pressing a fresh bandage to his skin and taping it in place. "Well, it's not completely healed yet, so just leave that bandage on there for a while, okay?"

"Yes, ma'am." He kept his hands on the wall as she threw away the bloody gauze. Her scent was becoming almost unbearable in the small room, and he put one hand over his mouth and nose as she tapped him on the back.

"Turn around so I can check the cut on your face."

He turned, and she shook her head in disbelief. "It's completely gone."

She eyed his broad, naked chest. Her face flushed, and he closed his eyes when the smell of her arousal filled the room.

"Bishop? What's wrong? Why do you have your hand over your face like that?"

Shit.

He dropped his hand and smiled nervously. "Uh, nothing."

"It's obviously something. Does your face hurt? Were you -"

"You smell!" he blurted out.

Her eyes widened, and a look of hurt flashed across her face. "Oh, um, I'm sorry. I'll just go."

She whipped open the bathroom door and cried out when it smacked him directly in the face. He staggered back, his hand cupping his throbbing nose, and she shut the door and crowded up against him.

"Oh my God! Bishop, I'm so sorry!" She pulled at his hand. "Let me see your face."

"It's fine." He kept his hand over his face and tried desperately to ignore the feel of her soft curves against him.

"Let me see it!" She yanked on his hand, and with a harsh sigh, he dropped his hand. Blood trickled out of his nose, and she moaned in dismay before wetting some gauze and wiping gently at the blood.

"Oh, God. I think I broke your nose," she said.

He reached up and straightened his nose with a hard twist of his fingers. She winced at the sound and pressed the gauze back to his nose as fresh blood trickled out.

"I am so sorry," she said.

He gave in to temptation and placed his hands on her full hips. She didn't seem to notice, and he held her firmly as she rechecked his nose.

"It's stopped bleeding. Thank God," she said with relief.

"It's fine." He smiled at her before inhaling deeply. "Doesn't even hurt anymore."

"Okay, good." She dropped the gauze into the sink and tried to step back. She made a soft squeak of surprise when his hands tightened around her hips, and she glanced briefly at them before staring up at him. "Wh-what are you doing, Bishop?"

"Nothing."

His grizzly was roaring at him to take the curvy redhead, and he was tired of denying the beast what he wanted most. Being trapped in the small bathroom, her intoxicating scent filling the small room and her soft body pressed against his had pushed all rational thought aside, and his grizzly half was firmly in control. Hell, a man only had so much willpower.

"Bishop, I should probably go," she said.

"Not yet," he murmured before burying his face in her neck and taking a nice, long sniff. His grizzly growled in approval, and he wondered if she could feel his erection.

Make her feel it. Show her how much we want her, his grizzly growled.

That was an excellent idea. His hands still on her hips, Bishop pulled Ava against him until every part of her soft body pressed against his.

"Oh!" she said, and he grinned against her throat before rubbing his cock against her.

"I love your freckles," he said. He traced the freckles on her upper chest with one rough finger. "Do you have them all over?"

She licked her lips, and he made a hoarse growl of need. "Do you, Ava? Answer me."

"Y-yes," she said.

"Good." He cupped the back of her neck and tugged her head back. She moaned in excitement when his tongue traced a wet path from her throat down to her collarbone.

He raised his head, and she stared up at him. "Bishop, I – you said I smell. Why are you doing this?"

He could smell her surprise when he licked her mouth with his warm tongue. "You do smell, Ava. You smell delicious."

"What do I smell like?" she whispered as his hand left her hip and wandered downward. He squeezed her full ass, kneading and rubbing it as he licked the line of her jaw.

"My favourite things." He bit at her earlobe, growling his approval when her hips jerked against him.

"What are your favourite things?" she asked breathlessly. Her hands clutched at his bare arms now, squeezing the biceps compulsively as he gently rocked his pelvis against hers.

"Chocolate," he murmured before licking her neck. "Sex."

She inhaled sharply, and he cupped the back of her neck and tugged her face upward. "You want me to fuck you, don't you, Ava?"

"I – I barely know you." She swallowed hard as his thumb stroked across her lips.

He pushed it into her mouth, and she sucked on it as he growled hoarsely. "I want to fuck you. I want to fuck you until every inch of your delicious body is covered in my scent, and that asshole lion shifter knows you belong to me."

He pulled his thumb from her mouth and rubbed her bottom lip roughly. "Let me fuck you, Ava."

"Okay," she whispered.

He grinned at her like the predator he was and then

kissed her. His tongue pushed past her parted lips and stroked against hers as he grabbed her ass with both hands and pressed her body into his.

She moaned into his mouth and slid her hands around his thick neck, gripping tightly as he kissed her repeatedly. He unzipped her dress, and she dropped her arms so he could rake it down to her waist. He groaned at the sight of her breasts barely contained in a black lace bra.

"So beautiful," he said.

He bent his head and licked the top of her breasts. She moaned again and threaded her fingers in his hair, clutching his head as he nipped and licked her soft flesh until the skin had reddened to a rosy glow.

He pulled down the cups of her bra, freeing her breasts to his gaze. She made a soft cry of need when he lifted one heavy breast and sucked her nipple into his mouth. He teased it with his tongue before biting it gently and pulling on it with his teeth.

"Bishop!" she gasped as his hand pinched and pulled at her other nipple.

"Mine, Ava. These are mine," he growled as he cupped her breast and kneaded it. "You taste so good. I can't wait to have my tongue in your sweet pussy. I'm going to make you ride my face until you're screaming my name."

"Oh my God," she moaned as he dipped his head and sucked on her nipple again. His erection was hot and heavy against her, and she squeezed her hand between their bodies and cupped it through his pants.

His breath hissed out between his teeth, and he bucked his hips against her as she stroked him. He reached for the hem of her dress and started to tug it upward. There was a sharp knock at the bathroom door, and he growled as Ava stiffened in his arms.

"What?" he roared.

"Mr. King? Mrs. Belfry would like to see you. Your associates and her sons are still missing, and she wants you to find them." Jeffries's voice was nervous and thin as it drifted through the door.

Bishop snarled before stepping away from Ava. "I have to go."

Her face flushed, Ava tucked her breasts into her bra and yanked up her dress. "Can you zip me up first?"

She turned her back to him, and he eyed her smooth, freckle-covered skin with regret before zipping up her dress. Without another word - he was hanging on to his self-control by a thread, and his grizzly was growling at him to finish what he started - he grabbed his shirt and jacket from the floor and left.

WILLOW SPRINTED THROUGH THE TREES. SHE COULD HEAR the heavy thudding footsteps of Mal behind her, and she blinked in surprise when Kat, her shoes kicked off, ran past her. The jaguar shifter moved with astonishing speed, and Willow envied her graceful movements as the lion brothers roared angrily somewhere ahead of them. Her heart pounding, she ran faster.

She dodged past a large tree and nearly knocked Kat flying when she ran into her back. The jaguar shifter stared in shock at the Belfry brothers. Keegan and Koren growled and snarled as rocks and branches came flying out of nowhere and rained down on their large bodies.

Keegan snapped at a branch flying toward his face and crushed it in his powerful jaws before backing up. Koren yelped in surprise and pain when a rock the size of Willow's head landed on his back and knocked him to the ground. Keegan roared again, the sound vibrating through the trees as Mal joined Kat and Willow.

"What the hell is happening?" Kat shouted.

"Ghost!" Willow shouted back. She darted forward, and Mal chased after her. He caught her around the waist and lifted her into the air as she kicked at him with her feet. "Mal, let me go!"

"No! You're going to get hurt." He backed away from the brothers.

She gave up struggling and instead shouted into thin air. "Hey! Hey, honey! Look at me! Stop, please! Just for a minute!"

The wind died down, and the rocks hovering in the air dropped to the ground with a soft thud.

"Mal, stop!" Willow pounded on his arm, and he stopped and set her on her feet but kept her tucked against his body.

"My name is Willow. Tell me yours, honey," Willow coaxed.

There was a soft, whispery moan, and Willow smiled. "Patricia. It's very nice to meet you, Patricia. Tell me why you're so angry at the Belfry brothers."

Keegan and Koren started to slink away, and Willow glared at them. "Don't you two dare sneak away!"

They growled at her and Mal, his eyes glowing and his body swelling snapped his teeth at them.

Kat joined them, and she grabbed his arm. "Cool it, Mal."

"Everyone cool it. Let me talk to Patricia," Willow said. "Mal, let go. You're holding me too tight."

He eased up on his grip around her waist but refused to release her as she smiled at a tree to her right. "Go ahead, Patricia. I'm listening."

The four of them waited as Willow stared at the tree. She frowned and nodded and then shook her head. "Assholes," she said before glaring at the Belfry brothers. "Okay, Patricia. No, I get it. You have every right to be angry."

She glared again at Koren and Keegan. "Shift right now, both of you."

They shifted to their human forms and gave each other uncomfortable looks before staring at the tree Willow had been talking to.

Koren cleared his throat. "Listen, I don't know what's going on or why you're talking to a tree, but -"

"Shut up, Koren!" Willow snapped. "Both of you owe Patricia an apology. A *sincere* apology. What you did to her was awful and selfish, and you know it. Say you're sorry."

"Say we're sorry to who?" Keegan stared at her in astonishment. "There's no one there, Willow."

"Patricia died! She was killed in a car accident shortly after you two tag-teamed her, promised her you'd be together forever, and then skipped out without saying a word. You broke her heart, and now she can't leave Earth because she's so upset by what you did to her. The two of you'd better get on your knees and beg for her forgiveness so she can move on. You owe her that much," Willow said.

"How – how do you know about her?" Keegan said.

Koren elbowed him. "Shut up, Keegan." He gave

Willow a grim look. "We don't know anyone named Patricia."

"Bullshit!" Willow said. Her head cocked, and Mal took a step back, bringing her with him as a cold wind rushed through them.

She slapped him lightly on the arm. "Don't, Mal. She won't hurt us."

She listened quietly as the Belfry brothers gave each other uneasy looks. After a few minutes, a small grin crossed her face, and she turned back to the brothers.

"You," she pointed to Koren, "like to be handcuffed to the bed and spanked. And you," she pointed at Keegan, "like to shift to your lion form after sex and have a woman brush your fur and braid your mane. You especially like it when she ties ribbons in it."

The Belfry brothers' mouths dropped open in identical looks of shock as Kat clapped her hand over her mouth to muffle her laughter.

"That's right," Willow said. "Patricia just told me all about your bedroom habits." She glanced up at Mal. "And that's the tame stuff. You would not *believe* how kinky these boys are."

She turned back to the lion shifters. "Should I go on? Should I mention how turned on you get, Keegan, when a woman lets you wear her -"

"No!" Keegan shouted. "Shit, Willow! Just – okay, we'll apologize, okay?"

"You have to mean it!" she said fiercely. "Do you understand how badly you hurt Patricia? What you did was awful, and you should be ashamed of yourselves. She loved you both."

Keegan's shoulders slumped. "We know, Willow. We're sorry."

"Don't say sorry to me, you big, dumb cat. Say sorry to Patricia," Willow said impatiently. "She's standing next to that tree."

Keegan licked his lips and turned toward the tree. "Patricia, baby, I'm so sorry. We shouldn't have just dumped you like that. It was stupid and immature of us, and I – I hope you can forgive us both."

Koren, his arms folded across his naked chest, snorted loudly.

"Koren," Willow said warningly.

He shook his head. "Willow, this is ridiculous. I can't apologize to someone I can't see, and besides -"

He gave a loud bellow of pain when a branch as thick as his wrist whacked him sharply across his bare ass. He dropped to his knees as Willow grinned.

"Patricia says there's more where that came from if you don't start apologizing. Of course," she stared up at Mal, "he's into that, so maybe she shouldn't threaten him with a spanking."

Mal, his face twitching and his body shaking, stared at the ground as he struggled to hold in his laughter. Kat didn't even bother to hide her wide grin as Koren's face turned a bright red.

"Fine!" he snapped. "I'm sorry, Patricia."

"Like you mean it," Willow said pointedly.

He sighed again. "I do mean it. Honestly, Patricia, I feel terrible for what we did. We were idiots to lead you on like that, and we should have been honest from the beginning. You were kind and sweet and didn't deserve to be treated like that."

"Not bad as far as apologies go," Willow said to Mal.

She leaned forward and listened intently for a moment. "Well, you're a better person than I am, Patricia, but I'll relay the message."

She stared sternly at the Belfry brothers as there was a soft rustling behind them, and Bishop appeared. His shirt was unbuttoned, and his jacket was slung over his arm, and he stood next to Kat and stared curiously at the others.

"Patricia's forgiving you. I think she should make you both beg a little more, but apparently, she's nicer than I am, so all is forgiven. She says she won't bother you again." Willow raised her eyebrows at them. "You should go back to the party. I'm sure your mother is worried about you."

With a final, uneasy look at the trees, the brothers shifted to their lion forms and loped out of sight. Willow tugged at Mal's arm. "Let me go, please. Patricia wants to talk to me again."

Reluctantly he let her go and watched as she walked a few feet away and leaned against a tree. She stared into the air in front of her with an intent look on her face as Kat and Bishop joined him.

"What just happened?" Bishop asked.

"Willow was right," Mal said. "It was a ghost at the warehouse. The Belfry boys hurt this woman's feelings, and when she died, she decided to take her revenge."

"You're kidding me, right?" Bishop said.

"I'm not." Mal shook his head. "Ask Kat."

"It's true," Kat said. "Be glad that you weren't here. We learned some personal and disturbing things about the Belfry brothers' sex lives."

"I don't even know what to say to that," Bishop said.

"How's your back?" Kat turned him around and lifted the back of his shirt. "Who bandaged it for you?"

"Uh, Ava. She's, uh, a nurse." Bishop turned bright red, and Mal stared at him.

"What's going on, Bishop?"

"Nothing. Nothing's going on. Ava bandaged it, and I said thank you and left. That's it," Bishop said. "Absolutely nothing else happened."

Kat laughed. "Really? Then why is there lipstick on your mouth?"

Bishop scrubbed furiously at his mouth as Mal rolled his eyes. "Just ask her out already, Bishop."

"No. Ava's a nice girl, and she deserves someone who doesn't just want sex. That's all I want, it's all I'll ever want, and humans don't understand that. I just need to find a nice grizzly bitch and get laid," Bishop said a bit desperately.

Kat patted him on the back. "You keep telling yourself that, Bishop."

CHAPTER 13

"Willow, I can wait for you. I don't mind," Ava said. "No, honey. Go on home. We need to convince Mrs. Belfry that her warehouse is still in trouble and who knows how long that will take. Mal said he would give me a ride home," Willow said.

"Are you sure?"

"I'm positive." Willow glanced behind her. Mal, Kat and Bishop waited patiently for her as she said goodbye to Ava. Bishop avoided looking in their direction, and Willow turned to AVa. "Is everything okay with you and Bishop?"

"Yes, why? Why would there be something wrong?" Ava said.

Willow arched her eyebrows. "You're hiding something from me."

Ava sighed. "Call me tomorrow morning, and we'll talk, okay?"

"Yes." Willow hugged her. "Thanks, honey. Be careful driving home."

"I will."

"Oh, and one more thing." Willow took her hand and squeezed it. "If Keegan asks you out on a date, say no."

"Why?"

"Just trust me on this. I'll explain later." Willow grinned at her.

"Okay. Bye, Willow."

"Bye, honey. I love you."

"I love you too."

Willow waited until Ava had driven away before joining the others. "Are you ready?"

They nodded, and the four of them returned to Mrs. Belfry's mansion. Marika, her husband, and her sons stood in the living room with a man Willow hadn't seen before.

"Mrs. Belfry, thank you for meeting with us. I know this is a bad time, but we need to speak to you about something very important," Kat said.

"That's fine," Mrs. Belfry said. She glanced at the man standing next to her husband. "This is Royce Darnell. He's the foreman for the warehouse and works very closely with Keegan in the day-to-day running of the warehouse. He's been on holiday the last two weeks."

The man nodded to them as Willow looked him over. He was tall and thin with yellow eyes and a bald, gleaming head. Before she could ask, Mal leaned down and whispered in her ear, "Snake shifter."

"It's nice to meet you, Mr. Darnell," Kat said.

"Please, call me Royce." He smiled at Kat, and the hair on the back of Willow's neck stood up.

The man had a slight lisp, and as she watched him walk across the living room and sit down on the couch, she told herself Royce was creepy because she hated snakes. It wasn't fair of her to judge him on that. He was probably perfectly nice.

"Well, what's the issue?" Mrs. Belfry said. "My sons tell me it's a ghost wreaking havoc in our warehouse, and while I'm fairly open-minded, I'm wondering if perhaps they're playing a joke on me."

"They're not, Marika," Willow said. She glanced at Mal, and he nodded for her to continue.

She took a deep breath and sat down beside Mrs. Belfry. "I have a unique ability. Since I was a child, I've seen spirits. These spirits are trapped on Earth, usually because they've been wronged or are upset, and they come to me for help. This particular spirit, Patricia, she was – well – she was wronged by your sons, and that's why she caused all that damage to the warehouse."

"What did they do to her?" Marika stared at her sons, and they both blushed and gave her identical guilty grins.

"It's not important," Willow said. "What's important is that your sons apologized, and Patricia accepted it. She's happy now and will leave our realm."

Mrs. Belfry frowned at her. "So, then what's the problem? Based on what you've just told me, we should have no more issues at the warehouse then."

"Before she left our realm, Patricia told me that she wasn't the one responsible for the violence at the warehouse," Willow said.

"What do you mean?" Marika asked.

"Well, she did some of the more harmless pranks – the window breaking, the dish smashing, that sort of thing - but she didn't set the truck on fire, nor did she hurt the bear shifter."

Mrs. Belfry stared at her for a long moment. "Do you believe her?"

"I do," Willow said.

"Well, if it wasn't her doing it, then who is? Did she tell you?"

"No, she didn't know," Willow said.

Garrett snorted quietly. "Marika, my love, surely you do not believe this nonsense?"

Willow glared at him. "It's not nonsense. It's the truth."

"Forgive me, Ms. Tanner, is it?" Garrett gave her a brittle smile. "Koren tells me you're the receptionist at the security firm. Why exactly are you even here?"

"I invited her, Garrett," Marika said sharply, "and you're being rude to my guest."

"Forgive me, my love," Garrett said. "It's just – we have a serious problem at the warehouse, and I refuse to believe that a ghost with a grudge against your sons caused it."

"Yes, you do have a serious problem," Mal said. "That's what we're trying to tell you. Thanks to Willow, the harmless pranks will end now, but the violence may not end. We need to find out who's responsible for it."

He turned toward Mrs. Belfry. "I know you don't want to hear this, Mrs. Belfry, but I believe that a staff member is causing the violence. Since our security team took over, there haven't been any violent outbursts. Our presence has made it more difficult for the staff member behind this. Obviously, they'd need to be more cautious with us around. If it was someone from outside your organization, they wouldn't know that you'd hired extra security and would continue their attacks."

Mrs. Belfry frowned. "Your persistent belief that one of my loyal staff members would betray me like this is starting to get on my nerves, wolf shifter."

"Mrs. Belfry," Kat said, "I believe Mal is right. It has to be an inside job."

Keegan cleared his throat. "Mother, they have a point. It might -"

"Quiet!" She curled her upper lip and hissed at him. "I will deal with you and your brother later." She glared fiercely at them, and despite their massive size and strength, they shrunk under her hot gaze.

She turned to Royce. "Royce, what do you think?"

He hesitated before sighing. "I agree with them, Marika. I'm sorry, I know you want to think the best of your employees, but I believe it would be wise to allow them to continue their investigation into the staff."

"They're a security company, not private detectives," Garrett said. "They were hired to keep the staff safe, not interrogate them."

"We're not going to interrogate them," Kat said. "We just want to speak with them again and take a look at their employee files to see if anything suspicious pops up."

"Absolutely not!" Mrs. Belfry said. "Those files are confidential, and I won't have you snooping through them. My employees deserve their privacy."

Willow stroked her arm. "Of course. You're right, Marika. But it wouldn't hurt if we spoke with them again, would it?"

"No, I suppose it wouldn't. Although," Marika gave her a doggedly determined look, "I refuse to believe that it's an employee and, in fact, I quite suspect that it is this ghost of yours who is lying."

Willow didn't reply, and Mrs. Belfry abruptly stood. "I'm tired, it's been a long night, and I have a headache. Would you mind showing yourselves out?"

"Of course not." Willow smiled at her as Mal stood.

"Mrs. Belfry, I'd like your permission to keep a larger team of security at the warehouse, just for another week or two until we can -"

"No," Mrs. Belfry said. "I'm certain the trouble is behind us now, so you can drop your team to one. I refuse to pay for extra men just because you think one of my staff is a violent sociopath. And I don't want you or Mr. King questioning the staff. Ms. Frost or Willow are the only ones allowed to question them. Do I make myself clear?"

Mal frowned. "Mrs. Belfry, that isn't -"

"That's perfectly fine, Mrs. Belfry," Kat said quickly. "Willow and I will be happy to talk to your employees. Thank you."

"WELL, THAT WAS SOME PARTY, HUH?" WILLOW SAID AS they walked down the hallway toward her apartment door.

"Yeah," Mal said.

He'd insisted on walking Willow right to her door, but he was starting to regret that decision. His wolf made it almost impossible to think straight, what with his howling and growling and downright demanding insistence that Mal pick up Willow and carry her straight to her bed.

"Thanks again for the ride home." She smiled sweetly at him as she opened the door to her apartment and flicked on the hall light. He stood in the doorway as she slipped off her high heels and made a soft sigh of relief. "God, that feels so much better."

He didn't reply, and she gave him another sweet smile. "Would you like to come in for a nightcap, Mal?"

Yes! Now is our chance to claim her.

He ignored his wolf. "That's not a good idea, Willow."

"I think it is." She smoothed the front of her dress. The rasp of her palms against the silky material was excruciatingly loud.

"It isn't," he said, while every part of him screamed to do what she asked.

"C'mon, Mal. I promise I don't bite. Unless you're into that sort of thing." She winked at him, and he clenched his hands into fists before backing out of her doorway.

"Goodnight, Willow." He swallowed thickly. "I'll see you at work."

Disappointment flickered across her face, but she nodded and gave him a strained smile. "Right. Bye, Mal."

"Bye." He walked away as she shut the door behind him.

What are you doing? Get back there, idiot! She wants you. Now is the time to take her and make her ours.

He pushed the button for the elevator, his head ringing with the insistent growl of his wolf. It wasn't a good idea. In fact, sleeping with Willow was the worst fucking idea in the world. The elevator doors opened, and he stepped into the small space.

WILLOW LOCKED THE DOOR AND SIGHED MOROSELY BEFORE heading toward the kitchen. Mal had rejected her again, and it was starting to be embarrassing. She kept acting like a total fool, and she needed to accept that Mal might want her, but he would never sleep with her. She couldn't blame him. His grandfather had told him how awful humans were and, truth be told, they kind of were. Humans had done some terrible things to paranormals, and it was unbelievable that there existed even a fragile type of peace between them.

She rubbed her lower back. It was time to stop being such a horny little tart and leave Mal alone. It wasn't fair to him. She started at the knock on her door, and, frowning slightly, she hurried over and peered through the peephole. She unlocked the door and stared up at the wolf shifter. "Mal? What's wrong?"

He pulled her into his embrace with a low growl and kissed her hotly. Her body reacted instantly, melting against his as she threw her arms around his neck and returned his kiss enthusiastically. He lifted her, and she wrapped her legs around his waist as he kicked the door shut with his foot.

"Bedroom?" he growled.

"Down the hallway, second door on the left," she said.

He carried her to the bedroom as she planted hot, wet kisses on his throat and tugged at his tie with one hand. By the time he'd brought her into the bedroom, she had removed his tie and was working on his shirt buttons. He set her gently on her feet, and she shoved his suit jacket from his broad body. His shirt followed quickly, and she licked her lips as she stared at his chest.

"God, Mal. You are so damn hot," she said.

He tugged impatiently at the sleeves of her dress, and she helped him pull off her dress. She wore nothing but panties and thigh-highs beneath it, and he growled loudly at the sight of her small breasts with their hard, pink nipples.

Without speaking, he bent his head and licked a warm path between her breasts before taking her right nipple into his mouth. He sucked hard on it as she gasped and reached eagerly for the button of his pants.

"Naked, Mal. I need you naked right now," she moaned.

He moved back and kicked off his shoes before standing on one foot and pulling awkwardly at his sock. She giggled when he nearly fell over, and he gave her a warning growl that she ignored.

"You look like a stork." She giggled again.

He pulled off his other sock and dropped his pants and briefs. The giggle dried up in her throat at the sight of his cock. It was huge and standing stiffly out from his body. She reached for it, wrapping her small hand around it and stroking lightly.

"Damn, Mal," she said in a quiet voice. "That's impressive."

"Thank you," he said politely, and she grinned at him.

He lifted her and dropped her on the bed. She squealed softly in surprise as she bounced on the bed, and he dropped between her legs and placed a wet kiss on her flat abdomen. Her hips arched up, and he wrapped his fist around her tiny lace panties and yanked. They ripped easily, and he pulled them from her body and threw them on the floor.

"Hey! Those were my favourite pair of panties!" She gave him a mock scowl that turned into a low moan when he kissed the small patch of dark hair between her legs.

"I'll buy you a new pair," he murmured as he pushed on her legs. She widened her thighs, and he stared at her swollen clit peeking out from between the wet lips of her pussy.

"Mine," he whispered before pushing her lips apart and licking the pink nub.

"Oh my God!" she cried out as her pelvis arched and her thighs tightened around his head. He sucked her clit into his mouth and slid a finger deep into her wet, tight entrance as she made soft noises of pleasure and thrust her hips against him.

He sucked on her clit until she moaned and squirmed beneath him. He placed his arm across her hips to hold her down and licked and sucked and teased her clit until she cried out with pleasure and came all over his face. He licked her clean as she twitched and shivered beneath him until, with a breathless cry, she pushed at his head.

"Enough, please, Mal!" she begged.

He grinned and rubbed his jaw along the soft, smooth skin of her inner thigh, marking her with his scent, before tracing the top of her stockings with his fingers. "Are you sure, Willow? I think you can take more."

"No, I can't," she pleaded. "I need you inside of me. Please!"

"Whatever you want," he said.

She made a low cry of distress when he left the bed, but he returned quickly. He ripped open the foil package he held and rolled the condom over his cock. She spread her thighs wide as he lowered himself into the cradle of her hips. He dipped his head and spent torturous moments licking and nipping at her breasts until she thought she would go mad with need.

He positioned himself at her entrance and pushed into her in one smooth motion. She cried out, her eyes squeezing shut as she stretched around his hard length. He kissed her, and she touched his tongue delicately with her own. They kissed slowly and deeply as she stroked his back with her soft hands.

"You feel so good, Willow," he whispered against her mouth. "So warm and wet."

She smiled at him and kneaded his back. "I need you, Mal. Don't make me wait any longer."

"I need you too," he said and slowly moved within her. She wrapped her legs around his waist and hooked her feet together in the small of his back as they moved against each other in a slow, deep rhythm. He buried his face in her neck and rubbed his stubble against her smooth skin, marking her repeatedly as he withdrew and surged into her with an unhurried pace.

She made small cooing noises of pleasure in his ear, and his hips started to thrust faster. He propped himself up on his hands and stared down at her as their bodies moved together. Their hips slapped against each other as he pushed a little harder and deeper, and she moaned her approval. Her hands clutched at his broad back, and she cried out when he slipped one hand between them and rubbed at her sensitive clit.

She bucked her hips against him, and he howled when her core tightened around him, and she shuddered help-lessly as she came. He plunged back and forth, burying his face into her long dark hair. He climaxed with another low howl, his large body shaking and twitching before he collapsed against her.

"Oof!" She made a soft grunt and pushed at his chest. "Can't breathe!"

"Sorry." He rolled off of her and stared up at the ceiling as she leaned over him.

"Hey, Mal?"

"Yeah?"

"That was awesome."

He laughed, and she kissed him lightly on the lips. "Were you holding back?"

"What do you mean?"

"You know what I mean." She stroked his chest. "You were worried about hurting me, weren't you?"

"Maybe," he said slowly. "You're little, Willow."

"I'm stronger than I look," she said before she curled into his embrace. "I'll give you a pass this time, wolf boy, because even holding back, you made my toes curl. But I don't want you to be afraid of hurting me, okay? You won't."

He didn't reply, but he pulled her closer and stroked her back with his fingertips as she sighed happily. "You're staying the night with me, right?"

"Yes. If you want me to."

She grinned up at him. "Oh, I definitely want you spending the night, Malcolm Burke."

CHAPTER 14

He woke up to the feel of her hot, wet mouth sliding over his cock. He cried out in the darkness, and she pushed him back to the bed when he tried to sit up.

"Willow," he moaned as she sucked him into an aching hardness.

"Yes, Mal?" She cupped his balls and stroked them lightly as she flicked her tongue over the head of his cock.

"Fuck, that feels amazing," he groaned.

"Glad you approve," she murmured before sliding her mouth over his cock again. She sucked firmly as her long dark hair tickled his thighs. He reached down and gathered her hair into a ponytail, watching as her soft lips slid up and down his aching flesh.

He cursed again when she squeezed the base of him with her tiny hand and sucked on the head of his cock. She grinned up at him, her mouth swollen and red, and he growled softly and tugged on her hair.

"Again."

"You're the boss," she said.

He pumped his hips against her as she used her mouth and tongue to torment and tease him until he was nearly frantic with the need to come.

"Willow! Stop!" he gasped out.

She gave him one last lick before straddling him and rubbing her pussy against his hard length. "Ready for round two, Mal?"

"Hell, yes," he moaned.

She leaned over him and rummaged through the drawer in the table beside the bed before pulling out a condom. She quickly rolled it over his cock and then slid him into her warmth. They both sighed with pleasure, and he gripped her narrow hips as she braced her hands on his chest.

"No holding back," she demanded.

He nodded, and she made a startled gasp when he thrust roughly back and forth. Her small breasts bounced, and her fingers dug into his chest as he plunged in and out. She reached down and rubbed firmly at her clit until she was making small breathless moans of pleasure. He watched as her back arched, and she bit down hard on her bottom lip as she came helplessly around his thick cock.

Before she could collapse against him, he flipped her onto her back, shoving her thighs apart and entering her again with one firm thrust. His entire body screaming for release, he pounded into her as she clung tightly to his hard body and made soft sounds of encouragement.

As his orgasm started, his fangs came out, and he bent his head to her shoulder.

Bite her, claim her as ours forever.

He groaned under his breath and forced his mouth

away from her smooth skin as his orgasm roared through him.

Bite her!

His wolf howled with anger, and Mal fought bitterly for control as his body shook with the force of his climax. After a moment, his human half won and the need to claim Willow lessened. He sagged in relief against her slender body.

She stroked his back and kissed his broad shoulder. "Mal, are you okay?"

"Yes. Are you?" He lifted himself off of her and stared anxiously at her.

"Just fine. I told you I'm tougher than I look." She smoothed his hair back from his face.

"I'm starting to realize that." He kissed her and reluctantly moved away from her warm body, disposing of the condom before curling up against her. She put her arms around him, and he buried his face in her throat.

"Mal?"

"Yeah?"

"Do you hate humans?"

He cupped her small breast and squeezed firmly. "I think it should be pretty obvious by now that I don't hate you, Willow."

"I don't mean me. I mean humans in general. Kat told me who your grandfather was."

He stiffened against her, and she immediately rubbed his back. "Don't be mad at her. Okay?"

"She shouldn't be gossiping at work."

"It wasn't gossip. She was trying to help me understand why you were so hell-bent on staying away from me."

He sighed, and she kissed the top of his head. "Tell me the truth, Mal. Do you hate humans?"

"No," he said. "I don't hate them. But I believe humans and paranormals are better off staying away from each other. Sooner or later, something's going to happen between us that creates enough tension to start a war. And the humans and the paranormals that are friends, or in relationships, they're going to be caught in the crossfire."

"I think you're wrong, Mal. I know there's tension between us, but there's enough good in humans and para-normals to keep war from breaking out," she said.

"Is there? The humans weren't exactly good to my grandfather," he said.

"I know." There was sorrow in her voice. "I'm sorry my kind was so awful to yours."

"It's in their nature," he said.

"So, what's happening between us is just a one-time thing then?" she said.

He hesitated. "I'm sorry, Willow, but yes – I think after tonight we shouldn't do this again."

"I thought that's what you would say," she said.

"I'm sorry. Do you want me to leave?" he asked.

She gave him a startled look. "What? No, of course not. If this is our only night, then I'm going to make the most of it."

"I don't want to take advantage of you," he said.

She smiled at him. "You're not, Mal. I'm a big girl, and I can take care of myself."

"Willow -"

"Enough talking," she said. "I think it's time I had another go at the big bad wolf, don't you?"

A small smile crossed his face. "Whatever you say, Willow."

WILLOW LEANED OVER THE FRESHLY BREWED POT OF coffee and inhaled. After a night of sex with Mal, she needed the caffeine jolt. Before she could pour herself a cup, there was a soft knock on her door. She walked to the door and checked the peephole before opening the door.

"Ava? What's wrong?"

Holding two coffees, Ava smiled at her. "Nothing's wrong. I just thought I would come by before work. You said you would call this morning, and I hadn't heard from you."

"Oh right. I'm sorry. I forgot," Willow said. "Here, come into the kitchen."

Ava followed her into the kitchen and sat down at the table. "So, how did it go with Mrs. Belfry? Did you convince her that there's still trouble at the warehouse?"

Willow sipped at her coffee. "Sort of. I mean, she accepted the whole ghost thing, but she believes that the issues will stop with Patricia gone. She's letting me and Kat question the staff again, but she's only allowing us to have one security guard at the warehouse now."

"So, this Patricia didn't do all that stuff at the warehouse?" Ava asked.

"She did some of the minor things, but she told me that she had nothing to do with the more vicious attacks, and I believe her. Unfortunately, we don't have a clue who -"

"Hey, Willow?" Mal strolled naked into the kitchen, holding a bottle of body wash and frowning at the back of it. "Are you seriously going to tell me that you don't have any other body wash besides this mango-vanilla crap? I can't shower with this. Men aren't supposed to smell like mango or vanil -"

He stopped, his eyes widening, as he looked up from the bottle in his hand to see Ava staring at him. Her gaze dropped to his dick, and he held the bottle of body wash in front of his crotch as Willow shook with laughter.

"Shit!" he said. "I'm sorry, I didn't realize you had company."

He continued to stand there like a deer in the head-lights as Ava, her face as red as her hair, looked away. "Good morning, Mal."

"Morning, Ava. Uh, how are you, uh, this morning?"

"Good, I'm good. How are you?"

"Uh, good, really good. I'm, uh, gonna go now and...."

Barely holding in her giggles, Willow raised her eyebrow. "Shower?"

"Yeah, shower. Uh, bye, Ava."

"Bye, Mal."

He backed out of the kitchen, still holding the bottle in front of his dick. Once he was gone, Willow laughed until tears came to her eyes. "That was awesome! Did you see the look on his face?"

"Honestly? I wasn't looking at his face," Ava said.

Willow laughed again. "Pervert."

"I'm not the one with a naked wolf shifter strolling around my apartment." Ava took another sip of coffee.

"That's only because you prefer bear shifters," Willow said.

At the mention of Bishop, Ava's face turned bright red

again, and Willow leaned forward. "Spill it, Ava. What happened between you and Bishop yesterday?"

"After he saved me from being wiped out by a flying table, I made him go to the bathroom with me. He had a piece of table sticking into his back, and he refused to go to the hospital. We were in the bathroom, and he freaked me out by just yanking the wood out of his back, but it started healing almost immediately. I've never seen anything like it, Willow."

She stared into her coffee. "I've seen paranormals start healing themselves at the hospital, but I've never seen it happen so quickly."

"Cool," Willow said. "Then what happened?"

"Well, his back was to me, and when he turned around, he had his hand over his mouth and nose. I asked him what was wrong, and he said I smelled."

Willow groaned. "Oh, Bishop. You moron."

"Naturally, my feelings were hurt, and so I tried to leave, but when I opened the door, it hit him in the face and broke his nose."

"Good. He deserved it," Willow said.

"No, he didn't," Ava said. "After his nose stopped bleeding, he told me that I smelled good. That I smelled like chocolate and," she hesitated, her cheeks flushing, "sex."

"Nice," Willow said.

"I told him I'd better go, but then he started touching me and then he – he said that he wanted to…."

She paused, and Willow leaned forward. "He wanted to what?"

"He wanted to make me ride his face until I was screaming his name," Ava whispered.

Willow's mouth dropped open. "Why that pervy little bear. I had no idea Bishop had that in him. I mean, he's so damn awkward and sweaty around women."

Ava didn't reply, and Willow grinned at her. "So, did you?"

"Did I what?"

"Did you ride his face?"

"Willow! No, I did not ride his face," Ava said as she glanced down the hallway toward Willow's bedroom. "And keep your voice down!"

"I think you should have at least considered it," Willow said.

"The bathroom was way too small for that," Ava said. "With my fat ass and his giant seven-foot body, there was no chance of that kind of acrobatic feat. Besides, I'm not going to – to just sit on his face like that – I'd suffocate him."

Willow rolled her eyes. "Bishop's a giant, Ava. I think he can handle your curves. What happened then?"

"Nothing," Ava said.

"Liar," Willow replied. "Don't skip past the good parts."

Ava sighed. "Fine. We might have started making out. Hell, Willow, he's an amazing kisser, and his hands are so big and so warm, and his tongue… he also told me that he wanted to fuck me until I was covered in his scent and that Keegan knew I belonged to him."

"Paranormals and their damn marking. What is up with that?" Willow touched her reddened throat. "Look at this. Mal must have marked me like fifty times last night. I'll smell like his wolf for months."

Ava studied her throat as Willow took a drink of

coffee. "So, did you and Bishop fuck like bunnies, uh, I mean bears?"

"No. That butler guy knocked on the door and said Mrs. Belfry wanted Bishop to find you guys, so he left."

"Ooh, that's bad timing."

"It's for the best," Ava said. "I've been doing some research on bear shifters, and they don't mate for life, Willow. They don't even raise their babies."

"I think Bishop might be different," Willow said.

Ava frowned at her. "You're only saying that because you know it's what I want to hear."

"No, I'm saying that because he does seem to have a thing for you. If all he wanted was sex, do you think he'd keep saving your cute ass from idiots like that guy at the farm and being smushed to death by random flying tables? Plus, he was super pissed when you danced with Keegan."

"I asked him to dance, and he said no," Ava said. "Every time I try to talk to him, he literally runs away. When I get him to stay in the same room with me, it always ends with him telling me he wants to fuck me. It's sex to him, Willow, nothing more."

"Ava -"

Ava shook her head. "I'm tired of talking about it. What's going on with you and Mal? Are you a couple now?"

"No. Last night was a one-time thing."

"Really?" Ava asked. "That doesn't sound like something you'd want."

Willow shrugged, but she knew Ava could see the hurt on her face. "I agreed to it. It's fine, Ava. Mal has his reasons for believing humans and paranormals shouldn't be in relationships, and I respect them."

Ava reached out and took her hand. "But you like him, Will, I know you do."

Willow nodded and took a glance down the hallway. "I do. I really do. We're the complete opposites. He's so organized and disgustingly neat, and he never wants to break the rules, and I – well, I'm me – but dammit if I don't really like him."

She sighed. "I'm an idiot."

"No, you're not," Ava said. "And I have a feeling that Mal isn't going to be able to stay away from you."

"Do you think so?" Willow brightened. "I tried to rock his world last night, and I'm pretty sure I succeeded. Maybe I should try seducing him over breakfast. I bet I could at least get him to stay the weekend."

Ava grinned at her. "That's my girl." She glanced at her watch. "Listen, I'd better go. I need to be at work in half an hour. Have fun seducing your wolf."

"Oh, I will." Willow hugged Ava and walked her to the door. She closed and locked it before returning to the kitchen.

She sipped at her coffee and drummed her fingers thoughtfully on the table before suddenly stripping out of her yoga pants and t-shirt. She sat naked at the table, crossing her legs and leaning back in the chair before jumping up and leaning against the counter instead. She thrust her small chest out and waited. After a moment, she frowned and dug through one of the drawers. She pulled out a colourful apron, tied it around her waist, and took some eggs out from the fridge. It probably wasn't nice of her to try to seduce Mal when he had so clearly indicated he only wanted one night with her, but hell, a girl had needs.

MAL SHOVED HIS TIE INTO HIS POCKET BEFORE BUTTONING his shirt. His wolf was growling at him to stay as Mal grabbed his suit jacket. Staying any longer with Willow was a bad idea. His wolf was already way too attached to her, and his human half was quickly catching up.

It wouldn't work between them, he reminded himself. Forgetting that Willow was human, she was also – well - odd, and two people as different as they were would never work long term. Besides, wolf shifters didn't mate for life with humans. At least the smart ones didn't.

Your mother would love her.

He shoved that thought out of his head. Yeah, maybe she would, but he was thirty-two years old and didn't need his mother's approval. She would just be happy if he settled down and provided her with a few grandpups.

He took a deep breath and left Willow's bedroom. He stopped in the hallway and listened carefully. It sounded like Ava had left and, still ignoring his wolf's very persistent growls, he walked into the kitchen.

"I should probably get going, Willow. I have…"

His voice trailed off in a low, breathless groan as Willow smiled at him.

"Willow, what -" he swallowed thickly, "what are you doing?"

"Cooking you breakfast," she said.

She stood at the stove cooking eggs in a pan, and his wolf made an almost frantic howl of need. He gripped the table in front of him and stared hungrily at her. She was completely naked except for a bright pink apron tied around her waist, and he gazed at her firm ass as she bent and pulled the toaster from a cupboard next to the stove.

"Willow," he whispered.

She turned to face him. He eyed her small breasts and growled softly as she pointed the spatula at him. "I know you need to go but at least sit and eat breakfast first, Mal. It's the most important meal of the day."

He crossed the kitchen and pulled the spatula from her hand before shutting off the burner. "You're going to burn yourself," he said.

"I'll be fine. I can't let my big bad wolf leave hungry, can I?" she said.

He lifted her and set her on the counter before pushing her legs apart. "I guess I'll need to eat pussy for breakfast then."

He pushed his face between her thighs and licked at her warm core. She moaned, and her hand gripped his hair and tightened as he licked at her clit. He marked her inner thighs again, rubbing his jaw repeatedly over the soft skin as she made a soft cooing noise. He growled when she pulled on his hair. "Mal, stop."

He straightened. "What's wrong?"

"Nothing's wrong. I just need to ask you something really important."

She gave him an uncharacteristically serious look, and he felt his stomach tighten. She was going to ask him what this meant and where they were going with this, and he knew without a doubt she would hate his answer.

"Go ahead," he said gruffly.

"Okay, and this is important, so be honest with me." She cupped his face and stroked the stubble on his jaw.

"Does that cheesy line about eating pussy for breakfast work on female shifters?"

He stared mutely at her, and she giggled. "I mean, not that I'm against you eating my pussy for breakfast but really, Mal? I had no idea you were such a cheeseball."

"You're going to pay for calling me a cheeseball, woman," he growled, and she shrieked in surprise when he hoisted her over his shoulder. He slapped her lightly on her naked ass as he strode down the hallway to her bedroom.

"Who's afraid of the big bad wolf?" She laughed and gave him a return slap on his ass. "Not this little Red Riding Hood."

He dropped her to the bed, and she giggled wildly as she bounced to a stop. He covered her body with his, and she wrapped her limbs around him and kissed him firmly on the mouth. He returned her kiss, deepening it as he untied the apron from around her waist. He cupped one small breast and kneaded it as she moaned.

"Mal?"

"Yes, Willow?"

"Stay the weekend with me?" she asked sweetly. "Just the weekend. That's all I'm asking for."

He studied her lovely face before stroking her hair. "Yes. I'd like that."

She gave him a brilliant smile, and he nuzzled her throat affectionately, kissing and licking the reddened skin as she squeezed him tight.

CHAPTER 15

"Don't take this the wrong way, Will, but you stink." Kat grinned at her.

Willow sniffed her armpit. "I showered this morning."

It was Monday morning, and she and Kat were on their way to Mrs. Belfry's warehouse to interview the staff. Kat rolled down the window before turning left off the highway.

"Showering isn't going to get rid of Mal's marking." She grinned again as Willow blushed.

"Is it really that strong?"

Kat nodded. "Yep. Don't even try to deny that you and Mal had sex, Willow."

"Oh, I'm not," Willow said happily. "We did it like bunnies all weekend. That wolf is insatiable."

"Gross." Kat glanced at the dark blue scarf around Willow's neck. "Is that why you're wearing a scarf today?"

"Yes." Willow unwound the scarf and showed Kat the

scratched, red skin of her throat. Mal got a little crazy with the marking."

Kat shook her head. "Shit. Did he ever. That'll take weeks to heal."

"You think my throat is bad? You should see my inner thighs," Willow said. "They're so red they -"

"Gross!" Kat repeated. "Seriously, Willow, I don't need to hear about Mal's bedroom performance."

"Are you sure? The guy is talented." Willow teased.

"I'm positive." She hesitated before giving Willow a casual look. "Did he, uh, bite you?"

Willow shook her head. "No. Why would he? A wolf shifter bites to claim his mate."

"I know, but they don't normally mark so heavily either," Kat said.

Willow shrugged. "It was just a one-time thing, Kat. We both agreed to it just being the weekend."

"Is that what you want?" Kat asked.

"Yes, of course." Willow smiled at her.

"Really?" Kat said. "Because I think you're lying, Willow."

Willow sighed. "Shit. Is it that obvious?"

"Eh, a little," Kat said.

Willow sighed again before looking out the window. "I like him, Kat. We're completely different, and he's so not into the idea of a long-term commitment with a human, but dammit if I'm not completely taken with the guy."

"I'm sorry, Willow," Kat said. "Listen, if it becomes too difficult, Bishop and I will understand if you want to find a new job. I mean, we don't want you to leave, but we also want what's best for you and -"

"I'm not going to quit," Willow said.

Kat breathed a sigh of relief. "Oh, thank God. I want to be supportive, but I'd hate it if you left. You're the most organized, competent admin person we've ever had, and I would seriously consider carving off Mal's balls if you left because of him."

Willow shrugged. "I like working for you guys, and besides, I'm a big girl. I knew what I was getting into when I agreed to Mal's terms. Although," she brightened, "he initially said just the night, and I coaxed him into the entire weekend so I might have a chance at winning him over."

"If anyone can win him over, it's you," Kat said.

"Big plans for tonight, Ava?" Ginger asked.

Ava shook her head. "Unless putting on my pajamas and watching a marathon of *The Bachelor* counts as big plans?"

"It doesn't," Ginger said as she sat down at the desk.

"Mr. Marson has been restless all day." Ava moved her neck from side to side, stretching the tense muscles.

"The poor guy. He's been in the ER for two days now. Why the hell can't they get him a bed already?"

"Respiratory keeps saying they don't have a bed," Ava said.

"They're full of shit," Ginger scoffed. "I'm at the point where I'm going to go up there and find a damn bed for…."

She trailed off, her eyes widening as she stared over Ava's shoulder. "Damn."

Ava turned and smiled hesitantly. "Keegan! What are you doing here?"

Keegan returned her smile. "I was in the neighbourhood. Thought I'd drop by and say hello."

"Oh. Well, um, hello," Ava said.

"Hello, Ava." He reached out and tugged lightly on a fiery strand of hair that had escaped her braid. "How are you, beautiful?"

"Good," Ava said. "How are you?"

"Better now that I see you. I'm sorry about the party on Friday night. I didn't mean for the night to end that way."

"It's fine."

"Hi, I'm Ginger." Ginger leaned over the desk and held out her hand.

"Hello, Ginger." Keegan flashed her a panty-melting smile. "I'm Keegan."

"It's nice to meet you, Keegan." Ginger held his hand a moment too long before blushing and releasing it.

"You as well," Keegan said. "Ava, I wondered if you'd like to have a drink with me. I know it's short notice."

"Oh, well, uh, I'm working so…."

"Another time perhaps," Keegan said with disappointment.

"Ava's shift is finished," Ginger said. "She was just on her way out the door."

"Come for a drink with me, Ava," Keegan coaxed. "I know the perfect place."

"I kind of have plans tonight," Ava said.

"What plans? Pajamas and bad reality TV aren't plans." Ginger smiled at Keegan. "Ava's just shy. She would love to go for a drink with you."

"Excellent. Do I need to take you home first to change?" Keegan eyed her blue scrubs.

Ava shook her head. "No, I've got a change of clothes here. I just need a minute. Do you want to give me directions, and I'll meet you there?"

"How about we drive together? I can bring you back to the hospital to pick up your car afterward," Keegan said.

"Sure."

"Great! I'm just parked outside. I'll wait for you by the entrance, okay?" Keegan said. "Goodbye, Ginger. It was a pleasure."

"Bye, Keegan," Ginger said.

As soon as the lion shifter was out of earshot, Ava glared at Ginger. "What the hell, Ginger?"

"Cork it, Ava! That guy is gorgeous, and there's no way in hell you're sitting home alone when you could be having drinks with him!" Her body nearly vibrating with excitement, Ginger stood and pushed her toward the locker room. "Go and change right now!"

Ava rolled her eyes and flipped Ginger the bird when the woman hollered, "And put on some damn lip gloss, woman!"

KAT HIT THE SPEAKER BUTTON ON HER CELL PHONE. "Hello, Mal."

"Hey, Kat. Where are you?" Mal's voice cut in and out, and Kat scowled as she turned right.

"Christ, Mal. Get a better cell phone, would you? Yours is a piece of shit."

"Yeah, yeah. You've been at the warehouse all day. Are you still there?" Mal asked.

"Willow and I are just headed back to the office. We'll tell you how it went when we get there," Kat said.

"Hi, Mal," Willow said.

"Oh, uh, hey, Willow." Mal cleared his throat. "Bishop and I aren't at the office. It's after five."

"Where are you?" Kat asked.

"Bud's."

"Great. We'll meet you there in ten minutes."

"What? No! Kat, don't bring Willow here. Do you hear me? It's not a good idea."

"Oh please, Mal," Kat said. "Do you think any paranormal in the place is going to go near her? She positively reeks of your scent."

There was silence, and Kat grinned at Willow. "Mal? You still there?"

"Yeah. Listen, Bishop, and I will meet you at the office," he said quickly.

"Nope," Kat said. "We're starving. We'll meet you at Bud's, and you can buy us dinner. See you soon!"

She hit the end button, cutting off Mal's protests as Willow said, "What's wrong with Bud's?"

"Nothing's wrong with it. It's just more of a paranormal bar. They don't outright ban humans from the place, but they don't actively encourage it either."

She smiled reassuringly at Willow. "It'll be fine. You smell like Mal, so none of the other paranormals will go near you. Don't be worried, okay?"

"Are you kidding me?" Willow grinned. "I'm not worried at all. I'm totally excited at the idea of being in a paranormal-only bar!"

Kat laughed. "You would be."

"THIS IS A TERRIBLE IDEA, KAT." MAL WAS WAITING FOR them just inside the front door of the bar, and he scowled at the jaguar shifter.

"It'll be fine." Kat waved at someone across the bar before nodding to the bouncer standing to her left. "Hey, Judd. How's it going?"

"Good, Kat." The bouncer, he was a large, solid mass of pure muscle, winked at her. "When are you going to take me up on my offer of dinner?"

Kat grinned at him. "Someday, I might just surprise you and say yes."

He clapped his hand to his chest. "Why ya gotta toy with me like that, sexy?"

Kat laughed and patted his hard chest as Judd gazed around her at Willow. "Who's your pretty little human friend?" He sniffed in her direction and then wrinkled his nose. "Christ, she stinks."

"Judd!" Kat slapped him on the arm, and Judd gave her a sheepish look.

"Sorry, but she does." He grinned at Willow. "Sorry, cutie pie. I didn't mean to offend. I'm Judd."

"Hi, Judd." Willow held out her hand. "I'm Willow."

"Nice to meet you." He reached for her hand. "If you ever get tired of wolf, you should think about switching to _"

He took a step back when Mal, his eyes flashing and his fangs bared, growled fiercely and yanked Willow into his embrace. He curved his arm around Willow's waist and glared at the bouncer. "If you're smart, you'll stay away from her."

Judd growled at him. "Are you threatening me, Mal? That's not a good idea, and you know it."

"Go anywhere near her, and I'll -"

"You'll what?" Judd said impudently. "You think you can take me on? I'll rip you apart."

"Stop it!" Kat made a low hiss. "You're both being ridiculous!"

She pushed Judd back before grabbing Mal's arm. "Come on. We're starving."

She marched toward the booth where Bishop sat, and Mal followed. He kept his arm around Willow's waist and stared at her in frustration. "You shouldn't be here, Willow."

"It'll be fine." Willow smiled at him. "I've got the big bad wolf to protect me."

"Right." Mal snarled at a man who stared at them, and Willow patted his arm.

"Relax, Mal. Seriously, you're going to have a stroke."

"I'm fine," he gritted out. "How, um, are you feeling?"

"Fine? Why?"

His voice was anxious. "I was rough with you this weekend. I just wanted to make sure that you're not hurt."

She sighed as they picked their way through the crowded bar. "I'm fine, Mal. You've got to stop with this belief that you're going to hurt me. I told you, I'm a big girl, and I can handle it."

He scanned the scarf around her throat. "Is your throat all right?"

"Yes. Just a terrible case of whisker burn." She lowered her voice. "My thighs are a lot worse. I swear you spent more time marking me than you did making me come, naughty boy."

He blushed at her words, and she grinned. "You're adorable when you blush."

"I'm not blushing," he said.

"Yes, you are." She slid into the booth. "Hey, Bishop."

"Hey, Willow."

Mal hesitated and then slid in next to Willow. Her scent already drove him to distraction, and he cursed inwardly. He wanted her again. He wanted to take her home and bury himself in her sweet warmth as she moaned his name.

Fuck! What was happening to him? It hadn't even been twenty-four hours since he'd taken her, and already his wolf was hungry for her again. He took a deep breath and jerked when Willow squeezed his thigh affectionately. "How was your day?"

"Fine," he said as Kat waved the waitress over. "Uh, how was yours?"

"Really interesting," she said.

"What did the staff say?"

Kat handed a menu to Willow. "Just let us order some food, and then we'll tell you."

Willow perused the menu as Mal took a large swallow of beer. Her hand still lingered on his thigh. He should have been doing the smart thing and moving it, but he liked the feel of its warmth through the fabric of his jeans. Of course, his cock was as hard as a rock, and if he didn't move her hand soon, he'd be suffering from one hell of a case of blue balls, but he'd worry about that later.

Kat and Willow ordered, and the waitress took back their menus as Willow scanned the bar. "So, this is a paranormal bar, huh? It looks pretty similar to a human one. Am I the only human in here?"

Bishop nodded. "Yep. It's why you're getting so many odd looks. Or maybe it's just the overwhelming scent of wolf."

He gave Mal a slight grin, and Willow laughed when the wolf shifter blushed again. "How adorable is he when he blushes like that?"

"Pretty adorable," Bishop agreed.

"Shut up, Bishop." Mal glared at him. "Besides, Willow and I aren't, I mean, we're not -"

"What he's trying to say," Willow said, "is that we had a weekend full of hot, passionate sex, but now we're back to being just friends."

Mal stared at her in dismay, and she shrugged. "What? There's no point in hiding it. We're all adults here. Although, if we're going to be just friends, maybe you could knock it off with the 'this is my woman, don't go near her' bullshit. Judd was kind of cute."

Mal immediately stiffened as his eyes glowed, and a dark beard grew on his face. "You stay away from that jackass bear shifter, Willow. If I catch his scent on you, I'll tear out his throat."

"So, which is he? A jackass shifter or a bear shifter?" She raised her eyebrows at him as Kat snorted loud laughter.

He cupped the back of her neck, forgetting entirely about Bishop and Kat, who watched them with avid interest and put his mouth to her ear. "I mean it, Willow. Judd's nothing but a man-whore, and if he so much as touches you, I'll -"

"Cool it, Mal." She glared frostily at him. "You lost the

right to tell me who I can and cannot date when you decided on a weekend-only sex fest. You might have marked the hell out of me, but I don't belong to you, and you need to remember that."

He blinked at her in surprise as she took her hand off his thigh and tugged free of his grip. There was a moment of silence that Kat finally broke. "Well, this isn't awkward at all."

"Excuse me." Willow pushed at Mal's shoulder. "I need to use the ladies' room."

He slid out of the booth, and she crossed the bar and disappeared into the hallway leading to the bathrooms. He returned to his seat, ignoring his anxiety that she was out of his sight. He took another drink of beer as Kat frowned at him.

"What?" he said.

"If she quits, I'll carve my initials into your balls, Mal."

"She's not going to quit," he said defensively.

"She might." Bishop shrugged. "You're kind of being a dick to her."

"I am not," he said. "I just – I don't want her getting hurt."

"Stop treating her like she's your property," Bishop said. "Women don't like that."

"You're one to talk," Mal said. "Willow told me all about your conversation with Ava in the bathroom."

Bishop blushed furiously as Kat glanced at him. "What's he talking about?"

"Nothing. Just drop it," Bishop said.

Eager to take the spotlight off his shameful behaviour with Willow, Mal leaned forward. "Bishop told Ava he wanted to fuck her until Keegan knew she belonged to him."

"Bishop!" Kat said in surprise. "You did not."

"He did," Mal said with satisfaction. "He also said he wanted her to ride his -"

"Shut up, Mal!" Bishop roared. He slammed one ham-like fist onto the table as the other paranormals in the bar glanced over nervously.

"Calm down, Bishop," Kat said soothingly.

"Jesus, is nothing a secret?" Bishop said.

"Ava and Willow are best friends," Mal said. "And Willow's terrible at keeping secrets."

As Bishop closed his eyes and took a few deep breaths, Mal sat back in the booth. "All I'm saying is that you're just as guilty of treating a woman like she's your property as I am. At least I'm willing to admit that I'm attracted to Willow."

"Oh, aren't you just a prince?" Kat rolled her eyes. "Yes, every woman loves it when a man boinks them for a weekend and then says, 'hey, let's just be friends'."

"She said it was fine," Mal said.

"You're an idiot, Mal," Kat said. Bishop chuckled, and she turned on him. "And so are you. Both of you need to keep your dicks in your pants when it comes to Willow and Ava."

Willow returned from the bathroom, and Mal left the booth and hurried over to her. He took her hand and squeezed it gently as he led her back to the booth. "Are you okay, Willow? I'm sorry."

"Yes, I'm fine," she said. "I'm sorry I snapped at you, but could you knock it off with the macho possessive bullshit?"

"Yes," he said. "I will. I promise, Willow. Just please promise me you won't go out with Judd."

"I won't." She smiled faintly at him and pulled her hand free. "I promise."

They sat down as the waitress brought their food over. Willow popped a French fry into her mouth as Bishop said, "So, how did the interviews go?"

Kat took a bite of salad and chewed delicately. "Fine. Honestly, we didn't learn much of anything. All of the staff seem on the up and up. Everyone seems to enjoy their jobs and didn't have anything bad to say about Mrs. Belfry or her sons."

"I think it's Royce," Willow announced.

Bishop stared at her. "Why do you think that?"

She shrugged. "He's shifty and slithery, and I just get a bad feeling about him."

"Just because he's a snake shifter doesn't make him a bad guy," Kat pointed out. "You have an aversion to him because you're afraid of snakes."

"You're afraid of snakes?" Mal asked curiously as Willow visibly shuddered.

"Yes, isn't everyone? Say, when he shifts, is he a normal size snake or bigger?"

"It depends. Some snake shifters are normal size, and some are much bigger," Bishop said. "If I had to guess, Royce is one of the bigger ones."

"Ugh." Willow shivered again. "I was afraid of that."

"I don't think it's Royce," Kat said. "He's been with the company for years and years, and none of the other staff have an issue with him."

"Think about it." Willow ate another French fry. "He's Keegan's right-hand man in the warehouse, and he's got access to the warehouse anytime he wants. He could easily be sneaking in there at night."

"Yeah, but, Willow," Bishop leaned forward, "there's no way in hell he could have torn up the bear shifter. He might be big, but snake shifters are no match for a grizzly."

"That's true, but a lion shifter might be able to," Mal said thoughtfully.

Willow frowned at him. "You don't honestly believe that it's Keegan or Koren, do you? Why on earth would they want to destroy their own company?"

Mal shrugged. "There could be a dozen reasons why."

"I know you don't like the brothers, Mal, but it can't be them. They would never do that to their mother. You can see how much she means to them."

"Besides," Kat pulled a notebook from her bag and flipped through it, "they weren't even in town the night that Bentwell was attacked. They were at a trade show."

"Maybe we need to start over," Bishop mused. "We're so certain it's a staff member, but we've got nothing to base that on. Maybe we need -"

He suddenly stiffened as a strange look came over his face.

"Bishop? What's wrong?" Kat asked.

He didn't reply as he turned his head and stared at the entrance. Mal followed his gaze.

"Oh shit," Mal said.

"What? What's wrong?" Willow's eyes widened as she stared across the room. "Dammit! I told her to stay away from him."

Holding Ava's hand, Keegan led her to a small table across the bar. He pulled her chair out for her, and his hand lingered on the small of her back. A deep growl starting in his chest, Bishop began to slide out from the booth.

Kat grabbed his arm. "Bishop! Don't you dare!"

Bishop glared at her, and she hissed at him. "Control yourself."

Breathing shallowly, he gripped his mug of beer and stared down at the table as Willow gave him a tentative look. "It'll be fine, Bishop. Ava's not into the one-night stand thing. She'll figure out pretty quickly that Keegan's not the guy for her."

"Whatever. I don't care who she dates," he said.

Willow turned to Kat. "What is with these two? Neither of them seems to be capable of admitting the truth to themselves."

"Honestly, I've never seen either of them behave like this before," Kat said.

"We're right here," Mal said. "Maybe you could stop acting like we can't hear you." He leaned forward and tapped Bishop on the arm. "You should go, Bishop. We can finish this conversation tomorrow at the office."

"I'm fine!" Bishop snarled. He took a few more shallow breaths before staring at the others. "Go on."

CHAPTER 16

A va studied herself in the bathroom mirror and straightened her shirt. "Okay, so you're on a date with a gorgeous man who seems to be into you. You can do this," she said to her reflection.

She stepped out of the bathroom and stared in surprise at the bear shifter pacing the narrow hallway. "Bishop? What are you doing here?"

He glared at her. "You shouldn't be here, Ava."

"What are you talking about? How did you even know I was here?"

"I told you to stay away from Keegan."

"No, you didn't," she said pointedly. "And besides, who I have a drink with is none of your business."

She tried to move past him, and he gripped her arm and pushed her lightly against the wall. "He only wants one thing from you."

His nostrils flaring, he dropped his gaze to her breasts. She pulled self-consciously at her shirt before clearing her throat. "You don't know that."

"I do," he insisted. "I don't want you seeing him."

She frowned at him. "Since when did you get to tell me what to do, Bishop? I barely know you."

He leaned forward and sniffed at her throat. "I can smell him on you," he said grouchily. "I don't like it."

She sighed as he gave her an irritated look. "Has he touched you, Ava? Has he tried to take what's mine?"

"One – that's none of your business, and two – it isn't yours."

He snorted in annoyance, and she pushed at his broad chest. "Let me pass, Bishop."

"I don't want you seeing him. He's only interested in fucking you and nothing else," he repeated.

"And you aren't?" she said. "Every time I'm around you, I end up half-naked while you grope me like some kind of - of horny bear! I know all about bear shifters, Bishop, and it's pretty damn hypocritical of you to be telling me that Keegan only wants sex."

She whacked him on the stomach. He didn't even flinch, and she rubbed at her throbbing hand and glared at him again. "Let me pass. I mean it."

"Ava, I just don't want you to get hurt," he said. "Keegan is -"

"I won't ask you again," she warned. "Unless you're going to ask me out, stay out of my dating life."

She tamped down the guilt rising inside of her at his wounded look. She refused to feel bad for hurting his feelings. She'd given the damn bear shifter plenty of chances, and he'd made it perfectly clear what he wanted from her.

He stepped back, and she slipped past him and hurried down the hallway without looking back. As she sat down next to Keegan, he smiled and pushed the wine glass toward her. "I figured you could use a second drink."

"I can. Thank you." She drained the glass quickly, and Keegan blinked in surprise before signaling to the waitress for another.

Bishop stomped across the bar. Ava's eyes widened when she realized that Willow, Mal, and Kat sat in a booth across the room. Willow caught her eye and waved wildly at her.

She gave Willow a weak smile and wave as Keegan turned around and studied the four of them. "Looks like your friends are here. Do you want to go over and say hello?"

She shook her head. "No, I don't. Unless you really want to."

Keegan took her hand and ran his thumb over the palm. "Definitely not. I'm a greedy lion, Ava. I want you all to myself."

She smiled tentatively at him as he continued to caress her palm.

"I THINK IT'S TIME WE LEFT," MAL SAID TO KAT. SHE nodded in agreement.

His chest rising and falling rapidly, Bishop was staring at Ava and Keegan again. They could hear him growling deep in his chest, and Mal tapped him on the arm. "Let's go, Bishop."

"No," the bear shifter snarled. "I'm not leaving her alone with him."

"Bishop, Ava doesn't need a babysitter. I'm not particularly happy about her being with the 'braid my hair and let me wear your underwear' lion shifter either, but we're not her parents. She can make her own decisions," Willow said.

"If he goes anywhere near her underwear, I'll kill him," Bishop growled.

"I'll talk to her tomorrow, tell her what he's like, okay?" Willow said. "Let's just leave them to their date."

Bishop's growling suddenly grew louder and the waitress walking by gave him a startled look.

Willow grabbed Mal's arm. "Uh-oh. He's making a move on her."

Mal turned to see Keegan, his hand cupping Ava's face, lean in and kiss her softly on the mouth.

"Fuck!" he said as Bishop shot out of the booth and ran across the bar. He was already shifting, his clothes tearing away with a thick ripping sound. Mal slid out of the booth and chased after him. "Bishop, stop!"

Willow was right behind him, and he abruptly stopped as Bishop shifted fully. He put his arm out and caught Willow as she tried to run by him. "It's too late, Willow. Don't get any closer to him."

"Ava!" Willow shouted. "Look out!"

With an angry roar, the giant grizzly grabbed the back of Keegan's jacket and tore him away from Ava.

"What the fuck?" Keegan shouted as Bishop, his claws tearing at the lion shifter's jacket, picked him up and heaved him across the room. Keegan crashed into the wall, dropping to the floor with a loud thud as Ava gave a startled scream.

His large shaggy head lowered like a bull, Bishop charged at Keegan. Keegan shifted to his lion form with a loud snarl and crouched on all fours. Roaring, he leaped at the grizzly. Bishop caught him and howled with pain and anger when Keegan dug the sharp, thick claws on his back feet into his stomach.

"Mal! Do something!" Willow cried.

"I can't!" he shouted. "Bishop will tear me apart!"

A large black bear ran by them, and Kat squeezed Willow's arm. "Judd will stop them. Don't worry, Willow."

She winced as Judd leaped onto the fighting shifters. With an angry snarl, he wrapped his arms around the lion shifter's body and tore him away from Bishop. He threw him carelessly to the side, and Keegan made a sharp yelp of pain as his head connected with the bar.

The two bears stood on their hind legs and roared at each other. The patrons in the bar clapped their hands over their ears as Bishop took a swipe at Judd. The bouncer snarled and snapped his teeth at him. Although Bishop was bigger and taller, Judd showed no fear as he moved toward the angry grizzly.

"This is so bad," Kat said. "Mal, we've got to do something. Bishop won't back down, and neither will Judd. If we don't stop them -"

She paused, her eyes widening in surprise as Ava suddenly stepped between the two bears. Her face was as red as her hair, and her chest rose and fell rapidly. She put her hands on her hips and glared at Bishop.

"Uh-oh! This isn't good," Willow shouted.

"Shit!" Mal started forward. "They'll rip her apart!"

He stared at Willow in confusion when she clamped her hand down on his arm. "Don't, Mal."

"Willow, are you crazy? They're pissed off, and they'll seriously hurt Ava. You just said this wasn't good!"

She shook her head. "I meant Ava. You think those two bears are pissed off? You haven't seen anything yet."

She took a step back and stuck her fingers in her ears as Ava took a deep breath and shouted, "ENOUGH!"

She stomped forward, and the paranormals in the bar gave a collective gasp of surprise when she reached up and poked the giant grizzly hard in the chest. "Stop this right now, Bishop King! Do you hear me? I don't belong to you, and I'll kiss whoever the hell I want when I want!"

She poked him again, and Mal's mouth dropped open when Bishop flinched back from the fiery redhead and shuffled backward.

"You shift right now, Bishop," she suddenly demanded. "Go on! Shift!"

He shifted immediately and smiled sheepishly. "I'm sorry, honey. I didn't mean -"

"Don't you honey me," she said. "You could have seriously hurt Keegan. And for what?"

"He touched you! He *kissed* you," Bishop said.

"So, what? What do you care? You don't date humans, remember?" She picked up a piece of his torn shirt and folded it in half before pressing it against the bleeding claw marks across his naked stomach. "Apply pressure."

"It's fine. I don't -"

"Apply PRESSURE!" She shouted at him again.

Bishop meekly nodded as he pressed the shirt against his flat stomach. "Okay, honey."

"Stop calling me honey," she said. "Making out with me in a bathroom doesn't give you the right to call me honey."

She glared at him before her shoulders slumped, and she rubbed at her forehead. "Are you going to ask me out on a proper date or not, Bishop? This is your last chance."

He hesitated. "I don't date humans."

"Are you sure she's a human?" someone shouted from the direction of the bar. "She's got bigger balls than an elephant shifter!"

Ava flushed at the loud chorus of laughter before stepping away from Bishop. "Fine. Goodbye, Bishop."

She crossed the room without looking at him and knelt beside Keegan as he shifted to his human form. "Are you okay?"

"Just great," he grunted as she helped him to his feet. He put his arm around her shoulders, and Bishop's loud growl was stopped before it started by Ava's fierce glare at him.

"Come on, Keegan. I think it's time we left." She led the naked lion shifter across the bar and out the front door, supporting him around the waist.

There was a moment of silence in the bar before Judd, who had shifted back to his human form, snorted. "And that's why we don't want humans in here."

"I don't care, Boris!" Mal's angry shout could be heard even through his closed office door. "You do a walk-through of the building every hour on the goddamn hour or find a new job!"

Kat stood near Willow's desk. "What's that about?"

"Oh, Boris thinks the shopping mall doesn't need an hourly walk-through, and he wants to drop it to every two hours," Willow said. "He picked the wrong day to phone Mal about it."

"Would there be a good day?" Kat arched her eyebrow at Willow, who shrugged.

"He has been kind of grumpy all week."

"Kind of? Kind of?" Kat said in exasperation. "He's been a dink. Why the hell won't he give in and date you?"

Willow's face fell, and Kat said, "I'm sorry, Willow. That was stupid of me."

"It's fine." Willow forced herself to smile at her. "It's just... I thought I'd be able to – I don't know – tempt him into forgetting about his ridiculous idea that humans and shifters shouldn't date."

"He's a stubborn, stupid wolf," Kat said. "And between his grumpiness and Bishop's moodiness, I'm about ready to toss both of them out the window."

Willow nodded. "I don't think Bishop's said more than two words all week."

Kat rolled her eyes. "He's lucky that Mrs. Belfry didn't fire us when she found out what he did to Keegan in the bar."

"I don't think he told her," Willow said. "At least that's what Ava said."

"Have he and Ava gone on another date?"

Willow shrugged. "I don't really know. I think they had coffee, but I'm not sure they've gone on an actual date. I warned her about his, um, sexual preferences, but she didn't seem to care one way or the other. She's been pretty damn moody herself this week."

"What a mess," Kat said.

"I'm sorry. This is all my fault," Willow said.

"No, it isn't. Bishop said that Mal was lusting after you

during the interview. If it's anyone's fault, it's mine and Bishop's for hiring you. Of course, we had no idea that Mal was going to go all alpha wolf on you."

Willow sighed. "The worst part is that he's ignoring me. I miss him."

Kat squeezed her shoulder sympathetically before returning to her office.

Willow stared blankly at her computer screen. She really did miss Mal. He'd spent most of the week in his office with the door shut, and she tried her best not to take it personally, but the shifter's rejection stung. Hell, it did more than sting. It hurt her feelings tremendously, and she'd spent her evenings sitting in her apartment feeling sorry for herself. To make things worse, the ghost activity had been oddly quiet lately, and she couldn't even use that to distract herself from thoughts of the sexy wolf shifter and his warm hands.

The front door opened, and she forced a cheerful smile at the tall, elegant-looking woman who entered. "Hi there. How can I help you?"

"Hello. You must be the new receptionist. My name is Mara. I'm Malcolm's mother."

Willow stared in surprise as the woman held out her hand. She stood up and hurried around the desk to shake the woman's hand. "It's so nice to meet you. I'm Willow."

"What a pretty name," the woman said y. "It's nice to meet you, as well. How are you enjoying the -"

She stopped, and her hand squeezed Willow's tightly before she leaned in and inhaled. "Oh my," she said softly, "it seems my boy is rather fond of you."

She studied Willow's throat. The redness of her skin had faded to soft pink, but tiny scratches still covered it, and Willow blushed as Mara smiled at her. "How long have you and Malcolm been dating?"

"Oh, um…"

She trailed off as Mara gave her an expectant look. What the hell did she do now?

MAL STOOD AND WALKED TO HIS OFFICE DOOR. HE NEEDED to talk to Willow about work, and he was already dreading it. God, he missed her. But avoiding her was for the best for both of them. Pretending to study his phone to avoid her gaze, he stepped into the reception. "Willow? Can you call Mr. Tripke and ask him to -"

He caught his mother's scent and looked up. Shit! His mother stood next to Willow and held her hand. She gave Willow's hand a gentle squeeze before dropping it and smiling at Mal. "Hello, Pudding."

"Mom? What are you doing here?" Mal glanced at Willow before kissing his mother's cheek.

"What? Can't a mother stop by and say hello to her child? It's been ages since we talked," she said.

"I was just over for supper two weeks ago." He took her arm and tried to guide her to his office, but she dug her heels in and refused to budge.

"I know." She smiled at Willow. "I'm surprised you haven't brought Willow to meet us. She's so lovely."

"Thank you." Willow grinned at her as Mal turned a dull red.

"Mom, Willow is, well, she's our receptionist and -"

"Yes, Pudding. I figured that out," Mara said. "Now, I just popped in to say hello and invite you for dinner tonight. Bring Willow with you. I know your father and grandfather would love to meet her."

Mal twitched violently. "Oh, um, Willow's already got plans tonight. Isn't that right, Willow?" He stared desperately at her, and she smiled sweetly.

"Nope. No plans at all, P*udding*."

He glared at her as Mara smiled with delight. "Wonderful. We'll see you both around six then."

"Should I bring anything, Mrs. Burke?" Willow asked.

"No, dearest. Just bring your lovely self. And please, call me Mara."

She kissed Mal on the cheek and patted his face before walking toward the door. "Malcolm, don't be late, please. Oh, and tell Kat and Bishop that I said hello."

She waved at them as she left the office. Willow waved back as Mal groaned. "Willow! You cannot come to my parents' house for dinner."

"Why not? I've already said I would. It'll be rude not to go," she said.

"You don't understand. My mom, she, well she's fascinated with humans. She'll grill you the entire night about your life, about human cultures, and -"

"I don't mind," Willow said. "Besides, this is my chance to get to know the paranormal culture better too. I'm sure your mom won't mind if I ask my own questions."

"No, but my grandfather might," Mal replied. "He's not fond of humans, Willow."

"No, I imagine he isn't," Willow said. "Listen, Mal, if you don't want me to go, then I won't."

He hesitated and studied her face. She had a carefully neutral look on her face, but she couldn't hide the hope in her eyes. Knowing he was crazy but missing her so much he could hardly think straight, he said, "No, I'd like it if you came for dinner."

Her body relaxed, and she gave him her warm, sweet smile. "Can you pick me up, or do you want me to meet you there?"

"I'll pick you up at about five-thirty."

"Great. It's a date!" She shook her head. "I mean, not a date. It's a not date. I'm so excited to meet your family, Mal!"

He couldn't help but grin at her enthusiasm. "You may change your mind after you meet my grandfather."

CHAPTER 17

"How do I look?" Willow climbed into Mal's car and smoothed her dress down nervously.

"You look beautiful," Mal said. He wasn't lying. Willow had worn her hair down, and she wore a soft pink dress that hugged her tiny breasts and flared out around her narrow hips.

"Thank you." She smiled at him. "You look very handsome."

He glanced at his jeans and t-shirt combo as she buckled her seat belt and sat back in the seat. "Maybe I could drive on the way home?"

He pulled out into traffic. "What is with you and your need to drive my car?"

"I told you – I like fast cars. So, is there anything I shouldn't bring up tonight at dinner?"

"Not mentioning that you can see ghosts would be helpful."

She laughed. "Right. No ghost mentioning. Although I bet your mom would find that fascinating."

He sighed. "She probably would."

"Do you have any siblings?" she asked.

"Yes, I'm the oldest of six."

"Six! Holy smokes!"

"Wolf shifters like to have large families," he said.

"That makes sense. You like living in packs, right?"

He nodded, and she smiled again at him. "Will all of your siblings be at dinner?"

"I don't think so. My youngest sister, Becky, will be. She's only fifteen and still lives at home, but the rest of us have our own places. We usually do a big family dinner once a month, and then Mom has us over individually throughout the month. She's always worried that she doesn't give each of us enough attention, so she tries to spend quality time with us separately."

"That's nice. Do you get along with everyone?"

He nodded. "Yeah. I get along best with my brother Porter, he's only two years younger than I am, but our entire family is close."

"I'm jealous of your big family," she said. "I always wanted a bunch of siblings, but my mom had a hard time getting pregnant with me, and even though they tried for more, it never happened."

The sadness in her voice had him reaching for her hand. He squeezed it before stroking her palm with his fingertips. "I'm sorry, Willow. I can't imagine what it would be like to lose my parents so young."

"Thank you," she said.

The week had been hell. Every time he was around Willow his wolf threatened to take over and he was getting more and more difficult to control. He knew he should release her hand, but after avoiding her all week, even something as simple as holding her hand calmed his wolf down.

They were nearly at his parents' place, and he took a deep breath. "Are you sure you want to do this?"

"I am," she said.

"My grandfather will be rude to you. Don't take it personally, okay?" he said.

"I won't. I understand why he won't like me. Will you do me a favour, though? Will you at least pretend we're dating? I don't want your family thinking I'm some little tart who just had a weekend of sex with their son."

Mal nodded. "Of course."

"Great!" She smiled cheerfully at him.

He pulled into the driveway of a large two-story house, and Willow studied his childhood home. The house had a wide porch with lush flowerbeds surrounding it, and she smiled at Mal when he gave her a nervous look. "It'll be fine, Mal. Stop worrying."

"Right," he said as she climbed out of the car.

They started up the sidewalk, and he reached out and took her hand, holding it firmly as she gave him another warm smile. They climbed the steps as the front door was flung open, and his grandfather stepped out onto the porch.

His grandfather was tall and wide, his back bent a little with age, and he had long, gray hair that flowed down to the middle of his back. A faded scar marred his right cheek, and Willow smiled at him as he gave her a suspicious look, his bright green eyes glowing.

"You're late, Malcolm."

"Sorry, Grandpa," Mal said. "Grandpa, this is Willow Tanner. Willow, this is my grandfather, Amos Burke."

Willow held out her hand. "It's nice to meet you, Mr. Burke."

He studied her carefully before giving her hand a brief shake. "You one of those humans who can only get their rocks off by having sex with a shifter?"

"Grandpa!" Mal said.

"No, sir," Willow said solemnly. "I can get my rocks off having sex with a human too."

There was a bellow of laughter behind the old man, and Mal jerked in surprise when his brother stuck his head over Amos' shoulder. "Hey, Mal."

"Hey, Porter. What are you doing here?"

"Mom told me you were coming by for dinner, and I wanted to meet your new woman." He stepped around his grandfather and held out his hand to Willow. "Hi, I'm Porter, Mal's younger and better-looking brother."

Willow laughed and shook his hand. "Hello, Porter. I'm Willow."

Porter lifted her hand to his lips and kissed her knuckles. "Mom said you were gorgeous. Are you sure you want to stick with my brother? I'm much prettier and funnier."

She laughed again as Mal growled deep in his throat and put a possessive hand on the back of her neck. "Knock it off, Porter."

"That riled him up, didn't it?" Porter grinned at Willow.

"Frankly, it doesn't take much," she said.

"Says you. Mal's known for his iron-clad control. What have you done to my big brother, Willow?"

He winked at her as Amos snorted behind him. "Keep it in your pants, Porter. It's bad enough Malcolm is dating a human."

"Be nice, Grandpa," Porter said as he tugged Willow away from Mal. "Ignore my grandfather, Willow. His bark is worse than his bite."

He led Willow into the house, and Amos and Mal followed them.

"So, Willow, do you come from a large family?" Mara asked as she handed a bowl of steaming potatoes to Mal's father, Roland. Roland was tall and handsome with short, graying hair and a neatly trimmed beard.

Willow shook her head. She was sandwiched at the dinner table between Mal and his younger sister Becky – the girl was the spitting image of her mother - and she handed the roasted asparagus to Mal. "No. I'm an only child."

"How sad," Mara said. "That's one thing I will never understand about human culture. So many of them believe that large families are a bad thing. Or they cut themselves off from each other and go their separate ways. Family is the most important bond in the world. Your family will always love you, no matter your choices."

She smiled sweetly at Mal as Amos made a grunt of disapproval.

"I wish I came from a large family." Willow took a bite of roast beef. "This is delicious, Mara."

"Thank you, honey." Mara smiled. "So, you want lots of children then? Mal will be a great dad. He loves kids and was so helpful with his younger siblings when he was a teen."

"Mom!" Mal glared at her as Becky giggled.

"I would like a big family," Willow said.

"Wonderful!" Mara wiped at her mouth delicately. "But you should know that the Burke pups tend to be on the bigger side. You're awfully tiny, so none of us will think badly of you if you want to stop after a couple of babies."

"Oh my God," Mal groaned and buried his face in his hands. "Mom," his voice was muffled," Willow and I just started dating. Could you please stop pressuring her to have my pups?"

"I'm not pressuring, Pudding. I'm just warning her. She needs to know what she's getting into if she's going to start pushing out your big-headed babies."

"Gross." Becky ate a large mouthful of potatoes.

"I never thought I would see the day where half-breed pups are running around my house," Amos said. He eyed Willow's flat stomach suspiciously. "You're not knocked up already, are you? Trying to trick my grandson into marriage?"

"*Dad!*" Roland glared at him as Mal, growling loudly, started to rise from his chair. Willow yanked him back to his seat, giving him a pointed look and rubbing his back soothingly.

"I'm definitely not knocked up." She smiled at Amos. "And I promise you I won't force Mal into a shotgun wedding. Although, a shotgun-themed wedding would be a hoot. Don't you think?"

Amos grunted and stared at Mal. "Knowing the Burke luck, your pups would be fully human and as useless as the rest of -"

"Enough, Dad," Roland said. "Be polite to Willow or leave the table."

Amos scowled at him before shoving a large piece of roast into his mouth. He chewed defiantly on it as Willow squeezed Mal's leg under the table and gave him another pointed look when he continued to growl softly.

Mara handed the platter of roast beef to Roland. "Our children are our greatest treasures. Aren't they, love?"

"Yes." Roland smiled and squeezed her arm affectionately. "Even Porter."

"Hey!" Porter scowled at him good naturedly. "I'm sitting right here, Dad."

He grinned across the table at Willow. "Dad's just miffed because he thought I would become a lawyer like him."

"I'm only teasing, Porter," Roland said. "You know we're very proud of you."

"What do you do for a living?" Willow asked.

"I'm a bartender for a paranormal bar called Bud's," Porter said.

"I've been there!" Willow turned to Mal. "You didn't tell me your brother was a bartender there."

Mal cleared his throat as Porter blinked at him. "You took her to Bud's?"

"I didn't *take* her to Bud's." Mal scowled. "Bishop and I were there, and Kat thought it would be a good idea to bring her there for a business meeting."

"How is the lovely Kat? Has she asked about me?" Porter's eyes glowed.

"Forget it, Porter. You know she's not interested in wolves," Mal said.

"I know, but a guy can dream," Porter said. "So, what did you think of Bud's, Willow?"

"I liked it," Willow said. "I've never been to a paranormals-only bar, so I found it quite fascinating. I'd like to go back when it isn't for work so I can really check it out."

"No," Mal said immediately. "Promise me you won't go into that bar without me."

"I wouldn't," Willow assured him.

"He's right, Willow," Porter said. "Humans aren't always the most welcome at Bud's. Arlo, he just started bartending last week, was telling me that on his second night, some idiot lion shifter brought a human into the bar, and a fight broke out between him and a grizzly over her."

Willow gave Mal a guilty look.

"What?" Porter said.

"The grizzly was Bishop," Mal said.

"What?" Porter's eyes widened in surprise. "You're kidding me! Bishop fought a lion shifter over a human?"

"Her name is Ava," Willow said. "She's my best friend, and Bishop has a bit of a crush on her."

Porter burst into loud laughter as delight crossed Mara's face. "He does? That's wonderful! Although I must confess, I never thought my Button would want to date anyone. Grizzly shifters are such loners, and Bishop is no exception."

"He's definitely fighting it," Willow said. "He keeps telling Ava he doesn't want to date her, but every time they're in the same room together, he can't keep his hands off of her. It's kind of adorable."

"Oh yes, adorable," Mal said. "It was particularly adorable when he almost killed our client over her."

"The lion shifter was your client?" Roland said. "That can't be good for business."

"It all worked out," Willow said. "Keegan didn't say anything about it, probably because Bishop kicked his furry butt, and we've still got the contract with his company."

"So, are he and Ava going to date?" Mara asked.

"No," Willow said. "He's being a stubborn fool, and Ava's tired of waiting."

"Arlo said the woman was hot for a human," Porter mused. "Said she had gorgeous red hair, curves in all the right places, and she put Bishop in his place in front of a bar full of shifters. Maybe you should introduce me to her, Willow."

"God, Porter. Can you try thinking with your brain just once?" Mal said.

"What? I'd like to meet the woman who isn't afraid of an angry grizzly," Porter said.

"I imagine you'd also like to keep your head exactly where it is, and if Bishop finds out you're dating Ava, he'll remove it for you," Mal said. "He's obsessed with her."

"He kind of is," Willow said. "I can introduce you to Ava, but you can't hold me responsible for what Bishop will do to you."

"Maybe you'd better sit this one out, Peanut," Mara said. "You know how grizzlies can be."

Porter shrugged as Mara turned back to Willow. "Eat up, honey. There's plenty."

———

"It was so lovely to meet you, Willow. Don't be a stranger, all right? You're welcome back anytime." Mara hugged her firmly.

"Thank you, Mara. I enjoyed dinner and meeting all of you. Thanks for having me over," Willow said.

"Anytime, honey. I mean that," Mara said. She hugged Mal and kissed his cheek. "Bye, Pudding."

"Bye, Mom."

Mal took Willow's hand and led her down the steps as Mara waved before disappearing into the house.

"Sorry, Willow."

"For what?"

"My grandfather was rude."

"I don't mind." She smiled at him. "I liked your family, especially Porter. He's hilarious."

"Yeah, he's something." Mal glanced behind him at the house. "Do me a favour and don't introduce him to Ava."

"Why not?" she asked.

"Well, the whole Bishop thing aside, Porter's a playboy. He's a good guy," he said hastily, "but he's a little immature, and he's not really into the serious relationship thing. I don't think that's what Ava is looking for."

"I'll keep her away from him. Besides, she's already got Keegan if all she wants is a roll in the hay." She frowned. "I hope she doesn't sleep with him. Ava is sensitive about her looks, and I'm worried about how it will affect her if Keegan sleeps with her once and then drops her. Not to mention, I don't want to hear about him wearing her underwear."

Mal laughed. "He really likes wearing women's underwear?"

"He really does," she said. "And there isn't anything wrong with that, but I just don't think he's right for Ava. She needs someone who'll be in it for the long run."

"Why is she sensitive about her looks?" Mal asked as they stopped at this car. "She's beautiful."

"She thinks she's too chubby, and she hates her freckles. She doesn't embrace her curves and thinks men don't want to date her because of them. She's very shy, and I think her shyness often comes across as aloofness. And even when a man does make a move on her, she never really believes he's hitting on her. It's why Bishop's direct approach is good for her. He's not leaving any doubt that he's attracted to her."

She suddenly sighed. "I just wish he wanted her for more than sex. Ava deserves to find love. She's the sweetest, nicest person I know, and I hate that she thinks she's ugly. I'd kill to have her curves.

Mal shook his head. "You're beautiful just the way you are, Willow."

She grinned at him. "Aren't you sweet, Malcolm Burke. But I know the boys like the large breasts and booty."

He stepped closer and trailed his fingers down the inside of her arm. She shivered at his touch and licked her lips as he gave her a predatory look of need and bent his head toward her. "I like everything about you, Willow. Your small breasts, your tight little ass, the way you moan when I eat your pussy."

"Mal, please," she whispered.

His wolf howling loudly at him, Mal could barely control the urge to push Willow up against his car, tear off her panties, and take her right there. He missed her desperately, and the smell of her desire was a delicious, intoxicating drug. Breathing heavily, he forced himself to step away from her. "I'm sorry. That was inappropriate."

"Right. Inappropriate," she said.

He could see the hurt in her eyes, and feeling guilty as

hell, he fished his keys out of his pocket and held them out. "Here."

"Here, what?" she asked.

"Take the keys. You're driving."

"Really?"

He nodded, and she snatched the keys from his hand and hurried around to the driver's side. She climbed behind the wheel and adjusted the seat and mirrors as Mal sat down in the passenger seat.

She started the engine and grinned at him. "Buckle up, Mr. Burke. You're in for a wild ride."

WILLOW SCREECHED TO A HALT IN FRONT OF HER apartment building and shut off the car before smiling happily at Mal. "Wasn't that fun?"

"Never again," Mal said hoarsely as he continued to clutch at the dashboard. "You are never driving my car again, Willow Blossom Tanner. Do you hear me?"

"Why not?"

"*Why not?*" He turned toward her. "Don't give me that innocent look! You are not a safe driver!"

She laughed. "Maybe you just have nerves of jelly."

"You took that last corner on two wheels!"

"Is that why you were screaming like a little girl?"

"I was not screaming like a little girl," he said through gritted teeth. "And if I was, it was a perfectly acceptable reaction from a person who nearly died multiple times during a half-hour car ride."

"You're totally exaggerating." She laughed again as

she unbuckled her seat belt. "Do you want to come upstairs for a drink?"

"It's late."

She shrugged. "It's only ten."

I can't, Willow. You know I can't," he said.

She sighed. "You're right. I'm sorry – I shouldn't keep pressuring you like this."

"Willow, I -"

His cell phone rang, and he grimaced before pulling it from his pocket. "Hey, Bishop. What's up?"

His hand tightened around the phone as he listed to Bishop. "Shit! I'll be right there."

"Mal? What's wrong?" Willow asked worriedly as he ended the call.

"There was another attack at the warehouse. Fenton was on patrol, and he was hurt pretty badly. Keegan was in his office, and Bishop says he was also attacked. He's in the hospital and in rough shape. They don't know if he'll live."

"Oh no," Willow breathed.

"Bishop and Kat are at the hospital right now. I need to get over there."

"I'm coming with you." Willow buckled her seat belt and started the car.

"Wait, I'll drive," Mal said as Willow pulled out into the street.

"No time. We'll get there faster if I drive."

He muttered a curse and clutched at the dashboard again as Willow stomped on the gas pedal.

CHAPTER 18

"How's Fenton?" Mal ducked behind the curtain, Willow right behind him, and stared worriedly at Bishop.

The bear shifter stepped aside, and Mal breathed a sigh of relief as Fenton, a tall and lithe-looking cheetah shifter, nodded to him from the hospital bed. A large bruise spanned his forehead, and an ugly looking scrape was just above his left eyebrow. He touched his swollen nose, wincing with pain. Kat stood next to the bed, holding his other hand, and she pulled his hand away from his face.

"Don't, Fenton. It hasn't started to heal yet."

"What happened?" Mal asked.

"I don't know," Fenton said. "One minute I was walking through the warehouse, and the next, I was on the floor with a busted nose."

"They think he smashed his face into the floor." Kat brushed back Fenton's hair. "His nose was broken, and they think he has a concussion. He might even have a skull fracture. We're waiting for the x-ray results."

Fenton caught her hand and squeezed it. "I'm fine, Kat."

"You didn't see or hear anything?" Mal asked.

"No."

"What about before? What were you doing?"

"I can't remember," Fenton said. "I know I talked briefly to Keegan in his office. I was surprised to see him because he had already left for the day, but he said he had forgotten something. I left his office and was doing my rounds through the warehouse. The next thing I knew, I woke up on the floor, and I could barely walk or think straight. I smelled the blood and found Keegan in his office, beat to shit and bleeding and unconscious. I called 9-1-1, and then I think I passed out. I'm sorry, Mal."

"You have nothing to be sorry about," Kat said. "You did nothing wrong."

Fenton shook his head. "I fucked up, Kat. Someone got by me, and Keegan paid the price."

"Kat is right," Mal said. "It's not your fault." He glanced at Bishop. "I'm going to go check on Keegan."

"I'll come with you." The bear shifter shook Fenton's hand. "Glad you're okay, man."

"Thanks, Bishop."

"I'll stay with Fenton," Kat said before Mal could ask.

As Mal, Willow, and Bishop headed down the hall, Willow squeezed his hand. "Are Kat and Fenton dating?"

"They used to date," Mal said. They followed Bishop into the elevator.

The intensive care unit was quiet. No one seemed to speak above a whisper, and the sound of their footsteps felt intrusively loud. Still holding Mal's hand, Willow led them to the desk.

"We're looking for Keegan Belfry," she said to the nurse.

"Are you family?"

Willow shook her head, and the nurse pointed to a door just behind them. "Only family are allowed in the room. I'll let his family know you're here. You can wait in the quiet room if you'd like."

Bishop and Mal followed Willow into the room. Royce Darnell sat in a chair, staring at his hands. Mal sat down next to him. "Mr. Darnell, how is he?"

The snake shifter shook his head. "Not good. His chest and back were ripped to shreds, and he lost a lot of blood. He was barely breathing when the medics got there, and his skull was fractured. They think he was thrown head-first into the metal safe in his office. He's in a coma, they said."

"Fuck." Bishop said under his breath as Willow sat down across from Royce and Mal.

"Mr. Darnell, what kind of marks were on Keegan?" Mal asked.

"They're from a cat shifter," Royce said.

"Are you sure?" Mal asked.

"Positive." Royce stared at the floor between his feet for a few minutes as the others waited patiently. When he spoke, it was in a low, absent voice as though he had forgotten the others were there. "I knew Koren was upset, but I never thought he would go this far."

"What did you say?" Mal shook the snake shifter's arm when he didn't respond.

"What?" Royce gave him a startled look.

"What about Koren?"

"Nothing. I didn't say -"

"You did," Bishop growled. "Don't start lying to us, Mr. Darnell."

He moved closer to the snake shifter, and Willow shuddered when Royce made a low, hissing sound. His whole body shivered, and the pupils of his eyes turned to slits. She leaned back in her chair, her body breaking out in goosebumps as Bishop glared at Royce. "Stop your damn hissing and tell us what you know about Koren."

"You're just security. You have no say in this."

"One of our men was injured. We told Marika Belfry that we'd find out who was doing this, and that's what we're going to do. Now tell us," Mal said.

Royce stared at the floor again. "Koren is jealous of Keegan."

"Why?"

"He knows that his mother is leaving the majority of the company to Keegan in her will. She believes Keegan is more responsible than his brother. Koren's upset by that."

Willow frowned. "That doesn't sound like Koren."

"It kind of does, Willow," Bishop said.

"I know he's a bit on the wild side, but he would never betray his mother or hurt his brother. He loves them both," Willow said.

"People do crazy shit when they're desperate," Royce said.

"What do you mean?" Mal asked.

"Koren is swimming in debt. He's been talking to Craig Howell about selling the company."

Willow gave Mal a questioning look. The name was familiar, but she didn't know why.

"Boar shifter from the party," he said. He turned back

to Royce. "Does Mrs. Belfry know that Koren is talking to Howell?"

"I don't know for certain." Royce stared nervously at Mal. "Listen, I'm not entirely sure that Koren has anything to do with this. I mean, I know he's desperate for money, and I know he wants his mother to sell the company, but -"

"What does it matter if she sells the company?" Willow said. "He'll still be broke. The company belongs to Marika."

"Actually, it belongs to all three of them. Marika owns a quarter of it, and the boys split the difference. If the company were to sell, they'd make a lot of money."

"If they have majority ownership, why can't they just sell the company without their mother's permission?" Bishop asked.

"The contract isn't set up that way. The boys own a larger percentage of the company, but Marika retained control of all financial and operational decisions."

Before Mal could reply, the door to the quiet room opened, and Garrett and Koren stepped into the room. Garrett was solemn looking, and Koren was pale with none of his usual swagger.

"Koren? How is he?" Willow stood and patted Koren's back lightly.

"He's still in a coma. They," Koren's voice broke, and his throat worked convulsively for a moment, "they don't know if he's going to wake up."

"I'm so sorry, honey." Willow threw her arms around him and hugged him as Garrett sat next to Royce.

"Is Mrs. Belfry with Keegan?" Mal asked.

Garrett nodded but didn't say anything. Koren stepped away from Willow, wiping at his eyes with the back of his hand before clearing his throat. "She wants to see the three of you."

He led them out of the quiet room and toward Keegan's room. A nurse was leaving the room, and she gave them a dirty look. Willow murmured an apology as they passed by her.

"I thought it was only family allowed," she whispered to Koren.

"It is, but my mother insisted, and the nurses are no match for her," he said wearily.

He pushed open the door, and they followed him into the room. Bishop stopped abruptly in the doorway.

"Keep it together, Bishop," Mal said under his breath.

Bishop hesitated as Ava stared coolly at him from her spot beside Keegan's hospital bed. After a moment, she looked away. He swallowed harshly and entered the room, standing just beside the door and looking as though he might bolt at any moment.

Her face grave, Willow approached Mrs. Belfry. She sat in a chair next to the bed and stared blankly at her child. She touched Mrs. Belfry's shoulder delicately. "I'm so sorry, Marika."

The lizard shifter didn't reply as Ava squeezed Keegan's shoulder and then crouched in front of his mother. "Mrs. Belfry? I'll be downstairs in the ER. My shift isn't over for another five hours. Have a nurse call down to the ER if you need me. Okay?"

"Thank you," Marika said.

"I'll come back and check on you and Keegan in a couple of hours." Ava touched her knee gently. "He's going to be fine. He's strong, and his wounds are already starting to heal. He'll be awake soon. I know he will."

She stood and hugged Willow before walking toward the door. Bishop shrank back, his hand coming up to cover his nose. Ava stared at him in disdain, and he dropped his hand as his face turned bright red. She ignored his muttered apology and slipped out of the room.

"Marika?" Willow said. "Is there anything I can get for you?"

She didn't reply, and Koren touched her shoulder. "Mother?"

"What?" Marika spoke woodenly.

"You should eat something. Why don't you and Willow go to the cafeteria? I'll stay with Keegan."

Ignoring him, she finally turned her gaze to Willow. Her yellow eyes were bloodshot, and the skin under them puffy, and deep lines creased her mouth. "Are you positive this is not your ghost?"

Willow nodded. "It isn't, Marika. I promise you."

Marika studied her closely before turning to stare at Keegan. "This is my fault."

"It isn't. Don't say that."

"I didn't believe you. I didn't believe that it could be one of our own. I made Mr. Burke drop his team to one, and now my son has paid the price for my stupidity and my arrogance."

"It's not your fault, Mrs. Belfry," Mal said.

"Is your employee still alive?" she asked.

Mal nodded. "He is. He doesn't remember anything. I promise you that we'll find the person responsible for this."

"I'm shutting down the company," Mrs. Belfry said.

"What? No, Mother, you can't do that," Koren said.

"I can, and I will. Just until we figure this out. We can't risk someone else being injured."

"Mother," Koren knelt beside her and took her hand, "I know you're upset about Keegan, and I know you blame yourself, but you can't shut the company down, not even for a few days. Our customers aren't going to wait for their shipments."

"I don't care," Mrs. Belfry said.

"Mother, we cannot shut the warehouse down. We won't recover, and you know it."

"People are being hurt, Koren! Your brother may never wake up! I can't keep the warehouse open knowing that it puts our employees in danger."

Koren squeezed her hand. "Maybe it's time to cut our losses."

"What are you saying?" Mrs. Belfry frowned at him.

"I'm saying that I think we need to give up the company. We sell it, and we move on. You did what you set out to do, Mother. After Naden's death, you turned this company around despite what people said. You don't need to prove anything else."

She stared at him. "Sell the company? Are you mad, Koren? Naden put his life into this company, and I promised him on his deathbed that I would keep it in the family. He wanted you and Keegan to have it someday. You know that."

"I know, but -"

"Naden treated you and your brother as his sons, did he not?" Mrs. Belfry said.

"Yes, and you know we loved him."

"And this is how you show that love? By selling the

very company he struggled to build?" She hissed at him. "I raised you better than this, Koren."

"Mother," Koren said patiently, "I don't believe Naden would want you to suffer like this. You're barely sleeping. Your health is declining. You can't -"

"I'm fine!" she spat. "Besides, you can't just up and sell a company in a matter of days." She paused and studied Koren for a moment. "What? What aren't you telling me?"

"I've been speaking with Craig Howell. He wants the company, and he's willing to give us a fair price for it. I think we should take it."

There was silence, and Willow, still crouching on Mrs. Belfry's other side, gave Mal a look of alarm before touching her knee. "Marika? Are you okay?"

"You've spoken with Howell?" Mrs. Belfry's voice was barely audible in the room.

"Yes," Koren said. "I know you hate him, and I know you have a good reason for that, but we have to look at the big picture. Sell the company to Craig, let him deal with whatever the hell is happening in the warehouse, and we'll -"

"How long have you been sneaking around behind my back?" Mrs. Belfry's voice was icy cold, and a shiver went down Willow's spine.

She didn't protest when Mal put his hands around her waist and lifted her to her feet. He guided her back to Bishop. The two shifters moved in front of her without speaking, creating a comforting shield of hard muscle and warm flesh. Willow rested her hand on Mal's back and poked her head around his broad body to peer at the lizard shifter and her son.

"Mother -"

"How long?"

Mrs. Belfry stood up from her chair and pushed it away in a shocking display of strength. The chair flew backward and slammed into Bishop's legs. He winced as Koren took a step back.

"I did it for you, Mother."

"For me?"

The old woman's body rippled inside of her clothing. Willow watched as her arms turned a pale green, and scales appeared against her flesh. Her hair, pulled into a neat bun at the back of her head, as usual, thinned, and the rough green flesh of a lizard appeared through the strands.

"For me?" Mrs. Belfry hissed again as she raised her right hand. The ends of her fingers turned into dark claws, and Willow watched in fascination as the nails lengthened and thickened.

Mal glanced at Bishop, and moving as one, they herded Willow into the corner of the room.

"Mal?" Willow whispered.

"It's fine," he murmured. "Just stay behind us."

"She's just a lizard, isn't she?" Willow said in confusion.

"Yes, but a very pissed off lizard." Bishop barely moved his lips as he spoke. "They're crazy quick and can do a surprising amount of damage."

"Calm down, Mother," Koren spoke firmly enough, but his eyes darted around the room and trickles of sweat slid down his face. "Let me explain."

"Judas!"

Willow's sharp gasp of surprise was buried under Koren's howl of pain. Moving so quickly she seemed to float, Mrs. Belfry had darted forward and sliced him across the face with her nails.

"Get out! Now!" She hissed at him. Her tongue flicked out, long and black and forked at the end, and Koren shrank back as blood poured from the slashes on his face.

"Mother -"

"OUT!"

Mrs. Belfry was completely green now, and she was hissing and spitting at her son. Koren turned and hurried from the room, leaving a trail of blood in his wake. Mal and Bishop waited as Mrs. Belfry, her back turned to them, made a muttered sound of displeasure.

After a few moments, Willow whispered, "Should I go to her?"

"No!" the two shifters said in unison.

After nearly five minutes, Mrs. Belfry's skin lightened. The green faded to pale pink, and her hair thickened. It hung haphazardly, and she gathered it up and tucked it neatly back into a bun as Mal and Bishop eased forward.

"Mrs. Belfry?" Mal spoke quietly.

"Yes, Mr. Burke?"

"Are you closing down the warehouse?"

The lizard shifter sighed and turned to face him. She looked tired and defeated, and Willow slipped past Bishop and tucked her arm around Mrs. Belfry. "Sit down, Marika."

"I'm fine," she said absentmindedly. "Do you believe I should close the warehouse down, Mr. Burke?"

"No. We'll increase our security team to keep everyone safe, and there are a few employees we'd like to speak to again. We may have a lead."

"A lead?" Mrs. Belfry walked to the hospital bed and

placed a gentle hand on Keegan's forehead. She smoothed his shaggy blond hair away from his face and stroked his skin. "Who?"

"Leave that to us, okay? It may turn out to be a dead-end," Mal said.

"I want you to find the people who did this, Mr. Burke," Mrs. Belfry said. "I want you to find them and bring them to me. I'm going to make them pay for what they've done to my child."

Willow gave her an anxious look. "Marika, I know you're upset, but -"

Ignoring Willow, Mrs. Belfry stared coldly at Mal. "Do you understand, wolf shifter?"

"Yes, ma'am."

"Good. Now leave me alone with my son."

CHAPTER 19

"I t can't be Koren."

"Willow, I know you think he's a good guy, but you don't really know him," Kat said. "A person desperate for money can do almost anything."

It was early the following day, and Willow had arrived at work to find Kat, Mal, and Bishop in a meeting. She couldn't resist joining them and was secretly pleased when they didn't ask her to leave.

"Are you telling me that you would hurt your sister or brother if you were desperate for money, Kat?" Willow asked. "Because that's what you're saying Koren did."

"He probably didn't mean to," Bishop said. "Fenton said that Keegan had left for the day. Koren wasn't expecting him to be there. Keegan probably stumbled onto him, leaving Koren with no choice."

"You're acting like we know for certain that he's guilty." Willow frowned. "We're just taking that snake shifter's word that Koren is broke?"

"He does want to sell the company," Bishop reminded her.

"Because he's worried about his mother," Willow said. "Have we even looked into Royce Darnell? It's odd that he would just share that information about Koren with us. What if he's trying to use Koren as a way to throw off suspicion of him? Again, we don't know for certain that Koren even needs money."

"We do," Bishop said. "We pulled his financial records and his bank statements."

"Isn't that private information?" Willow raised her eyebrows at him.

Bishop cleared his throat before darting a glance at Kat.

Willow stared at the jaguar shifter. "Kat?"

"I've got a knack with computers." There was a tinge of red in Kat's cheeks.

"More like she's a damn computer genius," Bishop snorted under his breath.

"You hacked into his accounts?" Willow said. "You know that's illegal, right?"

Kat grinned at her. "Only if we're caught."

Willow shook her head. "I can't believe you did that. You're usually so, so… moral."

Bishop burst out laughing, and Kat hissed lightly at him before turning back to Willow. "There's a lot you don't know about me, Willow."

"I'm starting to realize that," Willow said.

"Sometimes rules are meant to be broken. Isn't that what you always say?" Her tone was defensive, and Willow reached out and squeezed her arm.

"Yes. I'm not judging, Kat. Honest, I'm not. I'm just

surprised and a little shocked that Mal is on board with this."

She glanced at the wolf shifter. He was unusually quiet, and she wondered if he was even paying attention. He stared at a file folder of papers on the table in front of him, and she reached out and touched his arm lightly. "Mal?"

"Rules are meant to be broken," he repeated Kat's words as he leafed through the papers. "How many cat shifters work at the warehouse?"

"Five." Bishop had his own file folder, and he scanned a list of the employees. "No, wait, six. But Mal, we can't take Koren off our list of suspects. You know we can't."

"I'm not," Mal said. "But I'm with Willow. I have a hard time believing that Koren would do something like this to his brother."

He shook his head at Willow's smile of triumph. "But I don't think it's Royce Darnell either. The injuries to Keegan are definitely from a big cat."

"He could be working with someone from the warehouse," Willow said.

"Maybe. But what's his motivation?" Mal asked. "If the purpose of this is to get Mrs. Belfry to sell the company, what does that do for him? He could lose his job if someone else bought the company. It doesn't make sense, Willow."

"I guess," Willow said.

"None of this makes sense," Kat mused. "Other than the theory that Koren is doing this to get his mother to sell the company so he'll have enough money to pay off his debts."

"We'll question the six cat shifters again, as well as

Koren," Mal said. "I've already increased the security team at the warehouse to six."

"Six? That only leaves us with three, and we've got the mall job, Mr. Barick's daughter, and we picked up two new clients for personal security detail." Kat said. "We can't afford to put that many people at the warehouse."

"I know, but we don't have much choice. I don't want to risk another incident like the one last night. I'll make a few calls today. I've got a buddy who knows of a couple of guys looking for work," Mal said. "And if we have to, the three of us can take a few shifts at the mall or watching Melissa Barick."

"Count me out." Bishop raised his hands. "That chick's got a thing for bear shifters, remember? She trapped me in the library and stuck her hand down my damn pants when we went to their house for the initial interview."

Willow laughed, and Bishop grinned at her. "It's true, Will. She's a rabbit shifter, and they're fast as lightning and horny as hell."

"Who's next?" Bishop asked.

He and Mal were crammed into Mrs. Belfry's office. Mal scanned the paper in front of them. "Raluca Jones. She's a tiger shifter, has worked for the company for seventeen years, and is fifty-seven. She's the last one."

"Great. We've come up empty with the other five. You really think a fifty-seven-year-old tiger shifter beat the shit out of Keegan?" Bishop said.

"Fifty-seven isn't old for a tiger shifter," Mal said as there was a knock on the door. It opened a crack, and a wide-eyed and frightened looking woman peeked through the opening.

"My name is Raluca Jones," she squeaked out.

"Please, come in." Mal and Bishop stood as the tiger shifter crept into the room.

"You wanted to see me." She clasped her hands together in a poor attempt to keep them from shaking.

Mal sighed inwardly. Like most tiger shifters, the woman was tall and powerful looking, but she had a prey animal's timid, frightened demeanor. There was no way this woman could have nearly killed Keegan unless she was a superb actress.

"Yes, have a seat, Mrs. Jones." Mal tried to make himself look as non-threatening as possible, but it was at Bishop that the tiger shifter kept staring. She practically collapsed in the chair across the desk and watched Bishop carefully as a single tear slid down her face.

"Mrs. Jones, we're questioning a few of the employees today regarding the incident that happened two nights ago. One of our employees was injured, and Keegan Belfry was attacked," Mal said.

"I didn't have anything to do with that," she said. "I was home all night."

"Can anyone confirm that?" Bishop asked.

Mrs. Jones's bottom lip trembled. "I live alone. My husband passed away a few years back. It's just Bam-Bam and me now."

"Bam-Bam?" Bishop frowned, and the tiger shifter made a sharp moan of fear.

Mal kicked Bishop under the desk as Mrs. Jones leaned back into her chair.

"He – he's my cat. I have a picture of him." She

fumbled in her pocket and pulled out her cell phone. They waited patiently as she tried to punch in her code. Her fingers shook badly, and it took her three attempts before she succeeded. "This is Bam-Bam."

Mal stared politely at the picture of the large orange housecat glaring balefully at the camera. "He's lovely. Mrs. Jones, how do you like working for Mrs. Belfry?"

"She's real nice," Mrs. Jones said. "And she's been real good to me. When Gerald - that's my husband - got sick, she gave me plenty of time off to take care of him and didn't dock my pay even when I ran out of vacation time. And she came to Gerald's funeral – both her and her boys. They're real nice people."

She eyed the bear shifter with something approaching pure panic. "I didn't have nothing to do with what happened to Mr. Belfry. I swear it. I have arthritis, and I can barely extend my claws anymore. I can bring you a doctor's note if you need one."

"That won't be necessary," Mal said.

Bishop's nose twitched, and he leaned forward and inhaled as he stared intently at her. More tears flowed down Mrs. Jones' face, and Mal kicked Bishop again. He grunted and sat back before smiling at Mrs. Jones. She inhaled, and her hands dug into the arms of her chair.

"May I ask what type of shifters your parents were?" Bishop asked suddenly.

"I, um, my father was a tiger shifter, and my mother was a deer shifter," she said.

Mal stared in surprise at her. It certainly explained her nervous demeanor for a tiger shifter. "That's unusual."

A small smile crossed her face, and she wiped away the tears from her cheeks. "Yes, it was."

"How did a tiger shifter and a deer shifter even meet?" Bishop asked. "They don't normally run in the same social circles."

"My father was injured in a hunt. My mother stumbled onto him and helped him. My father said it was love at first sight for him, but it took a while to convince my mother."

"How long did they stay together?"

"They were married forty-three years until my mother passed away. My father died six months later."

"Forty-three years," Mal breathed. "A tiger and a deer in love - that's incredible."

The tiger shifter smiled, her fear forgotten. "Love is blind. It's what makes it so powerful."

The three of them were silent for a few moments. Mal stared at his hands, ignoring the look Bishop gave him.

Bishop cleared his throat. "Uh, thank you, Mrs. Jones. I think that's it for now."

The tiger shifter jumped to her feet and hurried out of the office with a noticeable sigh of relief. Bishop poked Mal in the shoulder. "Mal? What's wrong?"

"What?"

"What's wrong?"

Mal shook his head. "Nothing. What time is it?"

"Just about five. Why?"

"I need to go."

"I thought we were going to Bud's to grab a bite to eat and discuss -"

"Tomorrow, okay? We can talk about it tomorrow. I gotta go, Bishop." Mal stood and nearly ran out of the office.

WILLOW KICKED OFF HER SHOES AND WANDERED DOWN THE hallway toward the kitchen. She stared absentmindedly into the fridge before grabbing the bottle of wine and a glass. She sipped at the wine and tried to ignore the depression creeping in. She sighed heavily. She was head over heels in lust with Mal, and it was driving her crazy.

Lust or love?

She shook her head. She wasn't in love with her boss. She just really, really liked him. Besides, Mal had made it clear what he was looking for and, now that it was over, seemed to find it remarkably easy to forget what happened between them.

There was a knock on the door, and she checked the clock. Ava and Ginger were early for their girls' night. She called, "It's open," and took another gulp of wine.

"You shouldn't leave your door unlocked."

She whirled around with her heart thudding in her chest and stared in confusion at the wolf shifter. "Mal? What are you doing here?"

He stood in the kitchen doorway, dressed in his usual jeans and t-shirt, and her damn panties dampened just at the sight of him. She set her glass of wine on the counter. "Mal?"

She took an involuntary step back when he grinned at her, and his eyes glowed in the light of the fading sun. There was something different about him, something that hadn't been there earlier this afternoon when he left the office with Bishop. The look in his eyes and the way he stared so hungrily at her brought goosebumps to her flesh and the familiar, pulsing beat of lust through her body.

Keep it together, Tanner, she scolded herself fiercely.

"It's dangerous to leave your door unlocked." His voice was almost a growl, and a shiver of need tingled down her spine.

He lifted his head and inhaled deeply, a smile playing on his lips as Willow arched her eyebrows at him. "What's there to be afraid of?"

He stepped into the kitchen and gripped the chair in front of him. "Are you afraid of me?"

"You know I'm not," she said. "What are you doing here, Mal?"

"I miss you."

"You just saw me this afternoon." She took a deep breath and willed herself not to jump at the wolf shifter. She was about ten seconds from just dropping her skirt and inviting him to fuck her silly, and she was ashamed of her lack of self-control. Mal would have stopped by for something work related, despite the hungry way he eyed her.

He grinned again at her, his eyes dropping to her small breasts and then her core. This time there was no fooling herself about the reason for his visit.

"I miss your pussy," he growled. "I miss the way it clings to me so tightly, and I miss the sweet sounds you make when I fuck you."

A tidal wave of desire washed over her. It swept away all of her doubts and drowned her resolve to stay away. She stared at him with raw need in her eyes. "Please."

"Yes. God, yes," he growled again before lunging at her.

He pulled her into his arms, his mouth covering hers and his tongue sweeping between her lips. She moaned and threw her small body against him as he gripped her ass and squeezed tightly.

"Mine, Willow," he said against her mouth before tearing open her blouse and pushing it from her body. He cupped one small breast as he licked and nipped frantically at her throat. He marked her soft skin with a rough brush of his stubble, growling in satisfaction at the sound of her gasp before flicking open the clasps of her bra and pulling it off.

"Mine," he said again before sucking one nipple into his mouth. It hardened into a tight bud, and he sucked firmly on it as she cried out and gripped his head in her hands. She arched her pelvis against his erection, and he spun her around roughly, pushing her up against the kitchen table.

"Mal!" she moaned as he shoved her skirt up around her waist, tore her panties from her body and dropped them to the floor.

———

MAL'S WOLF HOWLED FOR HIM TO TAKE THE SOFT, SWEET-smelling human. Mal pushed his hand between her thighs and cupped her pussy. She was soaking wet, and he made a low growl of triumph before unzipping his jeans and pushing them and his briefs downward.

Take her! Give me what is mine!

His wolf snarled in need, and Mal pushed Willow down over the table and yanked her thighs apart as he stroked her smooth back and ass with one large hand.

"Mal," she moaned as she wiggled against the table, "I need you."

"I need you too, honey." He bent over her and sucked on her earlobe. She turned her head, and they kissed deeply as he rubbed his hard cock against her ass and pushed his hand between her thighs.

He rubbed her clit until she pulled her mouth from his and made a harsh, moaning cry of need. He straightened and guided his cock to her warm entrance. As the head of his cock pushed into her, a small voice of reason spoke in his head.

Condom, idiot.

She is our mate! his wolf snarled. *Put our pup in her belly.*

Excellent idea. He surged forward, pushing himself into her until he was fully sheathed in her smooth warmth. His mate gave another cry of need, and he placed a gentle hand on her back as he withdrew and thrust into her again.

"You feel so good, honey," he groaned. "I've missed you."

"I've missed you too," she gasped out as he pulled her upright until her hands were pressed against the smooth wood of the table.

He wrapped his big hands around her waist and held her firmly as he thrust back and forth. She moaned and shuddered wildly when he licked a warm path down her spine. His hand slipped between her thighs, and he pulled and caressed her clit as he plunged in and out of her. Her tiny body began to shake and her back arched as he rubbed her clit firmly. She cried his name, and his wolf howled with need.

Bite her! She is ours! Bite her now!

Mal howled as Willow's pussy tightened around him, and she came with a harsh shout. As his orgasm began, his fangs popped out in a smooth, easy motion, and he bent and sunk them deep into the back of his mate's shoulder.

She cried out as her entire body stiffened. He held her flush against the table with his teeth and his hard body as he came deep within her. Her pussy milked his cock eagerly, and he tasted the sweet saltiness of her blood as she cried out and climaxed again. Her body shook wildly under his, and he pulled his fangs free and licked the wound repeatedly until the blood had trickled to a stop.

His mate had collapsed beneath him, panting harshly, and he made a low growl of satisfaction as he studied the bite in her smooth flesh. She belonged to him now, was his forever, and no shifter would dare go near her. He would tear them apart if they did.

"Mal?"

His mate's soft voice broke through his haze of satisfaction. His eyes widened as his lust faded and reality set in. He had bitten Willow. His goddamn wolf had baited him into biting her, and he had done it. He had claimed her as his mate with no regard to what she wanted.

Feeling sick to his stomach, he stepped away from her. He reached with shaking hands for his pants as she straightened and touched the back of her shoulder. She winced and stared at the trace of blood on her fingers. She touched her back again, feeling the torn skin and the tender flesh before giving him a wide-eyed look of surprise. "You bit me."

"Willow, I…"

He trailed to a stop. He knew his face was pale, and he licked Willow's blood from his lips as he quickly buttoned his jeans. His eyes darted around the kitchen, and he swallowed compulsively. "I'm sorry. I – there was a tiger and a deer, and they fell in love for forty-three years, and they didn't care and…."

He trailed off again, and they stared at each other in silence for a moment.

"I'm so sorry," Mal said hoarsely and then turned and fled.

CHAPTER 20

Kat poured herself a cup of coffee and added a healthy spoonful of sugar. It was almost eight-thirty, and it wasn't like Mal to be late. Hell, even Bishop was here, and he never arrived before Mal did.

She thought about texting him just as the door flung open and Willow stormed into the office. Kat watched in surprise from the kitchenette as Willow marched across the reception area to Mal's office and flung open the door. His office was empty, and she slammed her hand against the doorframe in frustration as Bishop stuck his head out of his office.

"Where is he?" she snapped at them.

"He texted me and said he had a meeting this morning. Why?" Bishop asked as he joined Kat in the small kitchenette and poured himself a cup of coffee.

"Bullshit!" Willow shouted as she stomped over to them. "He's avoiding me."

Bishop dumped sugar into his coffee and stirred it

vigorously as Kat touched Willow's arm. "Will? What's wrong? Why do you think Mal is avoiding you?"

"Because he bit me!"

Kat's mouth dropped open, and the spoon slipped out of Bishop's hand to clatter noisily on the counter.

"He what?" Kat asked as Bishop joined them in the reception area.

"Last night, we were having sex, and he bit me," Willow said.

"Wait – are you saying he bit you? During sex? Last night?" Bishop said.

"Yes! What part of that was unclear?" Willow asked.

"Oh my God," Kat moaned, "this is bad. What was he thinking?"

"I have no idea," Willow said. "Because after he bit me, he ran from my apartment like a frightened puppy."

"Bishop, you need to find Mal right now." Kat grabbed the bear shifter's arm as Bishop shook his head.

"No way. I'm not getting involved in this."

"Bishop! You're his best friend!" Kat squeezed his arm. "You have to talk to him."

"Willow needs to talk to him, not me," Bishop protested.

"He won't talk to me. He didn't answer his phone last night, and I called and texted him repeatedly," Willow said. "I don't even know where he lives, so I couldn't go to his place and confront him. Then Damian showed up, and I -"

"Wait – who's Damian?" Kat asked.

"A ghost," Willow said impatiently.

"Right, of course," Kat said.

"Mal can't avoid me forever." Willow scowled. "Where does he live? Give me his address, Bishop."

"So, you're saying he just bit you and then left?" Bishop stalled nervously.

"He mumbled something about a tiger and a deer being in love for forty years, and then he ran, okay?" Willow said. "Give me his address."

"You should probably take a few hours to cool down, Willow. He'll turn up, and then you can speak to him," Bishop said.

"Bishop!" Kat glared at him as the room turned cold. She shivered delicately. "What the hell?"

"Ghost," Bishop said helpfully. "Right, Willow?"

Willow turned and glared at the wall behind her. "Yes, Damian, *I know*. And I asked you to give me a damn minute, remember?"

"Willow?" The hair on Kat's arms stood up, and her cat wanted nothing more than to hiss and spit.

"I will help you. Okay? Just let me take care of something first and then we'll find your stupid brother-in-law and tell him what a stupid jackass he was." Willow scowled at Bishop and Kat as a low moaning swept through the room, and the temperature dropped further.

"I do not have time for this," Willow snapped.

"Why don't you take the day off," Kat said. "Go and help your, uh, friend Damian, and Bishop will find Mal. As soon as he does, he'll text you. Right, Bishop?"

Bishop nodded with a remarkable lack of enthusiasm. "Sure will."

Willow stalked toward him and glared up at him. He was three times the size of her, but he shrunk back at the fury in her gaze. "You make sure you do. And Bishop? Give Mal a message for me."

His eyes widened as she relayed the message, and Kat pressed her lips together to stop from laughing as Willow turned and stared at the wall again. "C'mon, Damian. Let's go find your idiot brother-in-law."

She marched out of the office in a whoosh of cold air and indignation, and Bishop took a deep breath before staring at Kat. "Now what?"

"You find Mal."

"BAR'S CLOSED." JUDD FOLDED HIS ARMS ACROSS HIS massive chest and glared coldly at Bishop.

"I know it isn't closed," Bishop said. "Let me in, Judd."

The bear shifter stared impassively at him, and Bishop sighed. "Look, I'm sorry about the other night, okay? I don't know what got into me, but I shouldn't have attacked you like I did."

"You got a thing for the Red?" Judd asked.

"Not really," Bishop lied.

Judd snorted. "So, you didn't go after the lion because he had his hands all over her?"

Bishop remained silent, and Judd grinned at him. "Looked like she enjoyed it. I wouldn't be surprised if she took him home that night and helped him lick his wounds."

Bishop snarled at him, revealing long and razor-sharp teeth as his beard thickened and his body rippled.

Judd burst into loud laughter and slapped Bishop

roughly on the shoulder. "Never thought I'd see the day where you'd want to hump a human."

He stepped back, and Bishop followed him into the dim light of the bar. Although it was before noon, a few shifters already sat at the bar staring silently into their drinks. Porter stood behind the bar wiping down bottles, and he nodded to Bishop as he sat down on a barstool.

"You seen your brother?" Bishop asked.

"What's going on with him?" Porter wiped down the top of the bar. "He's acting weird."

"When did you see him?" Bishop asked. "I need to talk to him, Porter."

Porter pointed over Bishop's shoulder, and Bishop turned to see Mal sitting in one of the booths. He nodded his thanks and joined Mal, sliding his large frame into the booth.

"Hey, Mal."

"Hey, Bishop." The wolf shifter continued to stare at the cup of coffee in front of him.

"So, uh, Willow's really mad."

Mal didn't answer as Porter joined them. He sat down next to Mal and raised his eyebrows at him. "Why is she mad?"

When Mal stayed silent, Porter punched him in the arm. "Well, what did you do this time? You should know that Mom's going to be pissed if you ruined it with Willow already. She really liked her."

"It's complicated," Mal said.

"No, it isn't," Bishop said.

"Bishop, don't," Mal said.

"He bit Willow last night during sex," Bishop said to Porter.

"You're kidding me." Porter stared at his brother as Mal glared at Bishop.

"I'm not. He bit her and then ran away."

"Shut up, Bishop," Mal said wearily.

"You claimed Willow?" Porter gave him a look bordering on horror. "How long have you been dating this girl?"

"They're not even dating. They're just -"

"BISHOP!" Mal roared.

Bishop shut his mouth with a snap as Porter shook his head in disbelief. "What were you thinking, Mal?"

"I don't know," Mal said miserably.

"I do," Bishop said. "He was thinking about the tiger and the deer."

"The what now?" Porter blinked at him.

"Earlier in the day, we heard this disgustingly sappy story about a tiger and a deer who fell in love and were married for forty-three years. As much as he denies it, your brother is head over heels for our little human receptionist. He heard the story about these two opposite shifters beating the odds, and it got him all a flutter for *his* opposite object of desire," Bishop said.

"Oh my God," Mal groaned. "I'm such an idiot."

"You really are," Bishop said. "And Willow is furious with you. It's not a good idea to claim a woman you've only known for a couple of months, Mal."

"You think I don't know that? I don't know what came over me. I just – I mean...."

He stopped and stared in misery at his brother. Porter clapped him on the back consolingly. "Look on the bright side, big brother. Mom's going to be thrilled that you've claimed Willow as your mate. Of course, Grandpa will freak the hell out when he realizes he has a human for a granddaughter-in-law. We're in for a lot of awkward family dinners in the future."

"Do not tell Mom about this. Do you hear me, Porter? Keep your mouth shut!" Mal said.

"Okay, okay." Porter held up his hands. "Your secret is safe with me. But she's planning on having you and Willow over for dinner next week. As soon as she smells Willow, she'll know you bit her."

"I'll say we're busy," Mal said.

"You can't put her off forever. She'll find out eventually when you and Willow are married."

"I don't know that Willow wants to be with me."

"What?" Porter's mouth dropped open again. "Mal, is Willow even in love with you?"

"I don't know," Mal said.

"You don't know?" Porter shook his head. "You claimed a woman who might not even be in love with you. Do you know how serious this is?"

"It'll be fine," Mal said a little desperately. "If she doesn't love me, I'll just walk away and let her live her life. Just because I bit her doesn't mean she has to be my mate."

"Uh, it kind of does, you moron," Porter said affectionately.

"But it doesn't have to," Mal said. "If she doesn't want me as her mate, I'll let her go."

"Really?" Bishop said with skepticism in his voice. "I might be a grizzly shifter, but we've been best friends since we were kids, and I spent more time at your house than my own. I know plenty about wolf shifters, and I've never seen one walk away from their mate."

"We can't," Porter said. "Once we bite them, we're mated to them for life. Of course, normally, the woman agrees with us claiming them. I've never heard of a wolf shifter claiming a woman without asking her first."

"I can let her go," Mal repeated. "I can, Bishop."

Bishop nodded. "Okay, sure."

"You're fooling yourself, Mal," Porter said. "You honestly believe you'll be able to stay away from her now? That you'll do nothing the first time you see another shifter or human dating your mate? Kissing her? Hell, Willow's gorgeous and funny – maybe I should date her."

Mal growled, and his eyes flashed jade. "You will stay away from my mate, baby brother, or I'll tear out your guts."

"Told you so." Porter gave Bishop a wry look.

"Fuck," Mal muttered. "What am I going to do?"

"Just tell her you love her," Porter advised. "Women go crazy for that sappy shit."

"Do you love her, Mal?" Bishop asked.

Mal nodded. "Yeah, I do."

"Just like that, huh, big brother?" Porter grinned at him. "The irony of this moment is killing me. You, the shifter who thinks humans and our kind should stay away from each other, are in love with a human you've known less than three months."

When Mal didn't reply to his teasing, Porter squeezed his arm. "Hey, it'll be fine, Mal. Willow's fantastic, and it's about time you settled down and started giving Mom and Dad grandpups. I'm sure when you tell her that you bit her because you love her, she'll understand."

"Yeah?" Mal gave him a dry look. "So, if a woman came up to you after only a couple of months and told you she was in love with you and you were meant to spend the rest of your lives together, that wouldn't freak you out? Not even just a little?"

Porter paled. "Well, yeah, but I'm not Willow. She won't have a problem with it."

"You don't know that," Mal said. "Hell, I don't know that. I barely know anything about her. All I know is that I'm crazy about her. Whenever we're in the same room together, I need to touch her and be close to her. That I want to know everything about her, and the thought of my life without her in it makes me physically sick to my stomach."

He stared at Bishop in dismay. "Have I gone crazy? How did this happen? It's like I just woke up one day and decided I was in love with Willow. This isn't me. I don't do crazy, impulsive things like falling in love and claiming a woman I barely know."

He slammed his fist down on the table. "Willow is everything I'm not. I like order and rules, and she thrives on chaos. She's a hippie who does whatever the hell she feels like. She sees ghosts, for God's sake! What if after a few years, she -"

"Whoa, whoa, whoa." Porter held up his hand. "Did you just say that Willow sees ghosts?"

"Yes," Mal said impatiently. "Never mind that. What if, after a few years, she's tired of me? What if she never falls in love with me? What if I've driven her away forever? What if -"

"Mal, calm down!" Bishop suddenly barked at him. "You're freaking out, and you haven't even spoken to Willow. You need to take things one step at a time. First, get your ass to Willow's place and apologize for running out on her like that. She's super pissed at you for biting her and taking off."

Mal groaned. "I panicked. All I could think about was how much I loved her and that I couldn't live without her, and how weird she would find that. I'm in love with her, Bishop!"

"Yes, you are," Bishop said solemnly. "So, put on your big girl panties and deal with it."

Porter snickered as Bishop leaned forward and clapped Mal on the shoulder. "She wants me to give you a message."

"What is it?"

"She said to tell you that if you keep avoiding her and acting like a giant, spoiled baby, she's going to treat you like one and tell your mother what you did – in detail."

Porter snickered again as Mal groaned. "If Mom finds out that I bit Willow without her permission, she'll…."

"Kill you," Porter said.

"Yes." Mal dropped his head into his hands as Porter gave him a sympathetic grin.

"Then I guess you'd better find Willow and beg for her forgiveness."

CHAPTER 21

He was waiting on the front step of her apartment building when she pulled into her parking spot. She shut off her car, and he waited patiently as she took her time gathering her things before slowly walking toward him.

"Hi, Willow."

"Hello, Mal," she said coolly. "Finished with your meeting, are you?"

He winced. "Yeah. Were you at the office? Bishop said that you were at home, but I've been waiting a while."

"Oh, was I inconveniencing you?" she said.

"No," he said quickly. "I didn't mean it like that."

She fiddled with the strap on her purse. "I was with Damian."

His wolf sat up straight, his fur bristling and a low growl vibrating through his chest.

Find him and kill him for touching our mate.

"Who's Damian?" Mal demanded. Willow gave him another cool look before brushing past him and into the

245

lobby of her building. Mal followed and stared at her as she pushed the elevator button. "Willow? Who is this Damian guy?"

"What do you care?" she asked.

"I care because you're my ma -"

He stopped and took a deep breath. "I'm sorry. Would you please tell me who he is?"

She sighed as the elevator doors opened. "Relax. He's a little too old and a little too dead for me."

He followed her into the elevator. "I don't want you going off by yourself with ghosts, Willow. Don't you remember what happened the last time? If a ghost shows up, you call me immediately. Do you understand?"

She scoffed rude laughter. "That is so not going to happen, Mal."

She marched out of the elevator and down the hallway toward her apartment door.

"Willow! You could have been killed at that farm. If I hadn't shown up when I did -"

"I would have been just fine," she said. "I've been doing this for years. I don't need a babysitter."

She opened the door, and he made a grunt of surprise when she shoved him back. "What do you think you're doing?"

"I'm coming in." He gave her a wounded look.

"No, you're not. You owe me an apology, Malcolm Burke, and since it doesn't appear you're in the apolo-gizing mood, you're not coming in. Good night. I'll see you at work tomorrow."

She started to shut the door in his face, and he pushed against it lightly. "Willow, wait. You're right. Please let me come in so I can apologize and explain. Okay?"

She released her grip on the door. "Fine. But make it quick. You ruined my girls' night last night, so Ava and Ginger are coming over tonight."

He followed her into the kitchen and stared anxiously at her back. "Can I see your shoulder?"

"Why? Are you going to bite me and run again?"

He flinched. "No, I just want to make sure you're healing."

Her face softened, and she turned around before shrugging out of her shirt. She wore a thin camisole under it, and he brushed the narrow strap down her arm before carefully peeling back the bandage.

"It's healing," he said in relief.

She peered at him over her shoulder. "Did you think it wouldn't?"

"No, but I feel bad for hurting you."

"It didn't hurt that much. Or if it did, I didn't notice," she said.

He peeled off the bandage. "You should leave the bandage off for a little while."

"How big will the scar be?" she asked.

Shame swept through him. "Not very big. It'll just look like a, well, a dog bite."

"Great," she said. "What about other shifters? Will they know?"

He hesitated before nodding. "Yes. You'll smell differently to them now."

"You mean I'll smell like your wolf."

"Yes."

"Permanently."

"Yes. I'm sorry."

She gave him a thoughtful look. "Are you?"

Before he could reply, she crooked her finger at him. "Come with me."

She led him out of the kitchen and down the hall, and his heart leaped in his chest. She was headed toward her bedroom, and for a brief moment, he allowed himself hope that it would be that easy. His hope died when she stopped at the first door. It was a guest room with a single bed and a small desk with a laptop.

She pointed to the laptop. "Show me your records."

"What?"

"We didn't use a condom last night. I want to see your medical records, and I'll show you mine as well."

"I'm sorry," he said. "It's my fault. I should have used a condom, and I have no excuse for it."

She held her hand up. "Stop, Mal. You did many stupid things last night, but I'm an adult responsible for my sexual protection. I should have stopped you and told you to put on a condom."

She sat down, and he watched as she brought up her medical records. "Here, take a look. My records are negative."

"Willow, you don't have to show me."

"Look at them, Mal." She glared at him, and he took a quick, cursory look to appease her. When he was done, he logged in and showed her his records. She perused them carefully before logging out and closing the laptop.

She rubbed at her forehead. "I'm on the pill, so we don't have to worry about pregnancy."

He didn't reply, and she glanced up at him, an odd look crossing her face. He wondered if she could see the disappointment on his face and forced himself to smile at her. It was utterly ridiculous to be disappointed that there was no chance Willow was carrying his pup. "Okay, that's good."

"Right," she said.

"Willow, I…"

He wanted to take her hand. He wanted to sit down on the bed, pull her into his arms and tell her that he loved her, and he would spend the rest of his life doing whatever it took to make her happy. But she was giving him a strained look, and there were dark circles under her eyes.

She stood to move past him. Unable to help himself, he reached out and took her hand. "I'm so sorry, Willow. I shouldn't have left the way I did last night. It was a cowardly thing to do, and you have every right to be angry with me."

"Why did you do it?"

"I felt terrible for hurting you, and I panicked and ran. It wasn't my finest moment, and I -"

"No," she said. "Why did you bite me? Why did you claim me as your mate?"

He opened his mouth to tell her it was an accident and instead told the truth. "I love you, Willow. You're my mate, and I want to spend the rest of my life with you."

She dropped his hand and took a step back. Nausea swept through him at the cautious look in her eyes.

"It's the truth, Willow. I love you," he said.

"Last week," she spoke slowly as if she thought he wouldn't understand, "you were determined to stay away from me. You told me it would never work between us and all you were looking for was a weekend of fun. Do you remember that?"

"I know it's hard to understand, but -"

"Do you remember that?" she said.

He nodded. "I remember."

"Now you've claimed me as your mate without my permission and effectively ruined my chance at a relationship with another man."

His heart pounding in his chest, he said the last thing he wanted to say. "Human men wouldn't know that I claimed you."

"True," she said. "What about you? What if I'm not in love with you, Mal? Would you just move on to someone else? Find another woman to claim without her permission?"

He winced at the thought. "No."

She twitched a bit and stared up at him. "What do you mean, 'no'?"

"When a wolf shifter bites a woman, he's mated to her for life. There's no other for me, Willow. You're the only one I'll ever want or need."

She stared at him. "Do you hear yourself? We've known each other for less than two months. You hate humans! I drive you crazy, remember?"

"I know," he said simply. "I love you, Willow. I know I sound crazy, but I've denied my feelings for you because I didn't believe that shifters and humans should mate for life."

"And now?"

"Now, I don't care. Now I just want to be with you." He reached out and took her hand, stroking the top of it with his thumb.

She stared at their clasped hands. "I don't know what you want me to say."

"I know it's a lot to take in, and I'm sorry I bit you without asking your permission first. It was wrong, and I should never have done that." He brought her hand to his mouth and pressed a gentle kiss against it. "Take some time away from the office to think things through. I won't pressure you."

She stared up at him, and he leaned down and kissed her forehead before leaving the room. As he left her apartment, he tried to ignore the cold fear in his belly. He'd done and said everything he could. Now it was up to Willow.

"WAIT, SO LET ME GET THIS STRAIGHT — HE'S A SHIFTER who thinks humans and shifters shouldn't be together, but then he bit you, and now he's in love with you?" Ginger sat on the couch with a glass of wine in one hand, and her feet curled up under her. She stared curiously at Willow. "Why did he bite you if he knew it would make him fall in love with you?"

"Biting her didn't *make* him fall in love with her." Ava came out from the kitchen and sat down next to Ginger. She held out the plate of cookies she carried, and Ginger selected a cookie. "He was *already* in love with her. That's why he bit her."

"Oh." Ginger bit into the cookie and brushed some crumbs from the front of her shirt. "That seems quick. I've been dating Robbie for nearly six months, and he still hasn't told me he loves me."

"Willow? Honey, are you okay? You're being really quiet," Ava said.

Willow sighed. She was lying on the floor with her legs propped up against the wall and a pillow under her head. "I don't know. Mal spends weeks telling me that he doesn't want to sleep with me, then he sleeps with me but makes it clear it's nothing more than sex, and now the guy's in love with me and wants to be with me forever."

Ava leaned down and patted her shoulder. "You like Mal. I know you do."

"Yeah, I like him. I like him a lot, but do I love him? I don't know," she said.

"Sit up and let me see the bite," Ava said.

Willow did what she asked, and both Ava and Ginger leaned forward and studied the rapidly-healing wound.

"He just bit you last night?" Ginger asked.

At Willow's nod, Ginger gave Ava a look of surprise. "It's healing fast."

"I'll still be left with a scar," Willow said. "And now I'll smell like Mal's wolf forever."

Ginger sniffed at her. "You don't smell like a wolf to me."

"Only other shifters can smell it," Ava said.

"Oh." Ginger was quiet for a moment. "Maybe you should bite him back, Will. Make him smell like a human forever."

Ava and Willow stared silently at the small brunette before Ava burst into loud laughter. Even Willow had a grin on her face as she said, "I don't think it works that way, Ginger."

"No? Well, maybe you'd just feel better if you bit him." Ginger took another bite of cookie, noisily chewing before she grinned at Willow. "From what Ava tells me, your wolf shifter is pretty damn good looking."

Willow fell onto her back again and stared up at the

ceiling. "He's frackin' hot. He's also smart and sweet and has a steady job. And he's amazing in bed."

"Jesus, Willow, what's the problem then?" Ginger frowned at her. "Robbie is continually getting his ass fired because he can't keep his mouth shut. Plus, he couldn't find my g-spot if I gave him a flashlight and a map."

Ava laughed again as Willow shook her head. "Great sex isn't everything, Ginger."

"Says the woman who's having great sex," Ginger said.

Ava took a sip of wine. "On a scale of one to ten, how freaked out are you, Willow?"

"I'd say a six."

"That's not bad. I'd probably be at a nine." Ava grinned at her.

"Oh, please," Ginger said. "You're telling me if that delicious hunk of lion shifter came to you and said he loved you, it wouldn't make your heart go pitter-patter?"

"No," Ava said. "It wouldn't."

"Only because he's not a big old grizzly shifter who wants you to ride his face," Willow said.

"Willow!"

"Sorry. How is Keegan, by the way?" Willow asked.

"The same. The wounds on his chest and back have almost healed completely, but he still hasn't woken up. I don't think his mother has left his side since he arrived at the hospital."

"Poor Marika," Willow said.

Ginger leaned forward. "Not to be insensitive about your shifter friends and their troubles, but can we back up this conversation to the part about Ava riding a grizzly shifter's face?"

Ava blushed furiously. "It's nothing."

"Doesn't sound like nothing." Ginger took a drink of wine. "In fact, it really sounds like something."

"It isn't," Ava said. "Besides, we're talking about Willow and what she should do about Mal."

"It's simple." Ginger selected another cookie from the plate. "You either decide you love him back, or you let him loose and move on."

"It's not that simple." Willow frowned at her.

"Sure, it is. People are always freaking out about love. Are they in it? Is the other person in it? Is it too soon to be in love? Is it not soon enough? You either love them, or you don't. You've known him long enough to know whether you're in love with him or not, Willow."

Willow blinked at her. "Who are you? This is not the Ginger I know and love. I'm supposed to be the flighty, fall in love at the drop of a hat, get myself into trouble, friend, remember? You and Ava are the stable, do the right thing, friends."

Ginger laughed. "That's right. You *do* fall in love at the drop of a hat. Remember Philip? You were certain he was the one after one night at the bar."

Ava grinned. "They were confessing their undying love for each other on the dance floor."

"Ooh, and what about Seth?" Ginger said. "On their fifth date, they booked their flights to Vegas for a quickie marriage."

Ava winced. "Don't remind me. I nearly broke my ankle chasing her down in the airport terminal to stop her from getting on the plane."

Ginger nodded. "I remember. And we can't forget about Jared, Xavier, Gary -"

"Okay, okay," Willow said irritably. "So, I have a history of being impulsive about love. I would think the two of you would be happy that I'm being more cautious now."

"And why exactly are you being more cautious this time?" Ginger asked.

"Well, because I…." Willow stared blankly at the two women.

"Because you know this time it really is love, and it scares the hell out of you?" Ava suggested gently.

Willow groaned and reached for the bottle of wine and the plate of cookies. "Grab the second bottle of wine from the fridge, would you, Ava? I'm going to need it."

CHAPTER 22

Τhe moment Mal smelled her scent, he hurried out of his office. Willow was at her desk wearing sunglasses. She turned on her computer as he stopped in front of her. "Willow? What are you doing here? I thought you were taking a few days off."

"You said I was taking a few days off. I never said that," she said irritably. "And can you please keep your voice down?"

"Are you okay?" he asked in alarm.

"I'm fine," she said. "I just have a horrible headache."

He sniffed in her direction. "Are you hungover?"

"I might be."

"Willow, you don't have to be here. We can cover the phones."

"It's fine."

"Are you – did you come in because you're ready to talk?" he asked.

She shook her head. "No. I came in because it's my job

and I'm a responsible person. I know you think I'm irresponsible, Mal, but I'm not."

"I don't think that, honey," he said.

She frowned at him, and he gave her a sheepish look. "Sorry."

"I just, I need a few days at least, okay?" she said.

"I know. Can I get you a coffee? Maybe some water and Advil?"

"No, I can grab it myself. There are some voicemails I need to listen to, Mal," she said.

"Right." He walked back to his office, stopping in the doorway to glance at Willow a final time. It drove him crazy that his mate was in pain and wouldn't allow him to help. He forced himself to go into his office and shut the door. Willow just needed time.

***

WILLOW RUBBED AT HER FOREHEAD AGAIN AND SQUINTED at the computer screen in front of her. She didn't know why she was here. The phones weren't busy, and other than some correspondence she had typed for Kat, she had nothing to do. If she were smart, she would go home and go to bed. She was only torturing herself and Mal by being here.

"Willow?" Kat asked tentatively.

Willow looked up to see the cat shifter standing next to her desk.

"Why don't you go home? It's not busy."

"Because this is my job, Kat," Willow said. "I'm not going to let Mal and his declarations of insta-love stop me from doing what you hired me to do."

"We understand, Will. Really."

"I appreciate that, honestly I do, but I need to be here. Okay?"

"Okay." Kat squeezed her shoulder before heading to Bishop's office. The door was closed, and she could hear the faint sound of Mal's voice.

She looked away when Kat opened the door and studied the desk in front of her. When the door was safely shut again, she sighed and made her way to the kitchenette for more coffee. Her left eye throbbed dully, and the wine had given her an upset stomach. The coffee wouldn't help her stomach, but she had spent most of last night tossing and turning despite the amount of wine she drank. She needed the caffeine.

As she poured herself a cup of the dark liquid, the bell over the door chimed softly. Forcing a cheerful tone, she said, "Be right with you."

"Take your time, dear."

Her head snapped up, and she stared in horror at Mal's mother. "Mrs. Burke? What are you doing here?"

"I told you to call me Mara, dear. Remember?" Mara said as she walked toward Willow. "I've come to invite you and Mal to a barbecue this weekend. All of Mal's siblings will be there, and it'll be a wonderful opportunity for you to meet everyone. It sounds overwhelming but don't worry. We won't…."

She trailed off, her eyes widening in surprise, as she inhaled deeply. "Oh! Oh my goodness!"

Willow glanced nervously at Bishop's office. "Mara, I -"

She squeaked in surprise when Mal's mother pulled her

into her embrace. She kissed her cheek, and Willow groaned inwardly when she saw the tears on Mara's face.

"Oh, Willow! You have no idea how happy I am! Congratulations! This is so wonderful!" She took a step back and beamed at Willow. "So, when is the wedding?"

"Oh, uh, I don't, I mean we haven't -"

Mara grinned. "If you don't mind me saying so, you look a little shell-shocked. Of course, that's not surprising. I just knew that my boy would waste no time when he found the one. His father was worried about him, you know. Worried that he would never settle down, but I knew he'd be fine. He just needed to find the right girl, and now he has!"

She inhaled again before squeezing Willow's arms. "Oh, this is going to be so much fun! Malcolm told me about the loss of your parents - I'm so sorry - but if you'd like, I would love to offer my services to help with any wedding planning. I promise I won't be the overbearing mother-in-law who must have the wedding exactly the way she wants. I'll just be quietly in the background, doing whatever it is you need done. Okay?"

"Um, yeah, okay," Willow said.

"Wonderful! So? When's the date for the wedding?" Mara asked again.

"So, you told her you loved her?" Bishop asked.

Mal nodded. "I did."

"How did she take it?" Bishop glanced at the closed door of his office. "Judging by her mood, I'm guessing not very well."

"She's hungover," Mal replied. "She's in a bad mood because she's not feeling well."

"Yeah, sure. That's it," Bishop said. "Are you still up for talking with Koren today?"

"He finally returned your call?" Mal asked.

"Nope. He's avoiding us. But I figure he must be at the warehouse, right? His mother is still at the hospital with his brother, and she sure as hell doesn't want him there. Someone needs to be looking after the company."

"True." Mal sipped at his coffee. "So, what? We're just going to go there and force him to talk to us."

"I don't see why not," Bishop said. "While we're there, we can talk to Royce Darnell as well."

"You think Willow is right?"

"I don't know, but it can't hurt to find out what he was doing that night."

The door opened, and Kat slipped into the office. She closed the door and glared at Mal. "You need to fix this, Mal."

"I'm trying," he said. "Willow asked for some time, and I'm giving it to her."

"She's really upset."

"I know she is, and I feel terrible about it. I wish I had told her I loved her before I lost my damn mind and claimed her, but I didn't. Now, the only thing I can do is give her the time she needs and hope she loves me."

Kat sat down in the chair next to him. "I never thought you'd fall in love with a human."

"I didn't either," he said. "But Willow is special."

"What if she rejects you?" Kat asked.

"No offense, but I don't want to talk about it. Can we

just concentrate on figuring out who the hell tried to murder Keegan Belfry?"

Kat nodded. "Yes. Sorry, Mal. It isn't any of my business."

She set down the file folder she was holding. "I found some more information on one of the cat shifters that work at the warehouse."

"Which one?"

"Raluca Jones."

"The one with the tiger and deer for parents?"

"That's the one." Kat opened the file folder and tapped the top paper. "I dug a little further into her financial records. She owes a lot of money."

"For what?" Bishop asked.

"Her late husband had a problem with betting. He died owing a substantial amount of money to Craig Howell."

"What? Craig Howell? Why would he loan a bunch of money to some tiger shifter?" Bishop asked.

"Lion shifter. Mr. Jones was a lion shifter," Kat said.

"Whatever," Bishop said. "How did he get Howell to loan him money?"

"Apparently, in addition to his food warehouse, Howell owns a couple of restaurants. Mr. Jones was the head chef at one of them. He worked there for over twenty years. I'm assuming he went to Howell for money to pay off his gambling debts, and Howell was feeling generous that day."

Mal stared at Bishop, and Bishop shook his head. "No way, Mal. It isn't her. You saw her in the interview. She was barely keeping it together. She might look like a tiger, but she's a deer shifter through and through. There's no way she would have the balls to attack Keegan and Fenton."

"We don't know that for sure. We know that Howell wants the company - Koren confirmed that at the hospital - and maybe Howell told Mrs. Jones there was a way for him to forgive her husband's debt without her having to pay a dime."

"She doesn't have the guts," Bishop said. "She was practically crying in the interview."

"Maybe she's just an excellent actress," Mal said. "I think we need to speak to her again."

He stood and crossed to the window, staring down at the street below them. "We can speak to her and Koren." He paused and inhaled deeply before whirling around. Bishop and Kat gave him similar uneasy looks.

"Mal, I can smell -"

"My mother," Mal groaned and bolted for the door. He threw it open and ran into the reception area. His mother stood in front of Willow, and she turned and smiled proudly at him.

"Pudding! Congratulations, darling! I'm so thrilled. Willow is going to fit right in with the rest of the family." She hugged him fiercely and kissed him on the cheek.

His face red, Mal stole a glance at Willow. She stared at him with a pale face and worried eyes, and he sighed. He had to tell his mother the truth. She'd kick his ass, but he couldn't ask Willow to lie for him. "Mom, I need to tell you something."

"What is it?" Concern crossed her face. "Pudding? What's wrong?"

"The thing is, I claimed Willow as my mate, but -"

"I know," his mother said. "I was just asking her when the wedding was."

Mal didn't reply, and Mara gave him and then Willow a worried look. "Will one of you please tell me what's wrong? You both look like you're going to throw up."

"Mom, I claimed Willow, but I haven't, that is, we aren't -"

"What he's trying to say is that we haven't set a date for the wedding yet," Willow said. She stood next to Mal and put her arm around his waist.

Gratitude rushed through Mal, and he put his arm around her slender body. He hugged her close and kissed the top of her head, knowing it was an act on her part but unable to resist touching her.

"Why not?" Mara asked.

"I'm a little worried about Mal's grandfather." Willow's smile was strained. "Mal and I haven't known each other for very long, and I know how he feels about humans. We thought we would keep it a secret for a while – just until we figure out how to tell his grandfather."

"Oh, my dear. You mustn't worry about Amos. He'll get over it. Mal loves you, and Amos loves his family and wants them to be happy."

When Willow didn't reply, Mara caught her hand and squeezed it. "I promise you it will all work out, Willow. I'll have Roland speak with Amos about being respectful, okay?"

"Thank you, Mara. You're very kind," Willow said.

"You're a part of our family now, my dear. We want you to be happy. It'll take Amos some time, but you'll win him over. I know you will."

She kissed Mal on the cheek. "We're having a family

barbecue Sunday afternoon. It'll be a wonderful opportunity to introduce Willow to the rest of the family."

"Mom, I think we should hold off on introducing Willow," Mal said.

"What on earth for?" Mara frowned at him. "Stop worrying about your grandfather. Your father and I will break the news to him, so he has time to adjust. We'll see the both of you on Sunday." She kissed Willow's cheek and left the office.

"Thank you, Willow," Mal said. They were still standing together with their arms around each other, and he had to restrain himself from kissing her.

"Well, I figured your mom would flip out if she knew you bit me without my permission."

"Yes, flip out is an accurate description."

His pulse sped up when a small, teasing grin crossed Willow's face. "Is the big bad wolf afraid of his mommy?"

He grinned. "Would you think less of me if I said yes?"

"No. It's my personal opinion that a son should always be just a tiny bit afraid of his mother."

He laughed, and she smiled at him before growing solemn. "What do we do about Sunday?"

"I don't know," Mal said. "I should have realized the possibility that mom would drop by the office. She really likes you."

"I like her too," Willow said. She rested her head against his broad chest absentmindedly as Mal rubbed her lower back.

"How are you?" he asked hesitantly. "Did you – are you sleeping okay?"

"Is that your way of telling me I look tired?" she asked.

"You look beautiful."

"Flattery will get you everywhere."

"It's the truth."

She snorted softly. "In answer to your question, I didn't sleep that well last night, but it's mostly because there's something wrong with my air conditioning. It rattled so loudly I couldn't sleep. I called the landlord this morning, but he was evasive on when he'd get around to fixing it."

"You could stay at my place," he said. "I have an extra bedroom, so, you know."

"I know what?" she asked.

"I just meant that there wouldn't be any pressure for you to, uh…."

"Sleep with you?"

He nodded. "Yeah."

"Thanks for the offer, but it's probably not a good idea."

"Of course." Depression washed over him. He had lost Willow forever. He was a fool to think she would forgive him for what he had done. Hell, she *shouldn't* forgive him. What he did to her was reprehensible, and he would spend the rest of his life regretting his lack of control.

"Mal?"

Willow turned and wrapped both her arms around his waist. He pulled her into his embrace and buried his face in her hair. He inhaled deeply as she said, "Let's make one thing clear, wolf boy. Just because you freaked me the hell out doesn't mean I don't want to sleep with you. I really, really want to sleep with you."

Relief flooded through him, and he tightened his hold on her until she squeaked in protest.

"Sorry." He loosened his grip as she stared up at him.

"But I don't think it's a good idea for us to sleep together right now. It'll cloud the issue."

"I know," he said. "I just miss you."

"I miss you too, but you have to know how weird this is, right? You go from not wanting anything but sex to being in love with me. There's apparently no in-between for you, and it scares the hell out of me. You get how odd that is, right?"

"I do," he said. "I wish I could explain it, but I can't. This is all brand new for me too, Willow. I've never been in love before."

"Never?"

"No."

"Then how do you know this is love?" she asked.

He smiled. "I just do. I can't imagine my life without you. I know that makes me sound like a creepy stalker, but I can't lie to you about my feelings. I love you, Willow."

She didn't reply, and he kissed her forehead. "I'll wait for you, honey. As long as it takes."

"And if I never return your love?"

The whine slipped out of his throat before he could stop it, and her face paled at the sound. He took a deep breath. "Then I'll leave you alone."

"Will you?"

"Yes." He hoped he sounded sincere. He wanted to be genuine, but his wolf was howling over the thought of leaving his mate, and it was tough to ignore.

She studied his face for a few moments, and he could feel sweat breaking out on his forehead.

"Liar," she said softly.

"I'm not," he said. "I'll leave you alone, Willow. I promise."

"Is your underwear heating up?" she suddenly asked.

"What?" He gave her a blank look, and she smiled wryly at him.

"From your pants being on fire."

He wanted to laugh at her small joke, but his wolf was still protesting, and his stomach was rolling with nausea, and all he could manage was a slight grimace.

She rested her forehead against his chest for a moment. "If it's okay with you, maybe I will take the day off. I'm exhausted."

"That's fine." He kissed the top of her head again. "Why don't I give you the key to my house? You can go there and sleep for the afternoon. I won't come home until you text me that you're gone."

He was desperate to have her scent in his house, desperate to have something to remind him of her when she inevitably told him to take a hike. He hoped she would take him up on the offer.

To his dismay, she shook her head. "That's okay. I can stay with Ava until the air conditioning is fixed."

"Okay." He forced himself to smile at her. "Take tomorrow off, as well."

"We'll see."

She pulled away from him, and his wolf snarled at him to simply pick her up and take her home, to show her why she was his mate. He ignored it and let her go as the temperature in the reception area dropped a few degrees.

"Willow?" He stared at her in alarm and automatically pulled her behind him as he studied the empty area.

"It's fine." She patted his back. "It's just Damian again."

"Again? Why is he still bothering you?"

"Because his brother-in-law is a horse's ass and won't meet with me." She looked to her left. "Yes, Damian. I'm *trying*. He can't avoid me forever. We'll stop by his house tonight."

"No!" Mal said in alarm. "Willow, do not go to this guy's house by yourself."

"It's not a problem, Mal," she said tiredly. "Damian wasn't murdered, and his brother-in-law isn't some crazy-ass person after his money."

"What does he want you to do?"

"I can't tell you that. It's private," Willow said.

"Willow." He could hear the exasperation in his voice.

"It's a private matter between Damian and Raymond. Sorry."

"I'll come with you tonight."

"No, you won't," she said. "This is who I am, Mal. It's what I do, and if you can't trust that I can take care of myself, then this won't work."

"I do trust you," he said. "But you're my mate, and I won't let you put yourself in danger."

She moved away from him and scooped up her purse from behind the desk. "I appreciate that, I do, but your aura will mess everything up."

"I'll stay in the car." He was starting to feel a little frantic. "You can drive my car there, and I'll wait for you."

She eyed him suspiciously. "Are you using my love for driving fast cars to get what you want?"

"No," he said, arranging an innocent look on his face.

"I'll think about it." She moved toward the door, the blast of cold air moving with her, and smiled at him over her shoulder.

"Call me before you go over there," he called after her. "Okay?"

"Okay." She left, shutting the door quietly behind her, and he blew his breath out in a frustrated rush before returning to Bishop's office.

CHAPTER 23

"Willow? What are you doing here?" Ava peered at her from behind the nurse's desk.

"I came to yell at you. I have a headache from all the wine you made me drink last night."

Ava laughed. "Yes, the wine I *made* you drink." She leaned against the desk and studied Willow. "You look like shit, honey."

"Thanks."

"You're welcome. Did you see Mal this morning?"

"Yes."

"How did it go?"

"We didn't come to any decisions if that's what you're wondering."

Ava stared at her in disappointment. "Will, you need to tell him how you feel."

"I don't know how I feel," Willow said.

"Oh really?" Ava raised her eyebrow at her. "Because last night when I tucked your drunk ass into bed, you were babbling about how much you loved him and that his

271

biting you was the most romantic thing a guy had ever done for you. And that when he bit you, it was hands down the best orgasm of your entire life."

"Oh, God." Willow rubbed her forehead. "I thought I dreamed that."

"Nope. You're lucky I took away your phone. You were one glass of wine away from drunk-dialing him and asking him to come over and – I quote - 'put a furry little wolf-baby in your belly'."

As Willow groaned, Ava pulled her cell phone from her pocket. "That reminds me. Here's your phone."

"Thanks." She rested her elbows on the desk and stared at Ava. "What do I do, Ava?"

"I can't answer that for you, honey. I'm sorry," Ava said. "Besides, you already know what I think."

"Yes, yes," Willow said irritably, "that I'm in love with him and scared to death about it."

"Bingo," Ava said.

"His mom came to the office this morning, took one sniff of me, and went giddy with wedding planning," Willow said.

"You're kidding me!"

"I'm not. But she could tell something was weird, and she kept asking us what was wrong. I think Mal was about to tell her that he had bitten me without asking me first, but I jumped in and told her we were just worried about Mal's grandfather."

"That was nice of you."

"She would have kicked his butt," Willow said, "and it's not like I don't care about Mal. You know I do, Ava."

"What did his mother say?"

"She said we didn't need to worry about Amos, and

then she invited us to a family barbeque on Sunday to meet the rest of Mal's siblings."

"What did you say?"

"I said I'd be there. What else was I supposed to say?" Willow said.

"Well, I guess you know what that means," Ava said.

"What?"

"You have until Sunday to figure out what you want. If you're going to ignore what your heart is telling you and dump Mal, you'd better do it before you're supposed to meet his siblings."

"You're not biased at all," Willow said.

Ava squeezed her hand. "I love you, Willow, and I know you'll make the right decision."

"Thanks."

"Now, my shift isn't done for another half-hour, but I could probably leave a little early."

Willow shook her head. "That's okay. I'm going to go upstairs to see if I can sneak in to see Keegan."

"You won't have to sneak in. They moved him out of ICU this morning. He's on the third floor, room 303," Ava said.

"Is he awake?"

"No," Ava said. "But he's stable enough to be out of the ICU. Mrs. Belfry finally went home a few hours ago to get some rest."

"Maybe I'll stop by the house to see Marika when I'm done here."

"I think she'd like that," Ava said.

Beeping started, and Ava pressed a button before moving around the desk. "I gotta go, Will. Do you want to come by later tonight?"

"If it's okay with you, I might crash at your place tonight. My air conditioner is on the fritz, and my landlord is being slow about fixing it."

"That's fine," Ava called as she hurried down the hall. "You've still got your spare key?"

"Yes, I'll see you later."

Ava waved goodbye, and Willow left the ER and took the elevator to the third floor. Room 303 was a private room. Willow entered quietly and peeked around the curtain. Koren sat next to the bed holding Keegan's hand. He glanced up as she slipped past the curtain.

"Hello, Koren."

"Hello, Willow."

"How is he?"

"The same. His wounds have healed, but he won't wake up. Why won't he wake up?" he asked plaintively.

"He will soon, honey." She moved around the bed and put her arm around his shoulders. He leaned his head against her stomach, and she petted his thick blond hair as he stared at his motionless brother.

"This is my fault, Willow."

"What do you mean?" She stiffened.

"Keegan was only at the warehouse that night because of me. I asked him to go back and get the proposal we had drawn up for Mother. We were going to talk to her about it that night."

"Proposal?"

He nodded and held Keegan's hand a little tighter. "I had convinced Keegan that we needed to sell the company to Craig Howell. He didn't want to, but I bullied him into it."

"It's hard to imagine Keegan being bullied," she said.

"I'm his baby brother. It's ridiculously easy to get him to do what I want. I've taken advantage of that since we were kids, and this time, he was nearly killed because of it."

"It's not your fault, Koren."

"It is," he insisted. "I bullied him into helping me do up the sales proposal that would show Mother why it was best if we sold the company. I needed the money from the sale, and that's all I cared about. I didn't care that it was Naden's dream. I didn't care that my mother nearly killed herself trying to keep that dream going after he died. All I cared about was getting the money I needed so my life would be easier."

"We all make mistakes."

"Yeah," he said in a low voice.

She squeezed his shoulder. "What are the odds that Craig Howell is behind this?"

He frowned. "Well, slim, I would think. He knew I was keen to sell the company, and I had him convinced that I would get my mother to sell."

"Yes, but if it was taking too long or if he didn't believe you, it would make sense that he'd do what he could to speed the sale up, right?"

Koren frowned again. "He's a wealthy guy. He could afford to wait."

"Then that means it's someone who works at the warehouse," Willow said thoughtfully. "It has to be."

"King has left me a few voicemails," Koren said. "You guys think it's me, don't you? You think I would do this to my brother."

His body swelled as thick blond fur grew on his face.

Willow rubbed his back. "They aren't accusing you of anything, Koren. They just want to talk to you."

"Yeah, sure," he grunted.

Loud buzzing emitted from his pocket, and Koren pulled his cell phone from it. He glanced at the screen before sighing. "Well, shit."

"What's wrong?"

"There's something wrong with the computer system at the warehouse. It's crashed, and Royce is asking me to come in. Normally Keegan would take care of it, but…."

He stared at his brother before standing. He bent and kissed Keegan's forehead. "I'd better go."

"I'll come with you," Willow said.

He frowned at her. "What for?"

"I don't think you should be alone right now."

"That's nice of you, but the last thing I need is an angry wolf shifter trying to rip my insides out for being alone with his mate." He sniffed in her direction. "Congratulations, by the way. I assume I'll be invited to the wedding?"

She ignored his sniffing. "I'm coming with you. When you're finished, we'll grab a bite to eat."

"Why are you being so nice to me?" he asked.

"I'm assuming your mom is still pissed at you and, don't take this the wrong way, but I don't think you have a lot of friends."

"I don't," he said. "I had Keegan. I didn't need friends."

She looped her arm around his. "C'mon, pussy cat, I'll follow you in my car to the warehouse. When you're finished, I'll buy you dinner."

Ava stuck her head into the room. "Willow? I'm finished work. Do you want to grab a bite to eat?"

"I just told Koren I would go with him to the warehouse while he took care of a computer issue and then take him for dinner." She smiled at her best friend.

"Okay. Have fun." Ava entered the room and stroked Keegan's chest. "I'll stay with him for a while."

"Are you sure?" Koren asked.

Ava nodded. "Yes. Your mother said she would be back tonight. I'll wait until she arrives."

"Thank you," Koren said gratefully.

"You sure you don't have other plans?" he asked Willow as they left the hospital room.

"Nope."

Technically she did have plans, but Damian had disappeared for the moment, and she didn't like the way Koren looked so pale and sick. Besides, it would do her some good to stop thinking about her problems for a while and concentrate on something else.

"MRS. JONES? CAN WE COME IN?" MAL SMILED AT THE tiger shifter.

"I – I was just about to eat dinner," she squeaked out. Her eyes flitted to the massive grizzly shifter standing next to him, and Bishop smiled at her.

"It'll only take a few moments."

"I guess so." Raluca stepped back, and the two shifters entered the modest bungalow.

Bishop made a soft noise of disbelief, and Mal elbowed him discreetly as they followed the woman down the hallway and into the living room. The hallway and the entire room teemed with unicorns.

Pictures of unicorns covered the walls, various sized ceramic unicorns were displayed on every available space, and a giant unicorn, large enough to ride, stood in the corner of the room. A silver pole protruded from its back and rose to touch the ceiling.

Mal knew he was staring and being rude, but he couldn't help himself. Next to him, Bishop's face was bright red as he struggled to hold in his laughter. The tiger shifter gave them a defensive look. "I like unicorns."

"Right." Mal sat down on the couch. Bishop collapsed next to him and coughed into the crook of his arm as Raluca perched on a chair across from them. Mal pulled a unicorn-shaped pillow out from behind his back and set it on the arm of the couch as Bishop coughed again.

"Mrs. Jones, I'll get right to the point. Are you aware that Craig Howell wants to purchase the company?"

She blinked at him. "No, I wasn't aware of that."

"How much money do you owe Craig Howell?"

Raluca flushed bright red. "That's none of your business."

"Mrs. Jones, we -"

There was a heavy thud, and Bishop grunted in pain as a garish ceramic unicorn dropped onto his head. It shattered on contact, scattering bits of ceramic into his hair and on his shoulders. The two shifters looked upward. A large orange cat sat on a wooden shelf on the wall above them. It stared balefully at them, and at Bishop's low growl, it hissed loudly and bared its fangs.

"Bam-Bam, no!" Raluca said. "I'm sorry. He doesn't like strangers."

"No kidding," Bishop said as he shook more bits of ceramic from his thick dark hair.

"Come here, kitty." Raluca made a clicking noise with her tongue. With a final hiss at the two shifters, the cat jumped down with a floor-shaking thud and stalked to his owner. He leaped into her lap, and she stroked his fur anxiously as he cleaned his paws.

"Mrs. Jones, are you working with Craig Howell? Did he ask you to harm Keegan Belfry in exchange for releasing you from your dead husband's debt?" Mal said.

"No!" She stared at him in horror. "I've been paying Mr. Howell the money I owe him every two weeks like clockwork. He hasn't asked me to do anything!"

Her horrified look turned to defiance. "I wouldn't have even if he asked me to. I told you – Mrs. Belfry and her boys have been real good to me."

When they didn't reply, she stood up abruptly, dumping Bam-Bam from her lap with an undignified squawk. She hurried over to the desk in the corner of the room. She pawed through the papers as a few unicorn-themed sticky notes floated to the floor and then returned with a file folder.

She thrust it at Mal. There was a picture of a unicorn and its baby frolicking in a forest on the front of it, and Raluca folded her arms across her body. "My cheque stubs are in there. Go on – look."

Mal flipped open the folder and studied the cheque stubs. He handed it to Bishop who glanced over them quickly before closing the folder.

"We're sorry to have bothered you, Mrs. Jones. Thank you for your time." Bishop stood, and Mal followed him to the front door.

Raluca trailed after them. "I hope you find out who is responsible for hurting Mr. Belfry."

The two shifters walked toward Bishop's truck as Mrs. Jones closed her front door.

"Well, I think we can cross her off the list," Bishop said as he climbed behind the wheel.

"What time is it? Maybe we can catch Koren at the warehouse," Mal said.

Bishop shook his head. "It's close to seven, and Koren doesn't strike me as the type of guy who works late."

"Shit!" Mal reached into his pocket and groped for his phone.

"What's wrong?"

"Willow is supposed to be doing her 'helping ghosts' thing tonight, and I told her to call me before she went over there alone. I didn't realize how late it was."

He cursed again when he saw the missed call. "Dammit, I missed her call."

He called his voicemail as Bishop waited patiently. Mal frowned, and the blood drained from his face.

"Mal? What's wrong?" Bishop said.

Mal stared grimly at him. "I'm not sure. The message cut in and out. Fucking piece of shit phone!" He slammed his phone down on the dashboard, and it shattered with a loud crack. "I think Willow's in trouble."

"With her ghost?"

He shook his head. "No, she's at the warehouse. At least, I think that's what she said."

He suddenly howled in frustration, and Bishop started the truck. "Calm down, Mal. We'll find her."

"Hurry, Bishop." Mal stared out the windshield and held on to his self-control by a thin thread.

"HEY, WILLOW."

Willow smiled at the cheetah shifter. "Fenton, you're back to work already?"

He nodded, and she patted his arm. "Are you feeling better?"

"Yes. Don't worry about me."

"I'm taking good care of him." Garth, a broad and intimidating bull shifter, grinned at Willow.

"Shut up, Garth." Fenton rolled his eyes as he opened the door for Willow. "Mr. Belfry said you were on your way."

"Yeah, my car isn't quite as fast as his." Willow pointed to her battered Honda parked next to Koren's sleek and shiny BMW.

"Is there anyone else here?" she asked as she followed Garth and Fenton through the reception area and into the warehouse.

"Just you, Mr. Belfry, and Mr. Darnell," Garth said. "Apparently, there's some kind of problem with the computer system. Mr. Darnell says the whole damn thing crashed."

"Is it just you and Fenton on duty?"

Fenton shook his head. "No, Lee, Suzanne, Peter and Jake are here too. We're patrolling the warehouse in pairs. When Mr. Belfry said you were on your way, Garth and I decided to wait for you and escort you to his office."

"I'm sure I'll be fine." Willow smiled at him.

"We don't mind," Garth said. "Besides, Mal would kill us if we let anything happen to his mate. Hey, when's the wedding, by the way?"

"Oh, um, we haven't set a date yet." Willow blushed.

"Never thought the boss would marry a human, did you?" Garth nudged Fenton.

Fenton frowned. "You're being rude, Garth."

"Sorry, Willow. You're a great girl, and I know you and Mal will be very happy together," Garth said.

"Uh, thanks, Garth."

She followed the two shifters to Keegan's office. Koren sat behind the desk, typing on the keyboard and staring at the screen. She sat down across from him as Fenton and Garth disappeared into the warehouse.

"How's it going?" Willow asked.

Koren reached for his coffee and drank the rest of it in one large gulp. "Well, the system is truly fucked."

He sighed. "I'm going to reboot the server and hope for a miracle. If that doesn't work, I'll have to call Garrett."

He scowled at the computer as Willow crossed her legs. "Why do you dislike Garrett?"

He shrugged and, without looking at her, said, "He's an idiot."

"He seems to love your mother."

"Yes, I suppose he does in his own way. He's no Naden. Let's just leave it at that."

"Koren? Is it working?" Royce stuck his head into the office and stared in surprise at Willow. "Ms. Tanner, what are you doing here?"

"Just waiting for Koren." Willow forced herself to smile at the snake shifter.

"Oh. Can you fix it, Koren?" Royce fidgeted in the doorway before looking behind him.

"I don't know," Koren said. "I'm just about to go to the server room and reboot the system."

"Well, I'm going back to my office. Let me know if you need anything." With one last nervous look behind him, he disappeared.

"Do you trust him?" Willow asked.

"Who?" Koren asked distractedly.

"Royce Darnell."

"Of course, I do. He's worked at the warehouse for years. Naden always spoke highly of him, and he really stepped up when Naden died, and Mother was trying to save the company from going into bankruptcy."

Willow didn't reply, and Koren glanced at her. "He has nothing to do with this, Willow."

"Are you sure?"

"Positive." He stood, and Willow followed him out of the office and down one of the wide hallways of the warehouse. It was eerily quiet in the warehouse, and she scanned the aisles as they walked.

"Where is everyone?"

"Gone home." Koren gave her an odd look.

"No, I mean Lee and Suzanne and the others. There are six of our people patrolling tonight. You'd think we would have run into one of them," she said.

"It's a big warehouse, Willow." Koren stopped in front of a plain silver door with a small vent in the bottom half and unlocked it. "This is the server room."

She followed him into the room. It was on the larger side with a complicated looking bank of screens and computers along one wall. She stood out of the way as Koren tapped on one of the keyboards, and the screens began to go black one by one.

"Koren? Are you okay?"

The lion shifter swayed on his feet, and he turned and stared at her in confusion. "Willow? I feel so strange."

"Koren!" She ran forward and caught the shifter as he crumpled toward the floor. He was extremely heavy, and she grunted loudly as his weight drove her to the floor, and he collapsed on top of her.

"Koren!" She wheezed and pushed at his large body. "Wake up."

There was no response, and she cursed and wormed her way out from under him, wincing when his head hit the concrete floor with a loud thud. She rolled him onto his back and felt for his pulse. It was weak but steady, and she pried open one of his eyelids. His eyes had rolled back into his head, and she pulled out her cell phone and hurriedly dialed Mal's number. She waited impatiently as it rang and cursed in frustration when it went to his voicemail.

"Stupid voicemail!" she muttered as Mal's voice came on the line. She waited for the beep and spoke rapidly, "Mal? It's Willow. I need your help. I'm at the warehouse with Koren, and I think he's been drugged. I think -"

The phone was pulled from her hand, and she fell back on her butt, scooting across the slick floor. His face pale, Royce Darnell smashed her phone into the wall and dropped the broken pieces to the floor.

"I knew it was you! I knew it!" Willow jumped to her feet and backed away as Royce gave her a foul look.

"Shut up. You weren't supposed to be here, you nosy little twit."

He glanced at Koren's body lying on the floor and shook his head. "You've ruined everything."

"Mal is on his way," Willow said. "He's only five

minutes away, and if you're smart, you'll get the hell out of here."

Royce hissed laughter. "Sounded to me like you got his voicemail, sweetheart. Now, get your skinny little ass over here. You're coming with me."

"Why are you doing this?" Willow said. "Koren said you were loyal to the company. He trusted you. Mrs. Belfry trusted you."

"Trust doesn't pay the bills, does it? I've worked my ass off for this company for nearly twenty years, and where did it get me? I'm a glorified foreman. That idiot Keegan gets promoted to warehouse manager, and he doesn't know shit about the company. It should be me running the warehouse - that was the way Naden wanted it," Royce said.

"Naden wanted Keegan and Koren to run the company. You're delusional." Willow backed up to the wall and felt the smooth cylinder of a fire extinguisher press into her back.

"You know nothing of what Naden wanted," Royce said. "Now stop your fucking talking and get over here."

"What did you do to Koren?" Willow asked. She glanced behind him, hoping and praying that Fenton or one of the others would show up. She opened her mouth to shout for them, and Royce shook his head.

"Don't bother. Your little security team is just as incapacitated as Koren."

"What did you do?" she repeated.

"What does it look like?" he scoffed. "I drugged them. A little bit of liquid in their beverage of choice, and half an hour later, they're useless."

"That's how you got past Fenton the last time," Willow breathed.

"Oh, you're a smart one, aren't you?" Royce rolled his eyes.

"Tell me who the cat shifter is that's helping you. Which of the employees did you convince to help you?"

"Move your ass, bitch," Royce hissed at her. His skin was starting to darken and turn to scales, and Willow swallowed down her fear as his long, forked tongue flicked out of his mouth.

"Tell me why you're doing this," she said. "This isn't going to get you Keegan's job."

"Isn't it?" Royce asked. "Mrs. Belfry is going to sell the company."

"No, she isn't."

"She will once they find Koren's dead body in his brother's office."

Willow's eyes widened, and Royce laughed. "Here's the thing, Ms. Tanner – do you think Marika Belfry will keep this company once her son commits suicide in his brother's office? When she reads the note that says he's responsible for what happened to Keegan? One son lying brain dead in the hospital, and another, full of remorse and guilt and drowning in debt, kills himself. She'll be falling over herself to get rid of the company."

"You're a spineless asshole," Willow said.

"Maybe. But once Craig Howell buys the company, I'll be a spineless asshole running the warehouse. He's promised me the position, and I've only got so many years left before I retire, Ms. Tanner."

"That's one hell of a retirement plan, you bastard."

He laughed. "I suppose it is a bit on the extreme side."

"You won't get away with it."

He bellowed laughter at that, his skin beginning to shine as more scales appeared. "Oh my God, could you be any more of a walking cliché?"

"Mal knows I'm here. He's going to be here any minute, and when he does -"

"When he does, he'll find your body, ripped to shreds, alongside Koren's. Poor Koren snapped and tore you apart before he killed himself. Such a shame, really."

"They'll know it was you," she said desperately. "You're the only one here."

He held up a small vial of liquid. "They'll find me in the warehouse, as drugged as the rest of your security team. Now, I'm going to ask you one last time to -"

He stopped as his breath plumed out in front of him. The room turned icy cold, and he frowned when there was a low, whispery moan.

"What is that?" He turned in a slow circle, staring at the wall behind him. "Who's there?"

"His name is Damian."

He whirled around. Willow stood directly in front of him, and he shrieked in shock and pain when she slammed the fire extinguisher into the side of his head. He fell to his knees, and she darted to the side as his body rippled and his clothes tore with a soft purr.

"Shit!" she shouted and raised the extinguisher to hit him again. Before she could knock him out, he shifted completely, and she screamed when his tail wrapped around her waist, and he lifted her off her feet. She screamed again as, with a flick of his tail, he threw her out the door of the server room and sent her crashing into a floor-to-ceiling shelf of clothing. The shelf tipped over, and Willow disappeared under a mountain of clothes.

ROYCE HISSED HAPPILY WHEN THE LITTLE BITCH WAS knocked flying by the clothes. He started to slither from the room, stopping when there was a noise behind him. He turned to see the fire extinguisher twisting and floating in the air, and he bared his fangs and reared his upper body. He swayed back and forth, staring at the extinguisher, and then hissed again when foam sprayed out of the extinguisher and hit him in the face. He fell back, twisting and sliding in the foam, his eyes burning. He slithered out of the room and shifted to his human form. He wiped at his burning eyes and cursed before squinting at the fallen shelf.

"Ms. Tanner? Come out, come out, wherever you are," he said. "There's no point in hiding. I can smell you, you know. Smell your stupid wolf mate all over your skin."

There was no reply, and with a loud hiss, he shifted back to his snake form and wound his way over the fallen shelf, his tongue flicking out to taste the air in front of him.

CHAPTER 24

"You're a very kind girl."

Ava turned to see Mrs. Belfry walking into Keegan's room. She smiled at the lizard shifter. "Did you get some rest, Mrs. Belfry?"

"Call me Marika. Yes, I slept and had a hot shower, and Jeffries forced me to eat some soup. For a chicken shifter, he can be quite bold when the situation calls for it."

Ava smiled again as Mrs. Belfry sat down beside her. "You need to keep up your strength."

"I suppose." Mrs. Belfry stared silently at her son. "Are you and Keegan dating?"

Ava shook her head. "No. Well, we went on one date, but…."

Mrs. Belfry eyed her. "But a certain grizzly shifter has caught your eye."

Ava blushed. "How did you – I mean, no, that isn't what it's about."

"Is it not?" Mrs. Belfry asked. "I am not blind, Ms. Lewis. I saw the way he protected you at my party."

Ava stared down at her lap. "It's complicated."

"Love usually is," Mrs. Belfry said. "It's a shame that Keegan couldn't make it work with you. He could use a girl like you to keep him on the straight and narrow. I love my boys, but they usually have such terrible taste in women. I would never admit this to them, but I'm dying for some grandchildren. I'm an old woman, and I'd like to hold a grandbaby in my arms before I die."

"There's plenty of time for that, Marika." Ava smiled at her. "Keegan and Koren will find the right women and settle down."

Ava reached out and squeezed Mrs. Belfry's hand when tears slid down her cheeks. "I wish he would wake."

"He will," Ava said.

They both looked up at the sound of footsteps in the room. Kat, holding a small bouquet of flowers, smiled at them. "I came to see how Keegan was doing."

"The same," Mrs. Belfry said.

Kat set the flowers down and pulled a chair over. "How are you feeling, Mrs. Belfry?"

"Fine. Have you figured out who did this to my son?"

"Not yet. Bishop and Mal are following up on a few leads. There's a tiger shifter, Raluca Jones, who owes a great deal of money to Craig Howell."

"It's not Raluca," Mrs. Belfry said.

"Mrs. Belfry," Kat said gently, "we know that Craig Howell wants to buy your company. Mrs. Jones may have been causing the trouble in the warehouse as payment for her debt to him."

"It isn't. That woman may be a tiger shifter, but she's as nervous as a long-tailed cat in a room full of rocking chairs," Mrs. Belfry said. "There isn't a chance that it's her. Trust me, I -"

"Marika?" Ava said.

"What is it?"

Ava stared at Keegan, and Mrs. Belfry followed her gaze. She gasped, her hand coming up to her chest as Ava stood and leaned over the lion shifter. "Keegan? Can you hear me?"

Keegan's eyes were open, and Mrs. Belfry grasped his hand and squeezed it. "Keegan? It's Mama. Say something, my darling."

Keegan's gaze shifted to his mother, and she smiled encouragingly. "Hello, my darling."

He opened his mouth and rasped, "Garrett."

Mrs. Belfry frowned. "Garrett's not here, darling. Do you want me to call him?"

Keegan blinked rapidly and then coughed. "Garrett," he repeated.

"My darling, I don't -"

Kat leaned over him. "Keegan, did Garrett do this to you?"

"Don't be an idiot, Ms. Frost!" Mrs. Belfry said. "Garrett did not do this. He would never hurt the boys."

"Mother," Keegan rasped again, "he did."

Mrs. Belfry sank back in her chair as Kat pulled out her cell phone. She hit a button and waited a few moments before cursing under her breath.

"Who are you calling?" Ava said.

"I just tried Mal. Now I'm trying Bishop." Kat tapped her fingers against the side rail on Keegan's bed. Ava heard the faint sound of Bishop's voice when he answered.

"Hey, Bishop, it's Kat. It was Garrett, do you hear me?

Keegan's awake, and it was Garrett who attacked him. Bishop?" She pulled the phone away from her ear and stared at Ava. "It went dead."

"What?" Ava's heart stopped then started again with a painful thud. "What do you mean?"

"Bishop said hello, and then there was nothing."

"Where is he? Do you know?" Panic settled in her stomach. "Kat, where is he?"

"I don't know for sure. He and Mal were going to stop by Raluca Jones' house and then try to find Koren at the warehouse."

She called another number. It rang repeatedly, and she pressed the off button. "That's Fenton's cell phone. He's on duty tonight at the warehouse. He should have answered."

She touched Mrs. Belfry's shoulder. "Where is your husband, Mrs. Belfry?"

"I – I don't know," she said. "He wasn't home when I woke up from my nap. I didn't think to ask Jeffries where he had gone."

Kat stood up. "I'm going to the warehouse."

"I'm coming with you." Ava stood as Kat shook her head.

"No, that's not a good idea, Ava."

"Willow and Koren are at the warehouse," Ava said. "They were stopping there to fix a computer problem. What if Garrett is there?"

"Ava -"

"I'm going with you," Ava said. "Either you let me drive with you, or I'll drive my car there."

Kat hesitated and then nodded. "Let's go."

"Stay with your son, Marika," Ava said. "He needs you."

Mrs. Belfry took Keegan's hand as Ava and Kat ran from the room.

"WHY THE HELL AREN'T THEY ANSWERING THEIR PHONES?" Mal said in frustration. "I've tried all six of them, and not one goddamn person answered. Where the fuck are they?"

"I don't know." Bishop turned the wheel sharply, and Mal grunted as his seat belt locked painfully against his chest. He clutched Bishop's phone tighter and tried to calm his wolf. He snarled and raged to be free. Mal's fear for his mate drove his wolf into a frenzy of anger. For the first time in years, Mal was dangerously close to losing control of the shift.

Be calm! We'll find her. Just be calm. Despite his fear for Willow, he spoke soothingly, and after a moment, his wolf retreated.

Bishop sped down the highway, weaving through the traffic as Mal tried Willow's cell phone. It went straight to voicemail, and he cursed again as Bishop took the off-ramp on what felt like two tires.

Five minutes later, they pulled into the parking lot of the warehouse. As Bishop stopped in front of the building, Mal leaped out of the truck and ran to the front door. It was locked, and he pounded uselessly on it for a moment before Bishop joined him.

Bishop pulled him back and slammed both fists into the glass door. The glass shattered, and Bishop pulled chunks of glass from his hands as Mal reached in and unlocked the door. He yanked it open, and the two shifters ran through the reception area and into the warehouse.

"Willow!" Mal shouted, his voice echoing. "Where are you?"

There was no response, and Bishop inhaled deeply.

"Can you smell her?" Mal asked. "I can't find her scent."

Bishop shook his head. "No, but her scent is harder to find now. Yours covers it."

"Fuck!" Mal scanned the large, dark warehouse. "We split up. Keep your eyes open. If you find Willow, get her the hell out of here. Do you hear me?"

Bishop nodded and melted into the darkness as Mal crept down the left aisle. He could see as well as a cat in the darkness, and he checked the tall shelving on either side of him as he moved silently in the dark. He sniffed the air, searching frantically for Willow's scent.

It was utterly silent in the warehouse. He couldn't even hear Bishop's footsteps. He paused and cocked his head, listening intently. He thought he heard the soft tread of footsteps to his right, and he moved quickly down the aisle and turned right. There was an open door in front of him, and he peered into the room. Koren lay motionless on the floor, and he checked for the lion shifter's pulse before standing and inhaling.

Willow had been in the room. Her scent was fading, but there was still a faint whiff of it. His wolf howled, and he struggled for control as a thick beard grew on his face. Adrenaline pumped through his veins.

Let me free! Let me find my mate!

He stripped off his shirt. His sense of smell was stronger in his wolf form. He would shift and –

He froze at the clattering noise in the warehouse. He dropped his shirt and ran down the aisle, staring at the tipped-over shelf with clothing scattered across the floor. He dropped to his knees and inhaled deeply. Willow's scent clung to the clothing, and he growled before leaping over the mounds of clothes and running down the aisle. He kicked off his boots and reached for the button of his jeans when he heard the hiss.

A giant snake, its skin shining in the dim light, rose before him. It hissed at him, and Mal growled. His body swelled, and he took a deep breath as his fangs popped out and hair sprouted on his back. The shift was happening. He would force the snake shifter to tell him where his mate was. And if he had hurt her, if he had dared to touch her, he would –

A sharp prick pierced the back of his neck, and he yelped and clapped his hand to the flesh. A numbness immediately crept into his bones, and his wolf retreated with a soft whimper as the warehouse spun wildly.

"Marika is right. Wolf shifters are the worst." A mild voice spoke behind him, and he staggered around to see Garrett Finnegan standing behind him. He held a needle in his hand, and he dropped it indifferently to the floor before smiling at Mal. "Sorry, wolf shifter."

"What did you do to me?" The numbness seeped into his lips, making it hard to talk. He stared hazily at Garrett as the snake shifter wound its way toward them.

"Just a little something to put you down. That is what you do with wild dogs, isn't it? Put them down? Of course, this isn't powerful enough to kill you, but it will render you useless while we decide what to do with you."

The snake shifted, and Royce stared unblinkingly at Mal. "I still can't find his girlfriend."

Garrett rolled his eyes. "She's one little human girl. How difficult can it be? I can smell her scent. She's close. You can smell, can't you?"

"Yes!" Royce hissed at him. "But her fucking scent is all over the clothes back there. That's what you're smelling."

Garrett sighed. "I'll take care of the grizzly. Once the dog is out completely, you find the girl and bring her to me. I've got one hell of a mess to clean up, thanks to you."

"It's not my fault!" Royce said. "How was I supposed to know she would show up with Koren?"

Garrett ignored him and smiled at the swaying Mal. "How are we feeling, Mr. Wolf? Hmm? A little tired, perhaps? You go ahead and have a nice, long nap while I take care of your stupid friend and your annoying human girlfriend."

"Why are you doing this? She's your wife." Mal struggled to focus as the drug made its way through his body.

Garrett sighed. "Do you want to know, or are you just trying to keep me busy in the hopes that your grizzly friend will show up and save you?"

Mal reached out to catch the side of the shelving. His legs were ridiculously weak and trembling.

Garrett shrugged. "Very well, let me tell you."

"We don't have time for this," Royce said.

"We have plenty of time. Besides, if movies have taught us anything, it's that a villain does enjoy sharing his evil plans."

He winked at Mal. "I married Marika, not because I loved her but because I wanted to improve my circumstances. I spent years clawing," he paused and chuckled with amusement, "no pun intended, my way to the position I'm in now. My father was an ox shifter and a farmer. A farmer!"

He snorted in derision. "I have no idea what my mother was thinking when she married him. She died in childbirth, and my father raised me. He did his best, but what does an ox know of a jaguar? He expected me to take over the farm. As if I would want anything to do with his miserable way of life. I begged him to send me to university, but he didn't have the money, he said."

He stared at the floor. "I ended up going to a shitty community college for a ridiculous IT degree. I spent most of my life dreaming about something better, and when I met Marika, I knew I had found it. It didn't take long for me to convince her that I was in love with her. Her wealth and her connections afforded me the privileges I'd been looking for, but when Craig Howell approached me with his offer, I listened."

"What offer?" Mal asked hoarsely.

"To run the company, of course. He would buy the company from Marika and give me full control of it. Does that seem silly to you? To go to such lengths just for the opportunity to have my name on a door?"

He studied Mal. "Perhaps it was a bit silly, but the chance to run this company, to prove to my father and everyone else that the son of a stupid ox farmer could become something so much more, was too great to ignore. I agreed to help Craig and Royce."

"How?" Mal mumbled. "How did you hurt the security guard and the others?"

Garrett rolled his eyes. "God, wolf shifters are stupid.

Luckily for me, shortly after I agreed to help Mr. Howell, the computer system crashed. Marika called me in a panic, and I, thanks to that ridiculous IT degree, came in right away and fixed the problem. I also added in a few extra commands that gave me access to the entire system, including the security cameras."

He grinned at Mal. "It was easy enough to shut them off using my laptop, then sneak into the warehouse, drug the security guard's coffee, shred the clothing and set the truck on fire. Of course, that ghost business made it even easier for us. I thought it was one or two of the employees doing the pranks out of sheer boredom and decided it was a great idea to start the ball rolling on convincing Marika to sell the company. She's not a young lizard anymore, and the strain of running the company was already becoming too much for her."

He scowled. "Except then that idiot Koren approached Howell about selling the company. Howell told me to knock it off with the pranks and that he wanted to give Koren time to convince his mother, but I knew it wouldn't work. I know how stupid Koren is, and, more importantly, I know how clever and stubborn Marika is. She would never sell the company because Koren wanted her to. She loathes being told what to do. So, that's when I drugged the security guard and sliced him up."

He smiled at Royce. "Of course, we didn't expect Marika to hire a wolf shifter for security. I thought that having one of her employees nearly die would be enough to make her sell the company. She surprised me. Your security team made things a bit more difficult for us, but I think we've done well in accomplishing what we set out to do. There have been a few hiccups, of course, but what evil plan doesn't have the occasional hiccup?"

"Keegan? You tried to kill him," Mal said faintly.

"Unfortunate accident. I was at the warehouse, and Keegan overheard Royce and me talking. He wasn't supposed to be there."

Garrett patted Mal's shoulder. "When Marika realizes that Koren killed you and your friends and then killed himself in guilt over what he did to his brother, she'll be out of her mind with grief and sell the company. I'll divorce her and take charge of it. I'll be someone, wolf shifter. Someone better than just a farmer or the younger husband of a wealthy old woman. Don't you see?"

"You're fucking nuts," Mal slurred.

Garrett laughed. "I'm not the shifter who took a human as a mate. If anyone is nuts, it's you. Now, I'd love to stay and chat some more, but you're going to be asleep pretty soon, and I have so much to take care of before the evening is done."

He turned to Royce. "Remember, find the girl but don't kill her. We need to make it look like Koren killed her. Do you understand?"

"Yes," Royce said. Garrett disappeared into the darkness as Mal took a staggering step backward.

"I'm going to kill you," he growled. He squinted at the snake shifter as he took another step back. He tripped over his feet and fell to the floor as Royce laughed.

"I can't wait to see what Garrett has in mind for you, wolf shifter. I hate your kind. Always acting so superior to the rest of us. Garrett's right, you know. You're no better than a common dog."

"At least I'm not a slimy, dickless asshole without

legs," Mal said. Trying to concentrate and speaking clearly was becoming increasingly more difficult.

Royce's face turned red, and he glared at him. "What did you say about my dick?"

"What dick?" Mal taunted again.

With an angry hiss, Royce shifted to his snake form and slowly moved toward Mal. He bared his fangs and raised his head. He suddenly stiffened and made a high-pitched shriek before flattening himself to the ground.

Panting harshly, Willow gripped the steel rod and pushed it further into his body. The snake screamed in agony, and she scrambled back out of the way, her face scrunched up in a moue of disgust, as he twisted his upper body toward her and struck at her. His fangs hit the concrete floor, and he went into a frenzy writhing as they broke off and blood splattered across the floor.

Royce wrapped his upper body around the steel rod embedded in the middle of his body and tried to pull it free.

Willow stomped on his tail, digging the heel of her boot deep into his flesh and grinning maniacally when the snake hissed and shifted to his human form. Impaled through the back with the steel rod, Royce stared up at her.

"Help me. It hurts so much," he moaned as blood dripped from his mouth.

Willow slid past him and crouched beside Mal. He smiled at her and then closed his eyes. Christ, he was tired.

"Mal! Wake up, Mal! Hey!" Willow slapped him hard across the face, and his eyes blinked open.

"Willow?" he groaned.

"Yep, it's me. Get up, wolf boy. C'mon, I'm here to save your furry ass."

She helped him sit up and placed one of his hands on the metal shelving before shrugging her way under his other arm. She braced her tiny body and wrapped her arms around his waist. "Hang on to that and hoist yourself up. Do you hear me? I can't lift you on my own. You need to help. Mal? On the count of three."

He nodded, and she counted to three before lifting. Moving clumsily, Mal swayed to his feet and then held tightly to the shelving as he squinted at her. "There's two of you."

"Just more of me to love. C'mon, focus," Willow said. "We need to get moving."

"Okay." He swayed drunkenly, and she guided him slowly down the aisle and away from the dying snake shifter.

"Boy, that Garrett is a nutball, yeah?" she puffed as they staggered down the aisle. "I heard everything he said. If he wanted to get into university so badly, why the hell didn't he just take out a student loan like everyone else?"

Mal laughed faintly, and Willow squeezed his waist. "Stay awake. Not too much further," she panted as they rounded the corner. She led him to the staff room and winced when they crossed the doorway, and he crashed to the floor.

"Willow, so tired," he whispered.

"I know you are, honey. Try to stay awake for just a little bit longer, okay?" She patted his face and kissed his mouth before staring around the room. There was a first-aid box on the wall, and he watched blearily as she hurried over to it and ripped it off the wall. The lid popped open, and the supplies fell to the floor. Cursing, she dropped to her knees and searched through them.

"Yes!" She smiled triumphantly and grabbed the tube before darting back to Mal. She placed it against his thigh as he stared groggily at it.

"What is that?" he said.

"Blue to the sky, orange to the thigh," she said as she pulled the blue safety cap off. She jammed the orange tip into Mal's outer thigh and counted to ten before pulling it free.

"Mal? Can you hear me, honey?"

She shrieked in surprise and fell backward when Mal sat up with a howl. His heart was beating like a rabbit on speed, and adrenaline shot through his veins. He stared at her, his eyes bright jade and his fangs protruding from his mouth. "Willow?"

"Hey. How do you feel?"

"What the hell did you just give me?" he said.

"Epinephrine."

"What?" He stared at the Epi-pen in her hand. "Was I having an allergic reaction?"

She shook her head. "No, but I figured it was worth a shot."

"Worth a shot?" He stared at her. "You could have killed me."

"Don't be so dramatic, wolf boy." She grinned at him. "I saved your life back there, remember?"

"You scared the hell out of me, Willow." He staggered to his feet and yanked her into his embrace. He kissed her on the mouth, and she kissed him back, clinging tightly to him.

"Garrett," she said when he stopped.

"I just give you one hell of a kiss, and all you can say is Garrett?"

She slapped him lightly on the back. "We need to find him before he hurts Bishop."

"More like before Bishop hurts him," Mal said.

"Come on, Mal." Willow tugged on his hand, and he followed her out of the staff room. His heart still raced, and he felt sick to his stomach from the epinephrine. He took a deep breath as Willow suddenly stopped and turned to face him.

"Hey, Mal? In case things go bad and we don't make it out of here, I need to tell you something." She gave him a solemn look. His racing heart skipped a beat when she reached up and touched his face tenderly.

"Yes, honey?" he said.

"I told you it was the snake shifter."

He gaped at her, and she stuck her tongue out at him before taking his hand. "God, that felt good. Now let's go catch us a puddy-tat."

<hr>

HIS NOSE TWITCHING, BISHOP MOVED PAST THE SHELVING of boxes and peered to his left. He cursed under his breath and hurried forward. All six of their employees were lying on the floor, and he checked each of them before scanning the area. They were all alive but completely out of it, and he frowned as his cell phone buzzed.

What the hell was happening?

"Kat?"

"Hey, Bishop. It's… was … do you hear me? Keegan's … and it … attacked…. Bishop?"

"Kat? You're cutting in and out. Kat, can you hear me?" he whispered into the phone.

His phone beeped in his ear, and he stared at it in disgust. Thanks to the thick concrete walls, service was spotty in the warehouse. He sent Kat a quick text, letting her know where they were and what was happening. He could only hope it found a signal and went through.

He squeezed Garth's meaty shoulder. "Hang tight, guys. I'll be back."

He moved deeper into the warehouse, listening for sounds, and smelling the air. The Different scents filled the warehouse– the individual scents of the employees, Mal, Koren, the musty smell of fabric – and he closed his eyes and concentrated.

HIDING DEEP IN THE SHADOWS, GARRETT WATCHED AS THE grizzly shifter closed his eyes and lifted his face to the ceiling. He inhaled repeatedly, and the jaguar shifter pulled a needle from his pocket. Smiling, he moved toward Bishop. He would dose the grizzly, wait for him to fall, and then rip out his throat. He could easily blame his death on Koren as well.

He was behind Bishop now, and he eyed his thick neck before raising the needle. Lightning quick, Bishop turned and grabbed Garrett's wrist, stopping the downward motion of the needle.

A growl started deep in Bishop's chest, and warm and unpleasant fear rushed through Garrett. He made a soft whine of panic and let the needle drop to the floor. "I'm sorry. Please, don't hurt me."

"You're a fool," Bishop snarled at him. "You're nothing but -"

His fingernails turned to razor-sharp claws, Garrett swiped Bishop's stomach with his other hand. Bishop stared down at his belly in mild surprise as blood poured from his abdomen. Garrett hissed at him as his eyeteeth became long fangs, and he twisted out of Bishop's grip.

Bishop roared angrily as his body swelled and his clothes ripped apart and fell to the floor. He shifted completely and roared again, the sound echoing through the empty warehouse as Garrett stared up at the massive grizzly. Blood matted the dark fur on Bishop's stomach, and Garrett grinned. "Time to die, bear shifter."

He shifted to his jaguar and crouched down, snarling and hissing at the grizzly. Bishop growled viciously as Garrett leaped onto him and drove him backward into the metal shelves.

"KAT?" AVA STARED AT THE SHATTERED FRONT DOOR OF the warehouse.

"Stay in the car, Ava," Kat said.

"Like hell I am!" Ava followed the jaguar shifter into the warehouse. The warehouse wasn't far from the hospital, but Kat had gotten them there in record time, driving her bright blue Camaro like it was on a racetrack. Ava's stomach still spun.

They entered the warehouse, and Kat sniffed the air. "Bishop's here, and so is Mal," she murmured.

Fear blossomed in Ava's chest. "Where is Bishop? Is he hurt?"

"I don't know. C'mon, we -"

A loud and angry roar echoed in the warehouse. The two women froze and stared at each other.

"Bishop?" Ava said.

Without a word, Kat turned and sprinted toward the farthest aisle. Ava chased after her, but she was no match for the jaguar's speed. She forced herself to run faster as there was another angry roar and the loud clang of a metal shelf hitting the floor. She turned right and nearly ran straight into Willow.

"Ava!" Willow staggered to a stop as the dark grey wolf with her darted around them and disappeared into the darkness.

"Mal! Wait!" Willow shouted.

He barked sharply, and Willow grabbed Ava's hand. "C'mon, Ava!"

The two women ran through the warehouse. They could hear Bishop growling and snarling, and they hurried toward the sound as Mal barked again.

"Willow, hurry!" Ava nearly yanked the smaller woman off her feet. Her fear for Bishop grew by the second. As Bishop roared so loudly her eardrums vibrated, she turned down an aisle and staggered to a stop.

"Whoa," Willow said.

Kat and Mal, still in his wolf form, stood a healthy distance from the angry grizzly. Bishop paced back and forth, letting out a furious roar every few seconds. He stood on his hind legs and pushed at the metal shelf in front of him. It tipped over, and shoes flew from boxes to land in heaps around his feet.

Ava inhaled sharply. Just behind Bishop, she could see the body of a large cat. Its throat was torn open, and blood had pooled beneath its body. Bishop bellowed angrily again as Mal shifted to his human form.

"Mal, what's wrong with him?" Willow said.

"He's furious." Mal moved toward Bishop. "Bishop? Hey, big guy? Look at me. Time to calm down, okay?"

Bishop turned and roared at him. His large fangs dripped saliva, and Mal flinched and backed away. "Well, that's not going to work."

"He's bleeding, Mal," Kat said. "We need to get him calmed down so we can get him to the hospital."

"I know," Mal said. "But I can't go near him when he's like that. No one can. He's too angry to think straight, and he'll probably kill us without thinking twice about it. We need to walk away and give him some time to calm down."

"Ava!" Willow gasped.

Ava darted around Kat and walked toward the angry grizzly. Bishop growled at her, and she held out her hands to him. "Bishop, I need you to shift to your human form."

He snarled at her and stood on his hind legs. She stood directly in front of him, and Willow moaned in panic when Bishop raised one heavy paw, tipped with long, sharp nails.

Ava didn't move. "You're not going to hurt me. I know you won't. You're bleeding, and I want you to calm down and shift so I can examine you. Please, Bishop."

The grizzly stared at her for a long moment, and Ava released a trembling breath when his fur receded, and he turned into the familiar form of Bishop.

"Hi, honey," he said.

"Hi, Bishop. How do you feel?"

"Fine." He shrugged. "I feel -"

He paused and staggered backward before falling to

the floor amidst the sea of shoes. He stared at the wounds on his stomach as Ava rushed forward and knelt beside him.

"Don't move," she said as she looked around for something to stem the bleeding. With a snort of frustration, she whipped off her shirt and pressed it to the four deep slashes on his stomach.

"We'll get you to the hospital, and you'll be fine. Okay? Stay awake." She pressed firmly on his stomach as the others crowded around them.

Bishop's gaze dropped to her breasts in her dark blue bra. She flushed but continued to hold her shirt against his abdomen.

"Bishop? Are you okay?" Kat asked.

"Considering he can't stop eyeing Ava's rack, I'd say he's gonna live," Willow said.

Bishop blushed furiously and looked up at the ceiling.

"I'll call 9-1-1." Kat reached for her phone.

"It's starting to heal. I don't need to go to the hospital," Bishop said.

"You're going," Ava said.

"I don't need to."

"I said you're going." Ava's face turned red. "I don't care if it's completely healed by the time you get to the hospital. You're getting checked out, Bishop."

"Mal should probably go too," Willow said. "I gave him a shot of epinephrine after Garrett drugged him. Plus, we have, like, a dozen people all unconscious and a dying snake shifter."

"I'm fine. We'll call for the others, but I don't need to go," Mal said.

"You're both going. I don't want to hear another word from either of you," Ava said.

Mal started to protest, and after a glance at Ava's face, Bishop shook his head and gave him a look that was part warning and part fear. "Don't piss her off, Mal."

Ava smiled sweetly as Willow grinned at Mal. "Yeah, don't make her angry. You wouldn't like her when she's angry."

Mal pulled Willow into his embrace and hugged her tightly as Kat dialed 9-1-1.

CHAPTER 25

"Hello, Jeffries." Willow smiled at the chicken shifter when he opened the door.

"Ms. Tanner." The butler ushered her into the house and led her down the hallway and into the living room.

Keegan and Koren were sitting on the couch, and they both smiled at her. "Hey, Willow."

"Hello, Keegan. How are you feeling?"

"Better. A headache off and on, but the doctor said that should disappear in the next week or so."

"Good." She sat down in the chair across from them. "Koren, you look better."

Koren laughed. "Yeah, maybe because I'm standing upright and not drugged out of my mind."

Willow accepted the cup of tea from Jeffries with a nod of thanks. As the chicken shifter left the room, she sipped at the tea. "How is your mother?"

"She seems okay."

"She's just fine." Mrs. Belfry swept into the room and gave both her boys a stern look. "Keegan, you're supposed to be on bed rest. You just got out of the hospital yesterday."

"I'm on couch rest." Keegan grinned at his mother, and her face softened before she moved to Willow and gave her a peck on the cheek.

"How are you, my darling?"

"I'm well, Marika. How are you?"

"As well as can be expected, considering my husband tried to murder my children."

She sat down in the chair next to Willow and waved Jeffries away when he entered with another cup of tea. "How are your people?"

"They're good. All six of our team recovered from being drugged, and Bishop was only in the hospital for a couple of hours. His wounds were practically healed by the time the paramedics got him there."

"I'm glad to hear it. Your mate stopped by earlier this morning, but it completely slipped my mind to ask him how the others were."

"Mal was here earlier?"

"Yes, with the police. They wanted to go over every-thing that happened for the third time." Her face darkened. "I hated involving the police, but the dead bodies of Garrett and Royce left us no choice."

"Did they arrest Craig Howell?"

Koren scowled. "Unfortunately, there was nothing to tie Howell to the actions of Garrett and Royce. No emails, no texts, nothing. He was very careful."

"The police spoke with him, and he denied any knowl-edge of what they were doing. He tried to point the finger at Koren," Mrs. Belfry snarled.

"I was an idiot for even talking to him," Koren said.

"Yes, you were," Mrs. Belfry said.

At his wince, she relented and gave him a loving look. "You know I love you, Koren. You should have come to me for help in the first place."

"I know, Mother."

Mrs. Belfry turned to Willow. "When is the wedding?"

"We haven't set a date yet."

"Are you having a small or large wedding?"

"I hadn't thought about it. We haven't known each other for very long, so we're taking things slow." Willow set down her cup of tea.

"Very wise. Take it from me – it's never a good idea to marry someone you haven't known very long," Mrs. Belfry said as Willow stood.

"I'll keep that in mind. I should run. Thank you for the tea, and, Keegan, I'm glad you're feeling better."

Mrs. Belfry stood and hugged her. "Thank you, Willow. You've done so much for our family, and I won't forget it. I owe you a debt, and I always pay my debts. Remember that."

"Yes, ma'am."

Mrs. Belfry gave her a wry look. "And please, pass my thanks on to Ms. Frost, Mr. King, and that mate of yours. Perhaps wolf shifters aren't nearly as dreadful as I thought."

MAL PULLED ON HIS SHORTS AND THREW HIS DAMP TOWEL in the laundry hamper. He raked his hand through his wet hair and headed into the kitchen. He stared into the fridge, but nothing looked appealing for dinner. He grabbed a beer, twisted it open, and took a large swallow.

It had been three days since the incident at the warehouse. Willow hadn't come into work, and he hadn't spoken to her at all. He missed her terribly, and his wolf howled incessantly at him to go to his mate. Mal took another drink of beer. He told Willow he would stay away from her, but if he had to listen to his wolf constantly harass him to be with his mate, he would go insane. The barbecue was in two days, and he had a feeling that Willow wouldn't show, and he would have to tell his family the truth. His wolf snarled at the thought.

What would you have me do? I cannot force her to be our mate.

His wolf growled at his response, and Mal rubbed at his forehead. The doorbell rang, and he trudged wearily down the hallway and opened the door. Relief flooded through him. Willow stood on the front porch, but she looked tired and nervous.

"Hey, what are you doing here?" he said.

She hesitated, and he could have kicked himself. "Shit. I mean, come in, please."

She followed him into the hallway, and he took her thin sweater and hung it on the coat hook. She wore a tank top underneath, and his gaze roamed hungrily over her small breasts and flat abdomen.

She cleared her throat, and he forced his gaze back to her face. "How are you?"

"I'm good. I hope you don't mind me dropping by. Bishop gave me the address."

"I don't mind at all. Are you hungry? I was just thinking of making something to eat."

She shook her head and followed him into the kitchen. "No, thanks. Could I have something to drink?"

"Sure, I've got water and, uh, beer. That's about it."

She climbed onto the stool at the island. "I'll take a beer."

He pulled one from the fridge, twisted off the cap, and handed it to her. "I didn't know you drank beer."

"There's a lot you don't know about me," she said.

"I know, but I want to learn everything there is to know about Willow Blossom Tanner."

She smiled and took a swallow of beer. "Even the annoying stuff? The stuff I do that will drive you crazier than I do already?"

"Most definitely the annoying stuff," he said.

"There's kind of a lot, you know. We're so damn different." She glanced around his clean and tidy kitchen. "I'm a slob."

"I know. I've been to your place, remember?"

"I hate cleaning, and you'll hate living in a messy house."

"We'll hire a housecleaner."

"I talk too much."

"I like to listen," he said.

"I tell Ava everything. And I mean everything."

"I know."

"I see ghosts. They're almost always around. The house will be freezing," she said.

"We'll buy plenty of blankets."

"I won't always let you come with me when I'm helping spirits."

He hesitated, and she stared gravely at him as he gave her a small smile. "I just want to keep you safe, Willow."

315

"I know."

"What if I promise to work on my aura?"

A smile crossed her face. "That would help."

"I won't insist on going with you on every ghost expedition if you allow me to do some research on the spirits before you help them."

"I could probably work with that," she said slowly.

"We can start with this Damian guy. Can you ask him his last name?"

"I've already helped him," she said.

"Oh. What did he need?"

"It was a secret, remember?"

He grinned at her. "Your secrets are safe with me, Willow."

"Well, I have been dying to tell someone. It's so juicy, Mal! So," she leaned forward, her beer clasped tightly in her hands, "Damian's wife's sister was married to a man named Raymond. After nearly fifteen years of marriage, the sister left Raymond for another man. Raymond, of course, was devastated. Damian's wife asked him to spend some time with Raymond, you know, cheer him up and help him forget about his cheating ex-wife. Clear?"

"Mostly." Mal took a drink of his beer.

"It's confusing, but stay with me," Willow said. "Anyway, Damian and Raymond are getting pretty close. They're spending at least one day every weekend together doing guy stuff and going for coffee during the week, and Damian starts to have some feelings for Raymond."

"Feelings?"

She rolled her eyes. "Don't be naïve, Mal. Feelings! Feelings in his private parts for Raymond."

"Wait, isn't he married to Raymond's sister?"

"No, he's married to Raymond's ex-wife's sister."

"Right. But now Damian wants to hook up with Raymond? He was gay?"

"Well, I think bisexual. But he wanted more than a hook-up. It's six months later, and Damian's in love. In love like he's never been in his entire life. He wants to spend the rest of his life with this man. Isn't that romantic?"

"Very," Mal agreed, "except for the fact that he's already married."

"Yes, but get this," Willow said excitedly. "Damian can't take the guilt about his love for Raymond, plus he doesn't think his brother-in-law feels the same way about him anyway, so he decides he's going to honour his commitment to his wife and just forget about Raymond."

"That doesn't sound like a good plan."

"Right? How do you just stop yourself from being in love?"

"You can't," Mal said as Willow took a drink of beer.

"Except," Willow paused dramatically, "Damian comes home from work early one day to surprise his wife and finds her in bed with her sister's new lover's brother!"

Mal blinked. "What?"

"Damian's wife was having an affair! And had been for over two years. She introduced her sister to her lover's brother, and then her sister started having an affair as well."

"That's messed up."

"So, messed up. Anyway, Damian immediately goes to Raymond, even though he doesn't know that Raymond loves him and confesses his feelings. Raymond doesn't exactly confess his love, but he does admit his attraction to

Damian, and the two fall into bed and have hot sex for the next four days."

"Wow."

"Yep." Willow nodded and took another swig of beer.

"So, why did Damian need your help?"

"Get this. The two of them lived together for ten years. Ten years, and not once does Raymond say that he loves Damian. Then last week, Damian crosses the street to get to the subway and BOOM, he's hit by a taxi and killed instantly. Apparently, it was quite gruesome. At least, that's what Damian told me. Said his left leg was torn clean off his body, and his head was all smashed in like a pumpkin."

"Oh my God," Mal said. "Did he – I mean, was he all smashed in looking when you were helping him?"

"Of course not. It was his body that got smushed, not his spirit, Mal," Willow said.

"Right."

"So, Damian's dead, only he can't leave our realm because there's a part of him that's always been hurt by Raymond's refusal to acknowledge his love for him. He knows Raymond loves him, and he's pissed that the guy never said it."

"So, you had to go and tell Raymond that Damian was pissed and try to convince him to tell Damian's spirit that he loved him."

"Bingo!" Willow said triumphantly. "Raymond avoided my calls for a few days. Most of the time, they do because let's be honest, I come off sounding a wee bit crazy."

"No, not at all," Mal replied with an insincere smile.

She scowled at him, and he grinned and tipped his beer to her. "Go on, please."

"I finally cornered him in the grocery store, and after revealing a few things that only he and Damian could know, I convinced Raymond that Damian's spirit was with us. We went back to their place and -"

"Whoa, you just went to his place by yourself?" His wolf made an angry growl.

"It was fine, honey. Damian helped me escape that gross snake shifter back at the warehouse, remember? He's a good guy, and so is Raymond."

His heart skipped at the endearment, and a big goofy grin crossed his face. Willow, absorbed in her story, didn't notice.

"We get back to his place, walk through the front door, and poor Raymond just bursts into tears. We're talking full-on ugly cry. He was being eaten alive by his grief and regret for never telling Damian he loved him. He did love him, you know? Loved him deeply."

She stared silently at the top of the island before sipping at her beer. "Anyway, I hugged him and told him it was okay, and then we had a cup of tea while Raymond told Damian exactly how much he loved him and how sorry he was that he had never been able to say it. Then Damian asked me to tell Raymond he loved him, and I did, and then Damian went into the light."

She lapsed into silence. After a moment, Mal touched her arm. "Willow? What happened then?"

"Then I made plans to have dinner with Raymond next week and left," she said.

"You made two people very happy, honey."

"Yeah." She stood, dumped the rest of her beer down the sink, and stared out the window above it. "Hey, Mal?"

"Yes?"

"I've been thinking a lot the last few days. I'm sorry I didn't contact you, but I needed to sort some stuff out."

"I know. He reached out to touch her but hesitated and dropped his hand. "Did you?"

She nodded. "I did. Helping Damian, seeing Raymond's regret over never telling him that he loved him, it just …."

Mal, his heart pounding, touched the healed bite on her shoulder with a feather-light touch. "I'm sorry I did this to you, Willow."

She shivered at his touch and turned around. "Don't be. I love you, Mal."

He inhaled sharply as she stepped toward him and wrapped her arms around his waist.

"Say it again," he said hoarsely.

"I love you."

"I love you too." He bent his head and kissed her deeply, clutching at her like a man drowning as she kissed him back.

When he released her mouth, she gave him a slightly dazed look. He scooped her up and carried her toward his bedroom.

She kissed his thick neck. "I love you, Mal, but that doesn't mean we're getting married right away or I'm moving in with you or anything like that. Do you understand?"

"Yes." He bent his head and kissed her collarbone. "I know you need some time."

"I do." She cupped his face and gave him a solemn

look. "I'm not saying I won't marry you, but I'm worried that, after a while, you'll start thinking about how humans and shifters shouldn't be together. I'm having difficulty believing that you can just change your mind so easily. I think we should take it slow and really get to know each other before we start talking marriage."

"I know." He kissed her again. "I understand, Willow. Take all the time you need. I'll wait for you."

They were at his bedroom now, and she peered around the room with interest. "Oh dear God, you're one of those people."

"What people?"

"You make your bed. Lame." She rolled her eyes, and he growled playfully at her before dropping her onto the bed.

"Did you just call me lame? That's a spanking offense, you know." He grinned at her.

"Who's afraid of the big bad wolf? Not this girl," she said as he covered her small body with his.

"I love you, Willow. Always," he rasped into her ear.

"I love you too, Mal."

Keep reading for an excerpt from Elizabeth Kelly's next novel in the Shifters Series
"Ava and the Bear"

AVA AND THE BEAR EXCERPT

(THE SHIFTERS SERIES BOOK TWO)

It was two in the morning when she woke him with her screams. He rolled off the couch, a kink in his neck and his left leg asleep and stumbled toward her bedroom. His grizzly roared in confusion, and he soothed it as he limped into her room.

She screamed and thrashed in her bed, and he hurried over and sat down, grasping her shoulders and shaking her lightly. "Ava, honey, wake up. Wake up."

She screamed again. His grizzly growled in dismay at the sound. Bishop pulled her into his arms, rubbing her back roughly and ignoring her flailing limbs. "Wake up, honey. You're okay, wake up."

She woke with a startled gasp and tried to arch her body away from him. He tightened his hold on her and kissed the top of her head. "It's me, honey. It's Bishop. You're safe."

"Bishop?" Her voice was thick with tears.

He kissed the top of her head again. "Yeah, baby. It's me. You're okay."

She threw her arms around him and buried her face in his neck. "I was having a nightmare."

"It's okay. It's over."

"I was burning up, Bishop. I was burning up, and I couldn't…."

She made a gasping moan, and he rubbed her back through her thin nightshirt. "You're safe, baby. You're safe with me."

"Safe with you," she repeated.

"That's right." He shifted her on his lap and continued to rub her back as she trembled against him. It took nearly fifteen minutes for her to stop shaking.

"Better?" he asked when she finally relaxed in his arms.

"Yes, thank you," she said.

He started to ease her back to the bed, and she tightened her hold around his neck.

"Don't leave me." Fear laced her voice.

"I'm not. I'll lie down with you until you fall asleep, okay?" he said.

"Okay." She relaxed her grip and allowed him to place her on the bed. He climbed in beside her, and she plastered her body to his as he pulled up the quilt.

He wrapped his arms around her, and she snuggled into his chest.

"You have a comfortable bed," he said.

She made a small, choked sound of laughter and stared at the way his calves and feet hung over the end. "It's too small for you. I'm so sorry, Bishop."

"Don't be sorry, honey." He kissed her forehead. "Close your eyes."

"Don't leave me, okay?" she said.

"I won't." He shifted onto his side and pulled her closer until every part of their bodies touched and then buried his face in her long hair. She stroked his bare chest with her soft hands for a few minutes before settling against him.

The insistent buzzing of her phone dragged Ava from her sleep. She squinted blearily at the phone before picking it up. "Hello?"

She rested her head on the warm chest below her and ran her fingers through the coarse hair as she closed her eyes again.

"I'm fine, Willow. I was just sleeping," she mumbled.

There was a hard thigh between hers, and she made a contented moan as she rubbed her pelvis against it. The man beneath her made his own sound of contentment. She arched her back when his warm hands skimmed under her nightshirt and squeezed her ass.

"What? No, I'm fine. It's what time?" She pressed her lips against his firm flesh before nipping experimentally at it.

He groaned, his hand tightening on her ass. He pressed his leg against her pussy, rubbing his hair-roughened thigh against her panties.

"Willow, why are you calling me?" She tried not to contain her irritation. His warm hands slid inside her panties and kneaded and rubbed her bare ass, and she made a soft moan. "No, I'm fine. I just…"

Ava's eyes popped open. She struggled to sit up as she stared down at Bishop. His eyes were closed, and he bit his bottom lip before sliding his hand between her legs and touching the wet lips of her pussy.

"Bishop!" she gasped.

His eyes flew open, and he stared at her in confusion. "Ava? What's wrong?"

She pulled at his arm as Willow spoke rapidly in her ear.

Ava cleared her throat. "Yes, he's here with me. No, no, nothing's wrong. I just couldn't sleep last night, and Bishop came over and, uh, helped me sleep."

She pushed her way out of his arms and rolled to her side of the bed as she blushed furiously. "No! Not like that, Willow! He just, he made me a drink and then I went to bed."

Bishop sat up and pushed down the covers. He wore just a pair of briefs, and her eyes widened at the sizeable bulge between his legs before she forced herself to look away.

"Dammit!" Bishop suddenly shot to his feet and disappeared out of the room. She heard him fumbling around in the living room, and he cursed again when there was a loud thud.

"Bishop! Are you okay?" Ava glanced at the alarm clock. It was almost noon. She groaned and sat up, holding the covers up around her chest as Willow giggled like a madwoman in her ear.

"Fine." He reappeared in the doorway, his t-shirt on inside out and his hair sticking up everywhere. "I gotta go,

Ava. I'm late for work. Can you tell Willow I'm on my way into the office? I broke your chair, I'm sorry. I'll buy you a new one, okay?"

"Don't worry about it," she said.

He ran his hands through his thick hair. "I'll, uh, I'll call you later."

He left, and she collapsed on the bed with a harsh sigh.

"Ava? You there, or are you kissing Bishop goodbye?" Willow asked.

"Nothing happened, Willow," she said.

"Oh really? Because there was a lot of moaning and groaning coming through the phone," Willow said. "Did he sex you up last night to help you sleep or what?"

"No," Ava said. "I asked him to come over to keep me company for a while. He volunteered to sleep on the couch, but then I had a nightmare, and he crawled into bed with me because I was afraid. Then you woke us up when you called."

"Mal's been trying to get a hold of Bishop all morning." Willow laughed. "I can't wait to tell him he didn't answer his phone because he was in your bed."

"Don't you dare tell him, Willow," Ava said. "Nothing happened. Do you hear me? Nothing happened."

"Okay, okay. Don't get your panties in a bunch. Wait – you are wearing panties, right? You didn't give them to Bishop as, like, a trophy, did you?"

"I'm wearing underwear!" Ava said. "I swear to God, Willow Blossom Tanner, I'll break your arm if you tell anyone about what you heard."

Willow giggled. "Your secret is safe with me, honey."

"Like hell it is," she said.

"Listen, I've got to go. Are you feeling better?"

"Yes."

She was actually. She had slept well last night, and she had Bishop to thank for it. She climbed out of bed and went into the bathroom, staring at herself in the mirror before groaning.

"What? What's wrong?" Willow asked.

"Nothing." She stared at the sleep wrinkles on her face and her crazy bedhead. "I look awful in the morning, and today is no exception."

"I'm sure you have a lovely glow happening." Willow laughed.

"Willow," Ava said warningly.

"I have to go, honey. I love you! I'll talk to you later."

Willow ended the call, and Ava set her phone on the vanity before staring at herself in the mirror. "You idiot," she said and reached for her toothbrush.

ABOUT THE AUTHOR

Elizabeth Kelly was born and raised in Ontario, Canada. She moved west as a teenager and now lives in Alberta with her husband and a menagerie of pets. She firmly believes that a person can survive solely on sushi and coffee, and only her husband's mad cooking skills prevents her from proving that theory.

For more information about Elizabeth, check out her website at

www.elizabethkelly.ca

facebook.com/EKellyBooks
twitter.com/ElizabethKBooks
instagram.com/elizabethkelly_author
amazon.com/Elizabeth-Kelly/e/B00EOHZ0MS
bookbub.com/authors/elizabeth-kelly

Ava and the Bear (Book Two)

Katarina and the Bird (Book Three)

Porter's Mate (Book Four)

Bria and the Tiger (Book Five)

Rosalie Undone (Book Six)

The Dragon's Mate (Book Seven)

Rise of the Jaguar (Book Eight)

The Draax Series

Reign (Book One)

Rule (Book Two)

Rebel (Book Three)

Harmony Falls Series

Sweet Harmony (Book One)

Perfect Harmony (Book Two)

Forbidden Harmony (Book Three)

Redeeming Harmony (Book Four)

Individual Books

The Necessary Engagement

Amelia's Touch

The Rancher's Daughter

Healing Gabriel

The Contract

A Home for Lily

Saving Charlotte

Shameless

The Fairy Tales Collection

Broken

An Unlikely Seduction

Holiday Romance

The Christmas Wife

The Christmas Rescue

The Christmas Nanny

The Christmas Boss

Sordid Games